To Toby –
All the best
from the Greek
islands!

NEW WINE

a novel

John DeMers

2016

2365 Rice Blvd., Suite 202
Houston, Texas 77005

ISBN: 978-1-942945-08-6

10 9 8 7 6 5 4 3 2 1

Library of Congress Cataloging-in-Publication Data on file with publisher.

Editorial Direction: Lucy Herring Chambers
Managing Editor: Lauren Adams
Designer: Marla Y. Garcia

Printed in Canada through Friesens

John DeMers

ΔΕΛΦINOS

One Greek letter at a time, using what little I possessed of ancestral memory and a whole lot of college fraternity parties, I managed to confirm that this was indeed Delfinos. It was "that goddamn rock," as my father always described it—from which *his* grandfather had sailed to find his fortune in America, where the streets were paved with gold. Or at least they were in 1897, on the brink of a brand-new century. Somehow, our ever-wise patriarch had managed to land in Dayton, Ohio, where the family ran one and ultimately five coffee shops for a generation, until they set sail once again—to Lubbock, Texas. For guys who grew up beside the sea, they were never all that great at locating water.

My mother's frantic phone call had found me at my desk just over forty-eight hours earlier, glancing through (I'll never forget this little detail) my tasting notes from Vin Expo in Bordeaux and scribbling out my next wine order. I had not even headed home to pack. Unlike my great-grandfather on Delfinos, my last view of *my* homeland might turn out to be the glass and steel Houston high-rise that served as corporate headquarters for LRG Holdings Ltd., as my brother and several swarms of lawyers had recently re-baptized the Laros Restaurant Group, without consulting me. I had phoned my wife Bev on the company limo ride to IAH, but she was lunching with friends at Tony's and didn't pick up. I had a feeling she wouldn't. I also phoned my teenage stepdaughter Chloe, knowing all too well that she was in school. For both I left voicemails explaining what had happened on Delfinos, as best I could explain what *had* happened on Delfinos, and ending with "I love you."

Our travel department, usually adept at getting my brother Nick and/or me to Phoenix or San Jose or Chattanooga or either of the Portlands to check out some new location, outdid itself by locating Athens. The one *not* in Texas or Georgia. It even found a United flight via Frankfurt leaving in an hour and fifty-three minutes. My younger brother, who'd become CEO upon my father's retirement nine months earlier, was in the air on his way to or from somewhere. There seemed little I could do but try to get to our mother on the island. The United connection put me on the ground in Greece almost seven hours ahead of any other combination.

I'd spent the entire flight—two flights, actually—thinking of my father while trying not to think of my father. I'd picked up John Sandford's latest Virgil Flowers yarn at IAH, but Minnesota in the dead of winter seemed too far from Houston to engage me. In a half-hearted way, I chose and paid bits of attention to three Tom Hanks movies in a row, drifting off to sleep on the strength of gin and tonic just often enough to get the plotlines confused. It seemed liked Tom Hanks was a good enough actor. But I was definitely not a good enough audience. The only time I woke up fully was racing through Frankfurt airport after dragging through Passport Control to catch my flight, operated for United by Aegean logically enough, to Athens. Now, after several hours on the Aegean in rough weather, the airline's name was more than an idle threat.

It was cold on the ferry's wooden deck as rain pelted in thick sheets only inches beyond me and my dark suit—the clothes on my back, literally—a mid-level Italian-made fashion statement. I'd already lost the tie, probably on the plane somewhere, and it just struck me as one more damn thing I'd have to find and purchase in a place I knew nothing about. For the final hour of the crossing from

Piraeus, we had edged up against the small but mountainous island, which revealed only a lightbulb burning here and there in the rain, plus lots of wind and darkness, only to have each light snuffed out as though by the hand of God.

I was still thinking about my father, picturing him at various events, various ages and various amounts of hair—the progression that awaits so many of us, though I tried not to think about that. I tried to think of him at every event except one, but it was the one that kept hijacking all the rest. It was recent, I tried to console myself, so of course it still hurt. Still stung? No, it *hurt*. I was his oldest, after all, no matter what he'd decided, no matter what he'd told the board at our meeting at the Four Seasons. They'd been shocked, as several would comment anonymously to the *Houston Business Journal* in the days that followed. Our board had been caught off guard by my father's decision, as had I. Now, looking back without wanting to, I realized that only one other person in that private dining room, other than my father, had not been shocked. *He* was the one who'd not caught the first flight out of Houston, as any good son should. He was the one who'd not grabbed the first ferry out of Piraeus.

There was almost nobody on the ferry. It was merely going through the motions and burning up generations of fossil fuel months before whatever passed for the island's tourist season. At least it was getting me to Delfinos, which had no landing strip. I did not feel like a tourist, since nowhere in my shifting moods was there any excitement about discoveries that might lie ahead. I'd be here a week, ten days max, I'd told anyone who was interested at the office. A week out of my life, with a job to do. I felt no interest in making this journey anything more.

Reading the island's name—crudely hand-painted on a whitewashed wall that had no other apparent purpose—was difficult because of the February weather. As rain obscured my vision across the stretch of water between the ferry and the shore, shifting winds rocked a single bare bulb above the letters back and forth at the end of a long hanging wire, casting stuttering shadows. Violent gusts smashed the tiny illumination against the wall, as though trying to beat it into submission.

The sea calmed a bit as we rounded a promontory guarding the harbor—from which my great-grandfather and thousands of other starving, ambitious—what, *Definites*?—had voted to leave with their feet, hands and strong backs, and I caught my first official view of the place our family began. I could see a small strip of not-luxurious hotels along a dark beach that stretched west from the port and also, in the distance, the main town of Chora spread across the island's highest mountain. It was in that town that my father had rented a barely serviceable two-bedroom apartment and moved my mother—only temporarily, he insisted, while he got their *real* house "at the beach" fixed up—to the undying dismay of her friends back home in River Oaks.

I could almost hear my father preaching over the years to his forever-captive audience of my mother, Nick and me: When a Laros leaves a place, he *never* goes back. So why—goddamn it to hell, *why*—had my father done precisely that? I'd been warned that this was *Greece*—the Greece of the financial crisis and forced austerity, not the Greece of Pericles—so I shouldn't expect anything to make sense. As I prepared to climb off the night ferry onto the island of my ancestors, I figured the place was off to a mighty fine start.

The captain's voice over the scratch-infested loudspeaker barely cut through the drumbeat of rain. I heard *parakalo* and *efharisto*—the omnipresent Please and Thank you of modern, as opposed to classical, Greek. The two words almost exhausted my fluency. From what I'd seen at the four islands we'd touched that night so far, everything else he said meant "You people get your asses in gear. We won't be here long."

Five minutes—I think that's what the ferry was shooting for. And with few getting off on earlier islands and nobody getting on, it hadn't been a hard schedule to keep. These weren't really ports, I caught myself thinking: They were *bus stops*. And by the darkened welcome presented by Delfinos port and even by the town of Chora up on the mountainside, I gathered that basically no one was home.

Docking was tricky, thanks to surf driven in by the storm. The captain spun the ferry around in its ultra-tight anchorage, skillfully missing three small, tied-up fishing boats, and reversed to touch the concrete bulkhead once, twice and then three times. Each attempt was knocked aside by wind and waves. Finally deckhands in orange jumpsuits with reflective silver strips across their backs managed to loop ropes over steel spikes in the concrete and reel us against the dock. They lowered the car ramp, as they had at each of the islands before this one. No cars were leaving the ferry on Delfinos.

My mother had assured me, between bouts of hysterical crying, I'd be met at the boat by a man named Fotis. Hell, I couldn't even tell *what* the man was, much less *who*: an employee of my Dad's, or perhaps just a family friend? In either case, a glance around the port from the rain-battered deck turned up no one. It was too late to worry about that now, I knew. Too late, period.

Still, this Fotis was important to me. He spoke a little English. I spoke virtually no Greek. I understood barely enough to get through a baptism at our cathedral, and occasionally to mumble words to some song at our Greek Festival, where I could always be counted on to pour plastic cups of *moschophilero*. Yes, I repeated almost as a prayer to the stern Savior who looked down in almost any Greek church: *Yes,* Fotis would be important to me.

Several ship's officers, dark and hairy men in open-collared white dress shirts with no shortage of stripes on their sleeves, waved me brusquely toward the exit that led down to the ramp, as though at any second the ferry might splinter against the concrete. I forced a smile for each officer I passed, a legacy of my father's from-the-cradle training and my life in the restaurant business. The smiles were not returned.

"Delfinos," one of the men said to me without feeling, nodding toward the dark opening that reminded me, inevitably with my mood, as a coffin getting ready to close.

At the top of the final escalator against the ferry's wall—neither one was functioning, so they ended up being merely difficult stairs—I spotted two large black suitcases, the kind people take with them when they leave for a long time, or leave not knowing whether they'll ever return. The suitcases were scuffed, ripped in a couple places, and one of the handles counted on duct tape to keep it attached. More pressingly, the suitcases were blocking the escalator, my escape. I needed to move them aside to get off this ferry, and all signs said I needed to do it fast.

I had just set down my briefcase and bent to grasp the first handle when a voice behind spoke a word in English: "Please." A turn to locate the voice assured me that its owner and I were alone. A woman who seemed to be in her mid-30s, with ink-black hair tightly bound in a scarf, stood inches away—where had she *been*?—wearing a loose, sleeveless top of deep violet and a flowing, richly patterned wrap-around skirt that touched the tops of her brown leather sandals.

"Please. To help," she said, her pale face opening within the scarf to form something resembling a weak smile.

"Yes," I answered. "How can I help?"

"Surgery, I have." The woman's eyes, in the limited, false light offered by the ferry, seemed almost as black as her hair. "Knee. Is difficult." She gestured, somewhat miserably, toward the lifeless escalator. My brain kicked in about this time and I recognized the problem before her. Before us.

"You are visiting?" I asked, as though it mattered. Her intentions, her plans for a meaningful life, even her hopes for a better world, didn't matter at this moment. Only getting us off this damn ferry mattered. I glanced down at her bags and laughed as amicably as my sudden exhaustion would allow. "Maybe island... long time?"

Her laugh caught the tail end of mine, which was anything but unself-conscious. *There.* I had become another ugly American overseas, speaking to foreigners in *their* country in *their* version of *my* language. For the briefest of moments, I suspect we laughed together.

"Maybe," she said. "Job on island. In office. Not difficult." She looked to see if I understood, deciding I needed one more clue. "For knee."

"I understand," I said.

Gesturing to claim the work as my own, I nodded for the woman to head down the escalator ahead of me. This she did, taking slow, careful, sometimes shaky steps, her right hand gripping the rail. I followed with the first of her cases, setting it out on the dock in the rain before taking two steps up at a time to grab the second one. Obviously, I decided, this woman's business was importing rocks to Delfinos. I made sure both she and her bags were on solid ground, even as her scarf was soaking through and clumps of dark, saturated hair escaped onto her forehead, before I turned back for my briefcase.

"Thank you," I heard her say. Did a bemused tone sneak into her voice as she tacked on one more word: "*Sir?*"

I was only 52. Suddenly, I felt older than my father.

I was sprinting now, as a gaggle of deckhands appeared to argue amongst themselves as they untangled the ropes. A single impatient blast from the ferry's horn echoed around the port until it died. The engine rumble came up. By the time I made it back out onto the dock, I felt my eyes interrogate every street, every alley, every doorway. The woman and her two heavy suitcases were gone.

With a grinding that threatened to loosen my teeth, the good ship *Adamantios Korais* pulled away from Delfinos for Ios and Santorini, the last two islands I'd noticed on its posted nocturnal run. Within less than the minute that took, I was soaked through to the skin.

All the houses on the road up from the port were dark, seemingly abandoned, as though I'd landed on an island emptied by war, pirates or pestilence. There was one fading white building that seemed to have been a café in another life, but no other signs of a pulse, plus a grand total of three street lamps leading to the start of the dark mountain road to Chora. And then, I noticed. There was one more light, burning within a small wooden kiosk promising TURIST INFOS, its front shutter opened outward. Clutching my briefcase like the one thing that still made sense to me, I ran through the rain for the man whose shadow moved inside.

At first, he eyed my approach warily; but then again, it's hard for me to measure exactly how insane I must have looked. As soon as I was close enough to see the man's eyes, they brightened with recognition before I could form a single word.

"Hello, my *friend*," the man exuded, stepping out from the side of the kiosk and gathering me into a bear hug. "I am Fotis." As the rain cascaded from ledges formed by his tousled, salt and pepper hair, from his nose, his ears and his stubble-crusted chin, he opened into a broad grin that was missing two front teeth.

"Stelios," he said. "I am sorry. About your father. He was good man."

2

To my surprise—I'd have to get over being surprised, but after only thirteen minutes on Delfinos, how could I?—Fotis led me to his car that was actually a taxi. I knew because, for some reason, the plastic sign that rested atop the roof of the ancient, splotchy blue Toyota station wagon read ΤΑΞΙ, and I could read it. This was, he announced proudly, the only taxi on Delfinos.

The sign, it turned out, didn't light, and the front passenger seat belt was missing entirely, and the engine refused to start, flooding instead so we had to wait; but it was a vehicle that might, in a pinch, get me to my mother's apartment. Fotis and I sat there as the engine thought through its options. He had to sneak up on it, turning the key without warning, and the engine jumped to a start against its will.

"There," my new friend announced. "Victory."

"Victory is good," I said, mostly to fill silence.

"*Sigah, sigah,*" Fotis responded, waving the palm of his hand gently in my direction, moving it side to side as though the air were a much-loved kitten to be stroked.

"What's that mean? You know I don't speak any Greek, right?"

He nodded. "I say, *slowly-slowly*. But some say it means 'Take it easy.'"

"Slowly-slowly?"

"*Our* speed," said Fotis. "Here. You'll get used to it."

Turning from him to face the road, I watched as the Toyota's headlights—which did seem to function—picked out small shrines along the winding shoulder. Boxy plaster constructions with peaked roofs and crosses on top, they held something deep in their shadows. Our headlights left each shrine before I could figure out what.

Forcing my brain to organize, I said, "I won't be here long enough to get used to it."

Fotis grinned and turned to me, the left side of his face softly lit yellow-green by the dashboard. "Believe me, my friend. You *will*."

As the road wound upward from the port and its town, looping over the crests of scrub-covered hills before dipping briefly into greener valleys, I noticed the rain easing up. We'd traveled barely a mile from the sea and the clouds were already different, not black and violent but racing, like rolling smoke across the face of a bright full moon. It caught my eye, that moon, those clouds. But it was something I couldn't put into words, at least for Fotis with his quirky command of English. Forced to say something, I might have called it all—beautiful.

It was then, in the on-again, off-again light of the moon, that the ghosts began to appear.

They were tall and solid and utterly empty, angular gray shapes sketching in houses that never quite came to be. Some were barely started, somebody's cement mixer and a pile of shovels still strewn about the hillside. Others looked almost finished, two and even three stories tall, suggestions of plumbing and electricity visible amidst the tangle of concrete skeletons without any walls.

"The *cries*," Fotis said, seeing my curiosity.

"The what?"

"The cries. Here in Greece."

"I don't understand."

"It's everything now, my friend. It's why my son came home. With his wife and baby, to live at house. Why a lot of sons and daughters came home."

"The crisis? The *financial* crisis?"

"Yes," he nodded energetically, as though I was a slow child who'd finally made a breakthrough. "The *cries*." Fotis glared at the road, less to see the path ahead than to navigate in English through the sentences he felt coming. "So, rich guys from Athens come here. And to them, is paradise. Not like city, with traffic and noise. And pollutee. None. Like *paradise*. You know? So because they rich guys, they build rich-guy house. Like that one. And *that* one. But as they busy building and building some more, something bad is happening. You know, with the rotten, crooked bastards in charge. They are rich guys one night when they go to bed. And when they wake up, they are not rich guys no more."

"The cries?"

"Exactly," he said.

"So they just sit here? These *mansions?*"

Fotis shrugged, downshifting carefully then taking his attention from the road to make eye contact. "Where the hell are they going to go?"

At some point during our ride up to Chora, I let on that I hadn't eaten anything since shortly before the plane touched down at Eleftherios Venezelos, the airport in the middle of nowhere far outside Athens, now pushing ten hours ago. Since the time had to be nearing midnight, I mentioned this mostly to make conversation, not because I expected Fotis to do anything about it. Surely my mother would have bread and peanut butter, or whatever the Greek equivalent of those pantry staples might be. Instead, despite my efforts to stop him, Fotis pulled out his cell phone, speed-dialed a number and, though it took the person called quite a few rings to answer, got into what seemed a vicious argument. In Greece, I would learn, every conversation sounded like a vicious argument.

"We good," he said with no further comment as he broke the connection.

"I don't expect anybody to feed me dinner. It's the middle of the night, Fotis."

"We Greek," he laughed. "We prefer the middle of the night."

Apparently, he was speaking only for himself, not for Irini Vassilakis. When she opened the door of her grocery store/café on the outskirts of town, she was wearing what I think used to be called a housecoat. I'd never actually seen one before. The woman who wore it kept one hand holding it closed in front for modesty, the other hanging tiredly at her side. Fotis and Irini snarled at each other with impenetrable Greek phrases for a couple moments, then Fotis waved me toward the room's lone table.

"She is happy to see us," he reported.

The table was set with several small plates holding chunks of feta, dark purple olives and slices of something that resembled Italian salami but wasn't as dry. There was a crusty loaf of bread at the center for tearing off pieces—no knife in sight—and, after Irini paid one more visit to her kitchen, a large platter with something on it that resembled cooked ground meat. A dusty bottle also turned up on the table, which Fotis poured from into two small glasses of the kind we use for orange juice. This definitely wasn't orange juice.

"Tsipouro," he said, grabbing his glass and waiting for me to clink. I did and before I could even study the clear liquid, Fotis had downed his and gone back for a refill. "Or raki, if you prefer."

"Raki?" I really was confused. "Raki is Turkish, I think, and kinda like ouzo, yes? Licorice?" I hated licorice. I took a tentative sip. "This is more like—"

"Grappa. It's from the making wine." "High alcohol," I observed, ever master of the obvious.

"This is Greece," my friend laughed quietly. "We need it." He glanced from one side of the table to the other, then over at Irini, who was nodding off in a woven chair in front of a shelf filled with canned vegetables. "You *eat*, my friend."

I did.

I hadn't realized how tense I'd been, until the combination of tsipouro and company began to help me be less so. It had been a sprint, every plane and every cab and every ferry. It had been a sprint, filled with fear of failure, that somehow I had missed a step and would end up stuck somewhere with no way out. Oddly, I hadn't missed a step. Here I was, drinking Greek moonshine in the middle of the night and something delicious.

"What *is* this?" I asked.

Fotis embarked on another exchange with Irine—I kept wanting to say, "Come on, you two shouldn't fight"—but all he said when he turned back to me was, "She wants you to guess."

"Well, it's meat. I think."

Fotis grinned but only waved me to continue.

"It's a little like meatloaf, yet not like any meatloaf I've ever had in America."

"Meatloaf?"

"Like, yes, ground meat—usually beef, with seasoning, formed into a loaf. Then baked."

"I see. So?"

I tasted a couple more bites, then used my fork to pick apart some that was still on the platter. Looking for clues. And not really finding any.

Fotis shared my theorizing, my culinary detective work, with Irini, and I could tell they shared a good laugh at my expense. For once, they didn't argue. Was this one of those scenes that ended, "You, my friend, have just eaten the liver of a feral cat?" I hoped not. I'd tasted more than my share of weird, disgusting things during my years working with chefs in the restaurant business, but the older I got, the more I appreciated grilled chicken breast and a large pile of French fries.

"Meatloaf, you say?" offered Fotis, clearly enjoying the drama. "Well, maybe so. Or maybe... not."

"What's that mean?"

"It is ground beef, mostly. But you understand, this is Irini's specialty, people come from other villages, to enjoy. This is ground beef with chunks of *kotopoulou* mixed in."

"*Koto*—chicken? How odd."

"Even so. Then she forms a—what did you call it? loaf?—and wraps it in skin of *kotopoulou*."

"No wonder it's moist."

"And she puts in the oven. This what come out."

"Hmm, delicious," I enthused, serving myself another fall-apart slice. If an American meatloaf married the best-ever French country pate, their offspring would surely be a lot like this. In terms of presentation, it was hopeless, unfixable, ungarnishable. But it was one of the best things I've ever put in my mouth. I couldn't begin to figure out how to say this to Fotis, much less to Irini, so I simply kept serving myself more—each bite chased with olives, cheese and increasingly generous gulps of tsipouro.

It took me most of this midnight supper, well into wiping up the meat platter with my last chunk of bread, to realize I was eating alone.

Irini never budged from her seat against the shelf, drifting in and out of sleep. And Fotis merely drank and smoked, one cigarette after another. I realized I had not smelled cigarette smoke and food at the same time in years, since my earliest days of working in my father's restaurants. Just like everybody else in the dining rooms and kitchens of my father's restaurants, I'd taken up the nasty habit. It and I had parted company later, on the insistence of both doctor and wife.

This will kill you, they said in a kind of eternal evil chorus. As would, in later choruses, cholesterol from steaks. As would "white foods" like potatoes, pastas and rice, that, in some diabolical joke from the Almighty, managed to turn themselves into blood sugar. With thoughts of so many prohibitions, and ultimately, in the past year, the deep reality of all the damn *good* they'd done me, I wanted nothing on earth as much as a cigarette. I was about to ask Fotis for one, or three, when I noticed it was his last and opted for being humane.

Irini shook herself awake one last time, cleared the table of dishes that, thanks to me, wouldn't need much washing, and glanced at Fotis as though to ask, "Is he done yet?" Fotis nodded as affectionately as I'd seen him do anything. She glanced at me, pulled her housecoat closed at her throat and issued a shaky, *"Kali nichta."*

"*Kali nichta*," I parroted back. Then, it popped out: *"Efharisto."*

"*Parakalo*," Irini said, backing out of the retail area toward what I knew would be her small apartment in back.

I caught Fotis gazing at me, as though he wanted to speak but couldn't. As though he wanted to but didn't want to. Instead, he lifted the tsipouro bottle and divided the last few splashes between our glasses. He took hold of his glass, a bit uncertainly it seemed, and waited for me to do the same. "*Yassou,*" he said. "Means 'to health, my friend.'"

"Better late than never, I guess."

"What?"

"I mean—" I laughed without humor, pressing the truth aside with my hand. "Don't they all?"

"Even so."

"Then sure. *Yassou*, Fotis."

We finished off the tsipouro.

"You want for me," he said after a lengthy, uncomfortable silence, "to tell you? What happens, I mean. With your father."

"Yes."

For a moment, he obviously hoped I would tell him no. He pulled out his last cigarette, crumpled the pack and tossed it toward a waste basket in the corner, missing by two feet. Once the cigarette was lit, he took four quick, soul-deep drags from it, releasing the smoke. He shook his head, averting his eyes from mine.

"Is sad," he said.

That much I already knew. It was merely a matter of finding the best way to ask this man for more information. Between the language and the travel and my exhaustion and my occasional silent explosions of grief, I didn't have a clue.

"So," he said, "I work for your father. At his place by the sea. I do anything he need, anything he ask—clear land, dig hole, pour cement, paint wall. He see me when he first come here. Say he knew my family or that our families were close or something. It was enough. Plus, my friend, he pay me okay, and you know that helps. Like many, I have many jobs but little income."

I almost let a smile break through. Fotis had just defined, without knowing it, the universal human condition.

"He call me early on Wednesday. Two days ago, yes?" I nodded. "It is still dark, almost. And he say: Come here soon, I doing floor. Dining room. Yes, that is what he say. He say he will have cement ready, so I should not take too long. I understand him. He need my help. I throw on some work clothes. Drive my taxi to the port and take my boat—"

"What? I'm confused."

"The boat. You must take boat to get there. There is road over mountain, by old monastery, but it is broken. He will fix, he said. You will see, maybe tomorrow, yes? In this moment, you must take a boat. And pull it up on beach."

"Okay. How did my *father* get there?"

"He has boat also. Just so small. With motor, even so." Fotis stared sadly at the cigarette, figured it was done and crushed it out against the bottom of Irini's table. Seeing he'd never make the waste basket, he shoved what was left into his shirt pocket.

"I arrive as I always," he said. "I see his boat on beach. I see cement mixer by house. And I see it turning, and that is strange. I could not see ground, because the house is on hill and I am on beach. Lower?"

I nodded.

"But it is strange, so I walk faster. No, soon I *run* up the path. And then I find your father. A shovel is in his hand, and there is a—what do you say?—a *pile* of the cement, dry, by his feet. But he is lying, with the mixer turning and making scraping noise over and over. He is just lying there, Stelios. And he is not moving. Not breathing."

Suddenly, it hit me. The public truth of this very private death. By now, the *Chronicle* would be onto the story. "George Laros, Restaurant Empire Builder, Dies at 83." It would be on their website already, probably, in the print edition by morning. "My father died the way he lived," I could hear Nick saying in a statement released to the media. "He was doing exactly what he wanted, building something for his family."

"My" father? *Really,* Nick? I wasn't sure if I'd said this out loud. A glance at Fotis still trapped in his narrative told me I had not.

I tried to focus across the table. I tried to feel sorrier for this other man who was out of cigarettes, out of tsipouro, out of light bulbs for his ΤΑΞΙ sign. Considering all that raged through my brain and left me somewhere between clutching my own chest and collapsing in my own tears, it wasn't easy.

"Fotis," I said, "my mother told me it was a heart attack, that he didn't suffer at all?"

He struggled to find his way back into the story. Or forward out of it. "That is what doctor said. Yes, when he go there, to your father. But that took time. I had to go get him. From the port. In my boat." Fotis looked at me, holding both his hands out, palms-up. "It was, as I say you, very sad."

The fire started in my nostrils, just a series of twitches at the start, and then made its way into my dreams.

As I slept, I knew Dad and I were inside a building—one of our restaurants maybe, or one of the numberless houses and apartments our family had lived in when I was a child and my father was becoming an "Empire Builder"—and the building was catching fire. Flames were everywhere, but my father seemed so calm. He watched each piece of our shelter catch fire with only an accepting smile, which was hardly the smile he ever gave me, when he bothered to smile at all. I was hysterical, screaming for help and banging on walls, knowing there would be no help and that there, this being a dream, was no way out. I woke with a loud start on my mother's couch to the vision of Fotis sitting in silence across from me smoking a cigarette.

"Jesus," I shouted at him, trying to pivot from my nightmare. "My mother is going to freakin' kill you!"

"Why?" he asked calmly.

"Smoking in her house. She doesn't all—"

"George and I smoked here all the time."

"My Dad *never*—"

I stopped when it hit me. My father was a *person*, and as such he was a mystery, even to those who loved him, or feared him or at least assumed they knew him. This was an education, I realized, an education in my father. It was hardly a reassuring one.

"I, um, never saw him smoke at home in Houston." I started to lift my head from the pillow but decided to complete the act, sitting up and using both hands to rub my face until it felt awake. I had no idea how long I'd slept, but it definitely wasn't long enough.

It had to be morning. There was something early about the light making its way into my mother's small living room through the slats that shielded it from the street. We had come in after my dinner at Irini's and found a note from my mother. She was sorry, but she hadn't gotten the guest bedroom ready and now the doctor had given her a sedative, so now she'd be going to bed immediately. She hoped I would understand and help her do better for the following night. As I thought through these things, I heard good sounds and smelled good things from the kitchen, so I figured she was up. I shook myself upward so I could go and greet her, but Fotis waved to back onto the sofa.

"Please, one moment," he said. "You need to speak with your mother, Stelios. This I know. But I schedule some things for you this morning. Things that need to be done. And I must bring you, as you say, up to speed." He let a grin pop out, proud of his colloquialism. "You need to go see two people. About your father, so funeral can take place."

Did I know about that? No matter. Fotis knew about it.

"You must go see priest, so service can take place in church."

"Dad never went to church," I reported without thinking. I stopped myself before insisting, "And neither do I," and settled for a simple, "Why?"

"It was his wish."

"How do we know this?"

"Your mother says he told her. Many time."

"My father talked about dying? But he was *healthy*. He was building this new house and this new—"

Fotis waved me to silence. He knew what I was saying, but he also knew it didn't matter. "He tell me also, Stelios. So you must go to priest. I have set up for you, with priest who speak English pretty good." He shook his head. "Imagine that, right here on little Delfinos. Father Michael. I think you will like. And as I tell you, he is expecting."

"What time?" I asked.

"Morning." On Delfinos, apparently, *morning* counted as a time.

"Okay. Who else?"

"You must go police."

Something about this news, or at least the way Fotis delivered it, was disturbing. Like just about anybody who isn't a cop, I was basically afraid of them. No, I didn't know what I was guilty of, or whether it was a felony or a misdemeanor. But I knew that from the simplest traffic stop to look at my driver's license on up, I did not welcome that kind of attention.

"They don't think there was foul play, do they?" I looked closely at Fotis, hoping his expression would give something away. But it didn't. "From what you told me, it seems like your basic heart attack, yes?"

"Yes, my friend. It does. But there are papers to sign. All routine. We're still Greeks here, you know. We insist—*insist*, yes?—that everything we do make mountain of documents."

"Routine?"

"Even so."

"Okay," I said, letting go of a breath I didn't know I'd been holding in. "Sure, I'll go."

"Your mother said you would do this. She told police to wait for you."

I snickered. "Oh joy."

"It is always such a way, yes? Even in Houston, papers must be signed. I'm sure of it."

"I suppose."

"But one more thing, and then I must go. For the police, there are some fee to be paid. For filing. I spoke to the colonel—"

"Colonel?"

"Yes, is so. On Delfinos. Of police. He speak English also. He say you must bring one hundred euros. There is an ATM at end of street, by the big square. Both church and police station are convenient."

"Convenient *to the ATM*."

Fotis grinned fully this time, catching my drift. Then he led me to my mother, paid his respects, told me he'd pick me up on the square in the afternoon, and left the two of us alone to talk.

4

My mother had had her back to me when we walked into the kitchen, and for a moment I wondered who was cooking my breakfast. This woman in a nondescript black dress couldn't possibly be my mother—a woman who'd always dressed and fixed her hair almost nightly to be captured for the society pages. This woman's hair was almost white now, and she seemed shorter and more stooped than I remember her before Dad retired. And that was only months ago. It wasn't the island's fault, I figured—it wasn't the island that had substituted this old woman whose hand seemed to shake as she turned slices of bacon in the pan over a hot plate for the mother I remembered. But really, I wondered, as she recognized us behind her, whose fault *was* it?

Now that Fotis was gone, she took two weak steps in my direction, her face drained, her eyes empty, and I covered the rest of the distance between us, taking her into my arms. I felt something let go inside her and then a series of deep, heaving sobs, followed at last by stillness. "Thank you," my mother said from someplace behind my ear. "Thank you for coming here to help us." It clearly hurt to correct her mistake. "To help *me*."

"It wasn't easy, Mom. Or quick," I said, letting myself smile wistfully.

"I know, Stelios."

She stepped back and ran her left hand through her hair, pushing a few strands off her unexpectedly wrinkled forehead. Houston's humidity had kept her looking young, I realized, though I had no idea what combination of magic, makeup and cosmetic surgery had been in play all these years. All those things belonged to the past here in Delfinos, and I was shocked by what I saw in front of me. Apparently, the feeling was mutual.

"What's this?" my mother said.

"What?"

"Those *clothes*."

Only then did I look down. My creased white dress shirt was tucked in on one side and pulled out on the other, riding over the belt that held my pants in place. I was standing in black socks, my dress shoes probably somewhere near the couch I'd slept on.

"Best I could do, Mom. I was at the office. I figured I'd find a store."

"Store?" She seemed confused.

"Yeah, like a department store. Or anyplace that sells clothes that aren't business suits."

She glanced at her wrist, at her watch. And I thought I understood.

"What time do the stores open here?"

"Sit," was all she told me. "Eat your breakfast while it's hot."

There was something about being a child, even when you haven't been a child for decades, that makes you obey when your mother tells you to sit and eat. She served me the bacon from the pan—all seven slices of it—plus a scrambled mound of what seemed to be three, bright-yellow eggs, a completely deeper color than eggs were in the States. Both bacon and eggs had more flavor too, presumably from coming from local pigs and local chickens, as did the toast made in an oven from slices of crusty bread. My mother watched me eat, and didn't say a word until my plate looked like it had come out of a commercial dishwasher. She started to rise to clear it, but I waved her down and walked over to set it in the sink.

"How are you?" I asked, back in my chair and gazing at her across the table.

"Your brother called," she said.

"Good. I mean, I'm glad." It rankled. It always did, especially since the board meeting. I figured it always would.

"He doesn't think he can make it. But he promises he'll try. There's a restaurant opening, and—you know how it is. With you here, he said *somebody* had to stay and keep things moving. Somebody from the family."

Strange logic, I thought. Then again, our family was a bit famous for that. Publically, we'd made a fortune with strange logic. Privately, we had, well, our new CEO.

"Sure," I said. "Jacksonville."

My mother nodded. "He said it was going to be a great opening. Said your father would be proud."

"I'm sure, Mom."

"He said to call him if you need anything."

"Of course. I'll be sure to do that."

"And then there's the airport meeting in D.C.?"

"Airport—?" Almost as soon as I spoke, I remembered it. The group hoping to convince us to create a new version of ourselves for twelve to fifteen airports across America in the first year, and more after that. It was all just talk at this point, but just about everything worth doing in business was just talk at some point.

"Nick wanted me to tell you, Stelios, he could push back the meeting a few days, on the basis of your Dad's death. But only a few. He wants you there. It's a family thing, he says. And I think it is too. You need to think of what your Dad would have wanted."

That was feeling more and more like a fulltime job.

I was afraid there'd be nothing left to say, that my mother and I would be stranded in silence at the small kitchen table covered with a plastic table cloth with red and yellow flowers. But noise from the street filtered in as soon as we weren't talking. Someone was announcing something in Greek, seemingly with great urgency. I thought it might be some message about the crisis—something like "No more money until next Wednesday"—though in my worst fears it was an order to evacuate ahead of some natural disaster. I glanced at my mother, who rose to her feet and motioning for me to follow her.

On the narrow street outside the dark blue paint of my parents' front door, I couldn't tell where the sound was coming from. With the echo through the twisting streets of white plaster houses, one moment it came from the right and the next from the left. Finally, it settled into a position around the corner, my focus helped by a couple neighbors who pushed open second-story shutters, satisfied themselves who was coming and from where, then pulled the shutters tight. A gray van approached around the corner and started up the street to where we stood.

"The *store*," my mother said.

She waved the driver to a stop. With a quick and wordless nod in her direction, the man stepped around back, pulled open the back of the van and drew out a series of stainless steel bars that held pants, shirts and dresses. My mother spoke to the man in comfortable Greek, a language I didn't realize she knew at all, since we never used it around the house or at any of our restaurants—even the one serving Greek food. As I was living proof, we never used it anywhere.

"What do you need, Stelios?"

"Some pants, Mom, maybe shorts. Like, you know, cargo pants?" I didn't know the Greek word. Hell, I wasn't even sure what they were called in English. "With pockets. Plus, some kind of loose short-sleeved shirt. It's hotter here than it is in Houston."

"In the winter," she said.

"Which is, well, now."

More energetic Greek followed, she and the man tipping back and forth. For all the world, they were haggling over price, though maybe they were merely debating my size. It may have been that, since they kept looking at me like they were appraising a goat to make stew. Finally, the man reached into the van beneath the hanging items and uncovered a pair of khaki shorts that looked like they'd fit me, and an open-collared pale yellow cotton shirt to go with them. Canvas deck shoes came off the pile next. I tried them on, and somebody had done a rather impressive job.

My mother told me a number, and it virtually exhausted the number of euros I had left. I made a mental note, remembering what Fotis had told me, to find an ATM before going to visit with the Delfinos chief of police.

The man pushed his racks back into the van. But something I spotted rolled up deep in the shadows made me stop him with a wave of my hand. It was long and navy blue, and quite possibly the only thing of its kind on the island of Delfinos. I handed the man all the coins I had left, and he seemed satisfied. That was how I bought a tie to wear to my father's funeral.

Back inside, I checked the time—it was almost 10. And according to Fotis, I had places to go, people to meet and cash to distribute. Nothing could happen till then, he'd explained, and I'd certainly done enough business with local officials in different cities to get the message. I shared all this with my mother and went into the spare bedroom to change. I certainly felt like a new man when I did, and I figured I'd be even better when I finally had time for a shower.

I made sure I shoved my wallet with debit card into the right pocket of my shorts and my mobile phone into the left. I didn't seem to have service over here, but I simply wasn't ready to go anywhere without it. Getting ready to leave the house for my appointments, I noticed a white straw hat with a black band hanging beside the front door. The hat had been my father's. I slipped it on respectfully and turned to face my mother.

"Perfect," she said, lost somewhere between laughter and tears.

"At least till I find some sunblock." I smiled. "Unless there's some crazy van that comes around with that too."

"No," my mother giggled. "Pharmacy is a Greek word, you know."

"Of course it is, Mom. Of course it is."

I pulled open the front door, letting the sun pour in from the street. Something made me turn one more time, maybe something that came with my father's hat. I caught her watching me go out to settle my father's affairs, as though some darkest of dark truths had descended over her mind once again.

"Stelios," she said, her voice breaking slightly. "Are you all right? I mean, your *health*?"

The word cut through me, slicing deep despite my best efforts. "Mom, of course. Things are great. Why would you even *ask* me that?"

"Bev told me something about doctors."

And Bev didn't know the half of it. "I'm a man and I'm 52, Mom. There *will* be doctors. But everything is fine."

She gazed into my eyes, interrogating me in detail without saying a word. Then she shook herself, driving the last cloud from the horizon.

"I'm your mother, Stelios. I have to worry." She moved close and gave me an extended hug. "It's like your father always said: When you have your health, you have everything."

"Then I guess I have everything," I lied.

5

I made quick work of walking to the center of town. According to Fotis, both church and police station were there—as was the almighty ATM. I tracked it down first, asking first for 100 euros but cancelling that transaction and taking 300 instead. I had no cash left after clothes-shopping Delfinos-style, and I figured there'd be lunch and God knows what else between now and my pickup by Fotis at noon. I'd been told there were limits on daily withdrawls for locals. The ATM knew I was anything but one of those.

Happily, I found the church to be a town landmark, something I could steer by, heading around corners and along winding paths in any direction that kept its blue dome and golden cross in my vision. As promised, Father Michael was waiting for me. I had actually entertained some romantic notion of lighting a candle in front of some icon and saying a brief, confused prayer for my late father. But the priest came up behind me in silence before I could even kneel down.

I had counted on meeting someone old, fat and long of beard, the typical Greek Orthodox priest in any movie that bothered to feature one. Instead, he was young, slender and blessed with a closely trimmed black beard, making him resemble nothing so much as an ordained barista. He had bright, dancing eyes that looked like they'd see humor in life even when everything was hard and cruel, which it seemed to me it often was. Like any solid, American middle manager, Father Michael extended his right hand to take mine and quickly covered both with his left.

"I am happy meet you, Mr. Laros. Michael Koralis. I am truly sorry to hear of your loss."

"Wow," I uttered before editing myself. "All the words and all the grammar intact."

The young priest laughed. "University of Chicago," he said. "English is still the preferred language there."

"I would hope."

Moving before he'd let go of my hand, he led me back through the sacristy. The gold of icons—along with the gold and silver medallions attached to them asking the Creator to deliver a healed knee, a repaired roof, a new husband—faded as we found our way to his small desk topped with papers organized in manila folders.

"You see," he said, offering me a sympathetic grin. "I have your father's file right here."

"Do you have the body here?" I caught myself, realizing what a godawful question that was. "I mean, for the funeral. The burial."

"Heavens no. Bodies are matters for the police, up to a point. Of course, it will be delivered here from there, when it is time." He looked at me. "Respectfully," he added. He opened the top folder and turned through a page or two, apparently reading, though I didn't have a clue what would be recorded there. "So, Mr. Laros—"

"Please, call me Steve."

"Right. Steve. Your father has requested a church funeral within our Orthodox tradition. And your mother has deferred to you to do what is necessary to make that happen. Are you a church-goer back home, Steve?"

"Not really."

"I see."

"But I'm active at the church."

"Your church is a place for you to go and feel Greek."

"Well, yes. You may have a point."

"And I'm not judging. I just wished to know how much I would need to explain to you."

"I'd suggest we start with everything. If we can, we'll whittle it down."

"Amen," Father Michael said affectionately. "So be it."

"Exactly."

The priest turned a couple more pages, finding and frowning at a photocopy or perhaps fact of a document with two signatures at the bottom. "So, your father passed away... three days ago now."

I couldn't tell if his displeasure at that fact was theological or more, well, pragmatic.

"Yes," I said. "That is my understanding."

"I would like the funeral to be Saturday afternoon. For practical considerations."

"Practical con—?"

"You understand." He gave me a moment to do so. It took me an extra-long moment, but finally I nodded."It is Thursday now, and there must be time for your mother and her friends to prepare the *trisagion*—the first viewing, if you wish there to be one, with visiting and small foods and drinks—by tomorrow evening. And of course, there can be no funerals on Sunday."

"Never on Sunday?" I joked.

He laughed. "Exactly, Steve."

Father Michael closed the file folder and threaded his long, narrow, seemingly artistic fingers together to rest on top of it. "As for tone—"

"Yes?"

"As you may know, we Greeks view death as a happy occasion."

"Obviously you're not thinking of my mother."

"I understand. But no. It is happy for the deceased, who can now reside with God in spirit until the end of days, when he or she can be reunited with his body for eternity. That is why we frown on cremation." He paused, looking at me for response or at least guidance. Not getting any, he pressed on. "Or donating of the body to science. You understand, Steve, these are extremely traditional beliefs. Many modern theologians take a, well, looser view, not so black and white."

"I see." I bought a second or two, thinking. "My father didn't say he wanted either of those things, did he?"

"Actually, no. But I figured I would explain. Many from your country grow up without access to such traditions."

I raised my right hand and nodded: guilty as charged.

The priest looked at me sternly, and only after a split-second of feeling condemned to hell for unspecified moral failings did I realize he was taking in my new outfit. "The traditional dress for all funeral events, at home or at the church, is black. I hope you can understand that, Steve. At least at church, we must insist."

"It's okay, Father. I brought a suit. I *wore* it all the way here, in fact."

"Of course," he said, looking relieved. "Before and after the service on Saturday, you should count on neighbors bringing over brandy, coffee and small treats, including the funeral cakes called *paximathia*. Have you tasted those?"

I shook my head.

"They are not to be missed. Then again, they are sweets and it is Greece, after all." A question crossed his mind. "I trust you have met your parents' neighbors."

"All I've met is Fotis." I grinned. "He can bring whatever he wants."

"Yes, certainly," Father Michael said. "He can and he will."

For the next half-hour or so, we talked about Scripture readings. Or rather, Father Michael talked about Scripture readings, and I nodded my approval. Despite my early admission of non-observance, he rattled off passages by the traditional format of chapter and verse, as though assuming I would surely know each. Finally, like a teacher handing out a homework assignment, he gave me two sheets from the bottom on my father's folder and told me I'd need to get them signed by the police chief and then return them with the "appropriate paperwork." "So," Father Michael said, "We are on for Saturday."

"I gather that we are. I appreciate your help with all this. Sadly, I don't know most of these traditions. And I don't believe my mother does, either. We are Greek but we both grew up in America."

"I know your country very well," he breathed out with deliberation, as though to say, "May the Lord help you with *that*." I took my homework and walked through the church, deciding I didn't exactly feel like lighting a candle or saying a prayer anymore.

6

The sunlight was blinding as the door swung open and I stood there stunned, my eyes shut tight for a painful moment against it. As they adjusted—*slowly, slowly*, as Fotis would say—I spotted an official-looking square building halfway down a block that ran off west from the square. The blue-and-white Greek flag flew from a staff above the door, *not* the circle of yellow stars on a blue background used by the European Union. The plaque to the right of the charmless glass door set amid older white plaster assured me my ID of the Delfinos police station was correct.

Colonel Minos Petrakis, with icy military bearing and apparently the only human being inside the station, was waiting for me. Waiting was apparently what people did on Delfinos.

Petrakis, who seemed in his mid-40s, had a thick mop of bushy, black hair and a mustache that was even thicker and bushier, threatening to overrun all significant territory between his large ears. In the States, when we say someone is about to bust out of his clothes, we typically mean the person is fat. In the case of Petrakis, and indeed of many men on hard-living, hard-laboring Delfinos, we mean his muscles were taking over. You knew the chief of police worked out. A lot.

"You Laros," he said more than asked, glancing up from a log book of ruled pages splayed open atop a chest-high counter. "You will come with me."

I followed Petrakis around the end of the counter, through a doorway and up to the building's second floor by way of a stairway edged by peeling green paint. Again, I caught myself wondering about the financial crisis. Had this man had employees before? Deputies, secretaries? Probably? Had these stairs been painted before? Certainly. So many things had ground to a halt in Greece when the money ran out, when the money masters of Europe started turning off the spigot, and only a handful of them were visible unless you walked through a door and climbed up some stairs.

Petrakis settled behind a gray metal desk and retrieved an open pack of cigarettes from the top drawer. Starting to grab one for himself, he stopped them offered the pack to me. I declined with a hand and a meager effort at a smile. He shrugged, took out a cigarette and lit it with a small plastic lighter. Three deep drags came in quick succession followed by a long exhale that made the room look like fog had rolled in. Petrakis stepped over to the window, tapped around the edges of the frame and then pushed the thing open.

"Americans," he said. I could pick out no expression I could name. "You make things difficult."

The chief rocked his metal chair back against the wall, leaning precariously as he looked at me and smoked his cigarette in silence. I'm not sure why, but I got so uncomfortable with this treatment that I suddenly waved the two sheets from Father Michael in his direction and stretched forward from my chair to set them on the edge of his desk. From the way I felt, I was handing over my signed confession.

He gestured waved me back into inaction, closed his eyes as he enjoyed one last deep puff, then crushed the cigarette against the side of his desk, letting the butt drop to the floor. It had plenty of company.

"Your father," he said. "We have his body."

I took a moment to accept both the content and style of that announcement. "Yes," I said, trying to keep my gaze matched to his. "So I've been told."

"Typically, we do not keep them so long."

"I'm sorry. I didn't know. It took me this long to—"

"Yes, to get here from America."

"And my mother waited for me."

"America," he said dismissively. And I understood. A Greek widow would have delivered her husband's body to church by lunchtime, then brought in a crop of olives in baskets on her donkey by dark. She wouldn't even need to change her clothes, since she probably was dressed in black anyway, like her mother before her.

"There are," Petrakis said, "complications."

"Surely everything is clear? My father suffered a heart attack."

"Yes, that is what I am told. But—"

"But?"

"Mr. Laros, let me explain one small thing to you. Delfinos is not an important island. Some might say that, by being here, I make myself not an important man." He shrugged. "That does not interest me, what some might say. Finding the truth about things—now *that* interests me."

"What are you saying?"

"There is no foul play suspected. A man his age can have a heart attack and die. It happens all the time."

"Then—"

"No, Mr. Laros, our problem is paperwork."

"I understand. We must have a death certificate. I was told there is a fee, and I am prepared—"

"Death certificate? No sir, that is *easy*. That is the papers you brought for my signature. *That* can be done." His dark eyes drilled into me. "Have you brought from your Houston, Texas, your father's *birth* certificate?"

For a long moment, I didn't think I'd heard him right. Of course I had not brought a birth certificate for my father. Nor had anybody along the way suggested I might need one.

"To show what?" I asked, my exasperation pouring out. "To show that he was *born*? That he was alive? My father was here, Colonel, and he lived. And people saw him living."

Petrakis let his chair rock forward, settling his rough hands in a mound on his desk. "Yes, that is clear," he said. "That has no question. But we need one certificate to set, officially, beside the other."

"I'm sorry. But I've never heard of such a thing."

"Perhaps, Mr. Laros, you are not Greek enough." He didn't laugh, so I worked not to. "You do not know how important it is to us that such things are organized. For centuries, it was only the parish priest who knew anything, who wrote anything down—who *could* write anything down. But now, birth certificates must be filed with death certificates. So we can be certain who died. Otherwise, it could be anyone."

"I can identify the body."

"And with my respect, you could be lying."

It was all I could do not to fling my hands in the air. Then, maybe, I *would* be Greek enough. And then, for all the new and nonsensical information coming at me across that gray metal desk, even newer information grabbed onto the edge of my brain.

"Colonel," I said, "how much are we actually talking about here?"

"Administration. It is always necessary."

"And exactly what do you require?"

"The fee for the death certificate from my office, of course, which is one-hundred euros. And then the fee for researching your father's birth certificate in Houston, Texas."

"And how much is that?"

"It is very time-consuming process, Mr. Laros. That is *two* hundred euros."

"If I pay you now—I mean, the *fees* for both those things—you will have the body delivered to the church, so we can bury my father on Saturday?"

"Now *that*," he said, but stopped himself and forced a grin. "Yes, it will be done."

As Colonel Petrakis looked on, I retrieved my wallet from the back pocket of my shorts and counted out the six fifty-euro notes I had gotten from the ATM. He took them from me, folded them together along the center and placed them in his top drawer. Almost immediately, Petrakis excused himself, saying he had to make an important phone call, and that I could easily find my way downstairs and out. He, of course, was right. Yet it suddenly struck me, producing a bitter laugh that was louder than I wished, that I was penniless once again. I pushed open the glass door and stepped onto the sidewalk that led back to the square.

What happened next happened fast, and to this day I can't define how much I remember of the next thirty seconds versus how much I figured out later and pressed backward into my memory.

I spotted Fotis in his taxi at the corner and I saw a middle-aged woman walking a dog across the street and I felt the midday sunshine warming my face through the trim of my father's white hat. My ears filled with a buzzing that quickly became a whining that quickly became a roar. The woman screamed, grabbed her dog and ran against the plaster wall. I spun, two steps too late, to see a muscular shirtless man with a crewcut steering a motorcycle right at me, a woman with long blonde hair with her arms snug around his waist and her mouth open wide in laughter. As the bike roared past, I felt a handlebar slam into my chest like an artillery shell, and suddenly I was falling backward with the stones of the street coming up to meet me. I lost consciousness, only for a moment, since I also heard the man on the bike blaze off trailing a string of shouted curses in his wake.

Lying on the stones, I saw Fotis' face floating above me, and then the woman's face next to his, and then the form of Colonel Petrakis looking down from his second-floor window.

"Son of a bitch," I said, feeling my words cut off by blood filling my mouth. "Son of a bitch—"

"You okay," Fotis said, trying to calm me. I'm not so sure I wanted to be calmed.

"God knows what that stupid son of a bitch called me. I bet it was choice." I almost choked on my laugh. "But I fooled him, right? I don't understand any Greek."

I saw Fotis turn to glance up the road, to the place where the white walls opened into the square. Then he let his attention work its way back to me. And when he spoke, his voice was filled with resignation. "That, my friend, *was not* Greek."

7

"No, damn it, I want to go see it," I insisted, taking an anxious gulp of the *tsipouro* Fotis had ordered for me, along with one for himself, at the only open watering hole down by the port. It burned as it descended into me.

"We don't have to go," said Fotis. "We can sit here and get drunk. Is how you say—*roaring* drunk?"

"Yes, we say that. But I'll be fine."

I was telling something like the truth. That all-too-familiar band of—what, pain? discomfort?—that tightened around my chest and felt like it was pushing my heart out through my mouth had eased. Yes, the one that generally came on weekends when the only medical choice was the ER, and I'd been avoiding that. There was, by tradition now, the Monday morning EKG with my doctor, who assured me everything looked fine.

"I'm glad I wasn't having a heart attack," I'd told him after the first time.

"Me too, really."

"What do you mean?"

"If you had, you'd be dead by now."

Fotis and I were sitting outside, and the sun was warming the sand in a way that radiated heat in our direction. I looked at the blue-green water of the harbor, clear since no fishing boat or ferry was plowing it up, and I actually wanted to go for a swim. Right here, right now. In February. I made a note to self, a memo from my old, corporate life: go swimming in February.

The strip of hotels along the curve of the beach looked less foreboding now that they had when I arrived in the rain. But then again, so did most things in the bright sunlight. "I think maybe," Fotis said, "we should go another day."

"No!" I slammed the shot glass full of clear liquid on the table. I hadn't planned to, and I wondered if the overweight bearded barkeep inside had heard. Then again, I didn't care. "Look Fotis, I'm sorry. I came all this way to help my mother with my father's affairs. And he died working on this damn house he never told me much of anything about. There's no reason you shouldn't take me there."

He shrugged. Fotis was the master, I was learning, of the world's most versatile shrug. Then he lifted his glass, clinked it to mine where it rested on the table and downed the rest of his tsipouro. I did the same.

I followed him along the beach about a hundred yards—toward where he was "staying," he said, and I determined to ask him what that meant later since I knew he had a house in Chora—and found myself pretending to help him push a 16-foot skiff into water deep enough to lower the outboard motor. His other boat was larger, he explained, but his son had that one out fishing today. Trying to bring in some money, Fotis said, smiling sadly.

Once the outboard had settled into a consistent low roar, Fotis steered us out of the harbor past the promontory that had turned away some of the weather last night, hung a left and kept a respectful distance from the rocky shoreline as we headed north. The sea was choppy and I asked, trying to sound nautical after a couple Caribbean vacations, whether this was the island's windward side.

"It depends," he said. We left the ancient mariner talk at that.

Of course, the island was lovely. This was something of a shock. When you grow up hearing only of "that goddamn rock," you never quite understand (especially if you live in flat, hot, humid, green Houston) how breathtaking a *rock* can be. Wickedly sharp rocks pointed upward from pools of the blue, green and sometimes violet sea, having no problem showing how far they reached down. And then, past them, the island itself rose—gray, silver and pink stone with a thousand dried rivers carved by centuries of rainwater, sometimes the sheerest cliff for hundreds of feet, till it revealed only a suggestion of Chora along the top. Some houses had windows that opened onto the drop. Beginning where we were, there was incredible sea, incredible rock, incredible houses and incredible sky. My heart didn't know what to make of it all, except that I realized the tightness that often resided there had disappeared completely.

"Is good?" Fotis said, I thought as a question.

"Yes."

"No, the town. High." He pointed up the smooth face of rock.

"Yes, the town is high."

"No climb."

"Well, that's for sure. I'm a flatlander anyway. You know—*flatlander*?"

He nodded. "But no, they built up there. Centuries ago. Is good for people. Very *bad* for pirates on sea."

Perhaps twenty minutes into our journey, Fotis reached forward and tapped me on the back. I might have had my eyes closed, just enjoying the wind stinging my face. He was pointing up onto a rock-strewn hillside.

"See," he shouted above the motor. "The road."

"Okay?"

"The road to your father's."

"Ah."

"It is broken, but where you cannot see. And the church is not used anymore, so no one fix road."

"Church?"

"Agios Nikolaos. There!"

We edged around a bend in the island's stark contour, revealing a deep crease running up the mountainside. The town was two or more miles behind us by now, and this was country for goats and not much else. Goats or otherwise, at some point the islanders had climbed along this road to pray. To baptize their babies. To bury their dead.

The church, from where we were on the water, was little more than a blockish white building with a blockish white bell tower, with a sky-blue dome atop that, a gold cross above that, and a very large sky above that. It struck me as little more than a shrine like the ones we'd passed on the road from the harbor. But considering the distances and angles involved, I figured it was bigger than that. Plus, it had a saint's name. Shrines didn't usually have names—just an icon, a candle and occasional applications of fresh flowers.

"Very old," Fotis shouted. "I remember. The old ones talked about. Processions for Easter, many things. No more."

Had he spoken better English, Fotis could have said what he meant a thousand other, more eloquent ways. But the simple two-word statement "No more" came at me like the saddest thing I'd ever heard. Coming to Delfinos for the reason I was here, a lot of things about my life sounded too much like "no more."

Without a word, Fotis throttled down. The boat grunted into slow progress, feeling first the roll of our own wake and then the choppy seas. We passed a point jutting outward from the land and edged into a broad, deep lagoon, protected and calm, with what looked like a goat trail all the way up to the church. Something told me that was the last gasp of the road that came over the mountaintop and no longer made it down to this lagoon.

There was a small, brown sand beach at the center, with a weathered, sometimes crumbling concrete bulkhead following the shoreline to the left in front of a long, narrow concrete-block building. The building had a string of windows, but only two still showed any broken pieces of glass. The bulkhead ended in what appeared to be a dock, or what could be a dock: a straight edge out in deeper water, with rusty iron rings for tying up. Fotis pointed our boat toward that, though by this time all my attention was elsewhere.

On the far side of the lagoon, separated from what seemed the industrial area around the building, there was a whitewashed plaster wall looking out from the mountainside to the sea. A quirky, zig-zag of stone steps led down to the beach, and a rougher switchback led upward along terraced agricultural land. The white wall, as we moved closer to the dock, took on another corner, and then some suggestion of a roof. The roof was still open, though, merely dark beams in some places, attached in some *ad hoc* way to a back wall that—mostly—wasn't there.

As soon as Fotis tied us up, it was all I could do not to run. And as soon I noticed he wasn't following, I did break into a sprint. I can't explain my excitement, the heart-in-my-throat feeling that something among these rocks would explain something, perhaps would explain everything. Passing the building on its raised concrete slab, I jumped down onto the sand and raced to the start of the trail. By the time I started up the mountain, the white-hot burning in my throat reminded me that I was no longer young, and anything but the picture of health.

As usual, I vowed to go to the gym more often. As I stood in the wind heaving painfully, I saw that Fotis had settled on an edge of cracked wall by the industrial building and lit himself a cigarette. He, of course, wasn't heaving at all.

He knew I needed to be alone.

Especially now that my legs couldn't move.

I was standing at the start of a broad paved veranda in front of the house, a collection of flat stones gathered together by concrete. There before me was what I realized must be Dad's portable cement mixer—only a dad who moved home to Greece should even *own* a cement mixer!—and there, as described, was the pile of powder and small rocks he'd been stirring, and there was his shovel, lying abandoned where it presumably fell. No way to ease into it now. I was standing by accident, before going anyplace else, exactly where my father had died.

I hadn't expected this—though what, really, could or should I have expected? I hadn't prepared myself for the vision of him lying there, no doubt in his work clothes and heavy work boots, the former CEO of one of America's highest-grossing foodservice corporations. I mean, was he happy? Was he sad? Did he feel good about his life? Or did he simply... *die?* Like you're in a room without windows and somebody's unseen hand turns off the lights? At some point in all of this, I forgot to notice if I was asking about him, or about me.

I drew in a ragged mouthful of warm air and moved along the outer edge of the veranda. In some ways, this was close enough. I could see the empty rooms inside the house, picking out the kitchen and bathroom by the plumbing sprouting like weeds from the slab. There was a bathtub connected to nothing, floating in the middle of an open space, covered with brown paper held on by tape, and a commode in much the same condition. I was fascinated that the house had no roof, though I suppose my father had his reasons for doing things in the order he did them. He always had.

The house could wait till next time, I decided. At some point Fotis had told me that the property included the mountainside, almost all the way up to Agios Nikolaos, and I wondered what that was about. Other than making sure there were no neighbors, the ground here appeared more rough and unforgiving than anything else. The water lines on the rock seemed from rain that fell a geologic age ago.

The path showed signs that goats lived in the neighborhood, or at least knew my father's land as a terrific place to relieve themselves. At first I stepped carefully but, after twenty or thirty feet of difficult climbing, that seemed way more trouble than it was worth. Yes, it turned out, there were rough, unkempt terraces sweeping across the trail's incline, but they were covered with broken sticks and stones. The more I looked, and the more I climbed, the more I realized the sticks were what was left of long-dead vines.

This was unexpected, mostly since my father had never mentioned any such thing. Delfinos did turn out a small amount of wine, I knew, but generally only for local consumption and surely with quality to match. Winemaking, after all, was what gave us *tsipouro* as its inflammatory distilled next generation.

It took nearly half an hour, with stops for breathing, to reach that highest terrace on the mountain, just below the Church of Agios Nikolaos. I must have been looking at my feet and gasping for air, waiting for my dizziness to pass, for I clearly remember the moment I looked up. There, spread before me was one of God's loveliest things—a vineyard—undeniably abandoned and forgotten, but a vineyard all the same. And there was the broad curve of the beach with its lagoon, the white plaster house now to my left and the industrial building with the concrete dock to my right. Raising my gaze up and out from the brown sand, I saw only the sea, stretching until it disappeared into the sky.

Without at all intending to, I made Fotis wait a long time for me to come down from my father's mountain. Still, if you're a Greek man with a full pack of cigarettes and waiting is your only fulltime job, time doesn't really matter much.

8

We sat on the dock without speaking, me cross-legged on the concrete staring at my threaded fingers. And when Fotis broke the silence, it wasn't to ask me what I'd seen or how I felt or what I might want to do about any of those things. He started telling me about his family.

"My wife is happy now," he said, waiting, as though I had anything to add.

"That's good," I finally mumbled.

"She has my son—*our* son—home from Athens. She has the daughter she always wanted—his wife. And she has their baby to take care of. Like I said—everything, my friend."

"Were you," I struggled, "ready for so *much* family."

He laughed. "Not in any way. We knew things were bad. We saw the news. We heard what the big bosses in Europe were saying. About us. Nasty things, you know?"

I nodded, but I didn't know. Obviously I'd been reading the profit-and-loss reports that crossed my desk at LRG, not the latest news from the European Union.

"We were just some crazy goddamn Greeks," he said. "Lazy. Corrupt. Careless. Stupid. We need to be taught a lesson, to be punished."

I let myself grin and looked at him. He shrugged. "Well, okay. We *didn't* do such a good job. And then one day my wife gets call on the phone. And my computer genius says the big bosses in Germany are forcing the government to cut—austerity, they always call it, yes? My son's job is cut. His whole *building* is cut. And he says we should meet him, his wife and his baby at the dock." Fotis smiled. "Just like I met you. Except it was the day. And it was not raining. I am sorry for the not-so-nice welcome, my friend."

"Not your fault. Probably." I laughed to underline the point.

"So now I live at the boathouse."

"Boathouse? Like on your boat?"

"No, no. It's just a little house by the boat. By the port."

"Oh, where we *got* this boat."

"Exactly."

"Not enough beds. You know?" Fotis examined the glowing orange tip of his cigarette, then looked at me. "Besides, I'm old man. I'm just as happy having trouble sleeping here as having trouble sleeping there. Is same."

"Hey, at least you're happy."

"Happy?" He crushed his cigarette against the dock. "Did I say happy? We are *men*, Stelios. The women care about everything—what we eat, how much we drink, the way we talk, how much money we make, who we dance with. But if I were you, I think maybe you should not wait for them to care if we are happy."

Easy as that, on that dock and definitely on that note, I found myself telling Fotis about my life in Houston.

"Beverly and I have been married for seven years. Or, I guess, eight next month."

"One daughter," he filled in, apparently fearing I'd said all I was going to.

"Yes, Chloe. She is now fourteen. So yes, she was born during Bev's first marriage, what she likes to call her 'practice round.'"

"For *what,* please, are you practicing?"

"Excellent question, Fotis. Except she would tell you she was all the usual things back then—young, stupid, in love with love."

"Ah," he said with a theatrical sigh, "the most dangerous love of all."

"Exactly. She got married, got pregnant, got divorced. Do you know the word 'trifecta'?"

Fotis shook his head. It suddenly seemed too much effort to explain.

"By then, Bev was working as a pilates instructor at a fitness center, and she fell hard for the club's general manager. I've seen this guy, and one thing I can tell you is: He sure was *fit*. Still is, I suppose. They got married and did okay, as long as we define okay as equal parts arguments and vodka."

"I can picture, yes I can," he said.

"That didn't last, thank goodness. As GM, the guy fired her and they filed for *their* divorce. Meanwhile, Beverly started teaching at a different gym where, by chance, one slightly overweight restaurant executive fearing hair loss, and approximately everything else, was starting to attend pilates classes. He liked pilates, this executive, he thought. He was attending to appease—you know *appease*?" Fotis nodded. "To *appease* a pretty woman friend he was dating casually. I mean, *very* casually." I thought about my story, trying to remember if I'd ever told it before, other than when she and I told it together, the way couples do. And that was different. "So the executive thinks he really likes pilates. Until he realizes he really only likes the pilates instructor. He stops going to class, and she starts meeting him for coffee in the morning or wine at night. Or both."

"Is same."

I wasn't sure it was, but it felt like the best thing I could hear him say. "I had never been married, you see. For every reason and no reason. Just because. I was pretty busy. And in my business, if you can keep yourself from marrying one or more hostesses, you probably aren't marrying anybody." That was too inside-joke for Fotis. To his credit, he was happy when I forged ahead. "Beverly and I got married. Chloe got a new stepdad in a bigger, better house—it's the Houston way. And I got a beautiful life. I mean, wife."

"Maybe life too?"

"For a while. It hurts, though." I stood up and walked to the edge of the dock, the clear water deep beneath my feet. "It hurts when you wake up one morning, one normal-everyday morning, with everything the world says you need, and realize you are only somebody's means to an end."

"Money?"

"Well, partly, maybe. But no, I don't think so. Everything. Bev got a new last name, a new house, a new wardrobe, a new set of reasons to wear it, a new group of much better-dressed friends who meet for lunch." I turned toward Fotis. "I don't even think these are bad things, you know. And I certainly took pleasure in providing them. But it's that damned *morning*. The day before, you feel proud and successful and loved. The day after you feel like—"

"*Shit*, maybe?"

I laughed out loud. "Yeah, more or less." I took a couple steps closer but didn't like talking down, so I dropped to one knee. "Fotis, did my mother or my father tell you Bev and I are separated?"

He shook his head, and I suspect he was telling me the truth. This probably wasn't news my parents would want spread around, even six-thousand miles from the already-busy gossips of River Oaks.

"It's nothing *legal*—yet. My mother is convinced all will be well, mostly because that's what all *has* to be. My father didn't say anything at all, except for shaking his head in what I think was disgust." Disgust was a look any son of George Laros knew well. "Bev and I have both talked to lawyers, who have now talked to each other."

"Sounds bad," Fotis said.

"It is. And we've been to therapists and counselors, separately. I tried to get her to come see mine, who said he thought he could help us together. And you know what she told me? She said, 'You don't think I'm gonna talk to *your* guy, do you?'" I shrugged. "So then she said I should go and talk with *her* therapist, who apparently was telling her the same thing."

I felt like an idiot all of a sudden, remembering, but it was hard to back away from the truth now. "Of course, I said exactly what you'd expect. 'You don't think I'm gonna talk to *yours*, do you?' So we ended up not talking together to either. Or anybody. Or, least of all, to each other. And then she told me I had to move out of the house."

"Well," Fotis said, his jaw moving as he tried hard to think of something. Then he found it. "I hope that somewhere you have a boathouse."

We laughed awkwardly for a moment, especially the one of us who had no boathouse. He smoked another cigarette as I fumbled around in my own thoughts. And then he struggled to his feet, dusting the dirt from the dock off his jeans. Fotis glanced around the horizon, as though expecting an approaching storm, but the sky remained as blue as it had been when we set out from the harbor.

"Come on," he said. "There is someplace I want you to see."

After we'd spent forty-five minutes looping around the wild, windswept northern end of Delfinos, turning down along the west coast and covering the entire length of what struck me as the world's least expected vision, I shouted to Fotis above the roar of the outboard motor.

"I thought you Greeks lost all your *money!*"

Instead of shouting back, Fotis shut down the engine and sat in silence for a moment, letting our ears get used to the sounds of the sea.

"We did," he said. "But *they* didn't."

We were drifting perhaps half a mile off the shore, both of us looking back and me almost speechless. There was a white sand beach that stretched hundreds of yards in increments, each marked off by a fence or wall. Within each parcel, a white stone resort gathered every ounce of attention, three and sometimes four stories, hundreds upon hundreds of guest rooms with balconies facing the sea. On the beach there were restaurants and bars under thatched roofs, the faintest notion of music reaching us where we drifted, and there were water sports everywhere, from kayaking to parasailing and zip lining between outbreaks of rock. It was February in Europe, and the beaches were packed with people in very small swimsuits.

"Now that," I said when I finally stumbled onto a few words, "is something completely different."

"Yes," was all Fotis said.

It was strange, coming to this island—"that goddamn rock"—and then finding somebody's idea of Miami Beach by way of Atlantic City by way of Montego Bay. Nothing about the development struck me as Greek, and it surprised me how much that simple fact bothered me. What did I care? I fired back at myself. What did it matter? And most of all, who was I to feel something about somebody else's success. Hell, if this kept up, *we'd* probably be putting a restaurant here someday.

"I don't understand, Fotis. What's this all about?"

"They came here," he said, mostly staring at his knees, his hand tightly gripping the rudder. "One, now maybe two years ago. They came from Cyprus, many of them. It had been good there, but then it changed. The European bosses made the banks play by different rules, tougher rules. People lost money there. A lot of money."

"You mean, no bailout."

"No bailout. Some banks close, I mean just *close.* No insurance. So they decide not to *join* an island, like they did there, on Cyprus. They decided to *build* one."

"*Who*, Fotis? The Cyprus people?"

"No, my friend." He raised his eyes to meet mine. "The goddamn Russians."

I heard the wind in my ears and felt the lapping of waves against the boat, and I wondered for a second if I'd ever know enough about any of the things that mattered on Delfinos to understand.

"Russian money?"

"Yes. Russian money. And Russian tourists. And Russian music. And Russian language. And now—Greek furs sold to Russians."

I laughed because I thought Fotis was joking. "Hey, why not. Furs over your bikini, miss? The perfect outfit for your beach vacation."

"It's true. I show you."

"What? Furs?"

"Yes sir. And funny thing. We used to make furs in Greece, up north, and send them to Russia for the cheap selling. Now we get the pelts—you know, the skins—from the Polish, make the coats here, and then sell them to the goddamn Russians who come to us. Is crazy, I tell you. But money. Is all money, you know." He looked at me again, as though to explain the sublimely obvious. "We *need* their money."

I had heard of such things, maybe had read an article once, or a spy thriller, about Russians on the French Riviera or someplace. Russian *mafiya*. Russian oligarchs. Russian dirty money in search of a laundromat. But that was on the French Riviera. I didn't expect it in my father's backyard on Delfinos. I barely knew my father *had* a backyard.

The dark thoughts I was having needed a devil's advocate. And as long as I had Fotis to grill, I decided to be my own.

"So these guys come here—"

"Russians."

"Yes, Russians. And they bring money to spend. Maybe to invest. To put in the bank."

"Yes. For a while."

"Okay. They build these resorts at a time nobody here can build so much as an outhouse." I looked to see if Fotis knew the word, but he was following me whether he knew the word or not. "They spend money, they hire people maybe. *Greek* people?" Fotis nodded. "They bring jobs. At least for a while, right?"

"But," he said, "they're goddamn Russians. They don't give up, they don't give back, and they maybe never leave. And then our island is *their* island."

As the minutes passed and the sun began its slow descent toward the sea, Fotis answered my questions. The Russians could come because millions carried residence permits from the EU—they could travel freely throughout the Union. Many who came here already knew the ropes, having done much the same on Cyprus before the austerity measures. They had lost there, so they arranged to win here, to buy more real estate and more businesses, to control their destiny. A few brought their yachts, but most were second-tier bankers and lawyers, who handled the money for the big boys. And the tourists—the small figures of men and women we could see in the distance frolicking in these warm waters—they came here to buy furs.

"It's a deal," Fotis said. "They get their vacation almost free—one week or two weeks, sometimes more—as long as they agree to buy a fur. And the furs are cheaper here too, of course. Cheaper than in Russia. Everybody is happy. Everybody wins. It is all about the deal."

In my own career, I'd seen that when everybody wins, the deals tend to get done. But this was something new to me, something I obviously couldn't quite get my head around. For the first time in my life I found myself wondering: What if "everybody" doesn't actually include *everybody?*

Eventually, I ran out of questions, or at least mental energy. Fotis pulled the cord and the motor kicked to deafening life, and we headed in toward shore. There were large boats anchored just off the leach—small yachts, but large boats—and I could see topless, blonde women sunning themselves on several sleek decks. Cutting back on the engine, Fotis steered us safely past a cluster of bathers to a floating dock that helped mark the end of one resort and the start of another. After all I'd just learned, I was relieved that the guy who agreed to watch the boat for Fotis answered him in Greek.

As I followed Fotis up from the beach, music danced across the sun-struck open air. Music from different bars and cafes, like the Greek *bouzoukia* I knew from our festivals, but different. *Balalaika*, I think it was called. Like, *Doctor Zhivago*? It sounded tinny and mildly exotic, perhaps romantic. Especially the male crooners I heard exuding sex, and the females all loss and longing. It was sad music, I felt, trying to play soundtrack to an unrelentingly happy place.

The beach bars were full, with men in skimpy, thong-like swimsuits chatting up women wearing their version of the same. I spotted ouzo being poured, the occasional glass of white wine. But most of the revelers drank large schooners of beer. *Baltika,* according to the same sort of promotional flags that bars back in Texas might fly for Shiner or Bud Light. The language behind the laughter was impenetrable.

"Greek belly," Fotis snuffed, and I wasn't sure I heard him right.

"What?"

He nodded into a café beneath a bright red awning, where people feasted on platters of thick, red-tinged sausages with mounds of fried potatoes and dark, dense slabs of bread. "*Greek belly*. That what my tailor friends call it. These people come here. They eat and drink too much, and then they need the new clothes." This obviously gave Fotis a modicum of pleasure. "My friends, they call it 'Greek belly,' and they have to measure for it."

Fotis quickened his steps as we passed alongside the hotel itself, where all the signage was in Russian Cyrllic rather than Greek, following a sandy path between grass that led us to the road.

First off, I had a terrible flashback. As the sounds had announced before any sight, the road was abuzz with motorcycles cutting in and out among the cars. Any one of them could have been the guy who'd hit me, since all of them looked pretty much the same. There seemed an unlimited supply of blondes to hop behind each rider. The entire road, from one end of this new, invented beachfront town to the other, was retail. I stopped counting fur boutiques at thirty, and while I couldn't understand the deals being screamed from every window, they followed the international formula of numbers slashed and words with multiple exclamation points.

"Want some coffee?" Fotis asked.

"No," I answered without thinking. "What I really want to do is leave."

He laughed. "Good. You have learned well." He looked at me with a devilish grin. "Want some Rassol?"

"Some what?"

"Rassol." He nodded to a kiosk laden with cans than filled one corner so completely that you had to step out into the street to get past it. "To me and you, it is pickle juice. They drink it for their goddamn Russian hangovers."

Based on what I was seeing, there was about to be a worldwide shortage of Rassol.

Finally, we turned and headed back toward the boat. To my surprise, Fotis said he had to leave me here—"Anyplace but here," I wanted to shout, but didn't—and he would lead me to the bus stop for Chora. The bus was only two euros, he said, and only about three kilometers.

"You're kidding me," I said, my mood darkening. "This is only three kilometers from our town?"

"Exactly."

"That does not make me happy."

"I know. *We* are not happy. But really, is there anything we can do?"

"There needs to be." We'd pulled up at the bus stop, standing beneath the sign, and I could tell Fotis needed to be somewhere. But I couldn't stop myself. I felt my speech getting faster and higher, beyond my control. "For Christ's sake, we can't let Chora become like—like *this* shit!"

Fotis matched my over-the-top, anxious tone with flat, dead words, as though he were narrating a point of history that had been decided centuries ago. "Remember all the pirates, my friend. They came here to take what we had back then. And they are *still* coming here."

There was something cleansing, purifying even, about topping the first hill up from the beach on the minibus back into town. Fotis had given the driver instructions—amazingly long and detailed instructions, it seemed to me—on where to drop me, since he insisted I see something on the western edge. The driver looked at me, scanned me up and down in the jump seat behind him by the sliding door. All I could do was smile.

"See now," Fotis said, slowly pulling the door closed. "And we talk."

There was only one line of hills, though they were enough to obliterate even the suggestion of what was going on along the water. Just rock and dirt and low-slung vegetation. It was a windy place, I decided, and using a phrase I'd picked up as a Texan, everything learned young to *hunker down*.

Indeed, wasn't that what I should do? Everywhere you went in this world, bad stuff was happening. I mean, everywhere. Only the color of the skin, sound of the language and denomination of the currency changed. It was best to find your way within that, I think that's what my father taught, not by word but by deed. Work hard, play by the rules, take care of your family—there were simple rules a man could live by. And if he lived by them, he could have a good life. Yet was it really what I'd seen that had upset me so much, or the fact of seeing it after visiting my father's final dream?

I came out of my thoughts abruptly. The driver was speaking impatiently. And since I was the only passenger on the minibus, he was speaking impatiently to me. I smiled, slapped the side of my head to say something like "silly me," then grunted as I wrenched open the door. The minibus sped off, raising dust, as soon as my feet hit the ground.

"Bye," I said sarcastically. "Thanks for the ride."

It was only then I realized I hadn't paid the driver. And it was only then that I realized I didn't have any more euros.

I stood on the road in what seemed a plain. The town started perhaps a hundred yards from me now and, as Fotis promised, I could see the church bell tower on the main square. I could steer toward that when the time came. Yet with the thought that I was here to see something, I wasn't the least bit certain what I was here to see.

In the dust not far from the road, however, there was a deep grinding noise, the kind of huffing and grunting that might have belonged to dinosaurs had any of those still been around. No, I realized, these were mechanical behemoths. There was a low brick wall around what seemed a huge piece of land, stopping across a track with a silver chain across it. The chain, though, hung almost to the ground, which I decided was the international symbol for "Come on in." I stepped over it and, covering my mouth with my hand, pressed deeper into the clouds of dust.

The flat, smooth surface was long, maybe more than two football fields, but relatively narrow. It might have been a road, but there was no need for such a road on Delfinos, possibly ever. What it was, I realized suddenly, was a landing strip.

A sign I spotted ahead might have confirmed my guess. But as I feared with each step I took closer to it, it refused to give me any information. The sign held a lot of words, every single one of them in Russian.

Choking up moist dirt, I made my way back to the road and then toward the entrance to town. This was obviously a newer section of Chora—which in Greece might mean 17th century—since there was no wall around what was here or the remnants of a gate through the wall. There was simply the start of a gradual incline that got tighter as housing density increased, giving me small, low-lying houses that might hold one person comfortably but may well have held four. Many of the houses were clearly abandoned, but hardly all. Some front doors were open, with barely a colorful hanging bedsheet to keep out flies, and as the afternoon blurred into evening, cooking smells wafted out. Remembering the dishes Irini had served me what seemed a bizarre lifetime ago, it was all I could do not to stop and try to wrangle an invitation.

As I walked, an observation took hold. Though each house was separate, all were also connected, with some version of a shared wall, running unbroken the entire length of both sides of what was now a village street. The strip ran uphill to a small square with a waterless fountain at its center. I took note of this fact casually, but it meant nothing to me at the time.

Mostly I thought about dinner, wondering if I could find Irini's again. The cooking smells were getting to me. Failing that, though, it felt weird to do so for the first time in years, I wondered what, if anything, my mother had on the stove. I tried to guess if she was now serving Greek food or still dishing up some rendition of Texas food, like chili or enchiladas or chicken fried steak, all things we served in one or more of our LRG concepts. Since we first found success in Lubbock with such dishes, you'd better believe they retained a place of honor.

As it turned out, my mother wasn't cooking anything. The lights were out in her apartment when I let myself in—the door had been closed but not locked—and there was no sound of anybody moving around. I went to the door of my parents' bedroom, now my mother's bedroom, and it was locked, so I knocked. Softy the first time, then again a little louder.

"Mom." My own voice sounded strange to me. "Mom, are you all right?"

Listening closely, I heard some rustling of bedclothes and then some breathing, maybe the start of a slurred word. I was scared for my mother suddenly, and started glancing around for ways to get past the lock. But then, her words still muffled, she answered.

"Steve. I'm… I'm asleep."

And then it hit me. She'd taken more of the doctor's medication. It was barely—I checked my watch—barely 7, and she was in bed fast asleep. It would be cruel to wake her up, just to ask if she was okay. And I certainly wasn't going to ask her to cook dinner. No, that's why God created restaurants. My job was to track one down, by way of the ATM on the square.

"Love you, Mom," I said loud enough for her to hear, but I really doubted she heard. Then I stepped out onto the street and pulled the front door shut behind me.

It was dark by this point, well past winter sunset. The same narrow, twisting streets I'd taken to the square this morning, by way of the church and the police station, looked strange in the gas lamplight, and full of purple and ebony shadows. I couldn't see the bell tower, but I felt confident I remembered the way. There were no signs, no arrows and no names on any street.

I took three turns that felt right and then one that didn't, stopping to think about it and reluctantly turning back. There was the fork where I'd gone right, and I tried going left instead. But after the equivalent of a couple blocks, that didn't look right either. There was no one on any street to ask—no one, that is, until a door opened ahead of me and the familiar form of a woman stepped outside, turning her back to me so she could lock the door with a key. It was the woman from the ferry, I realized. Instinctively (though what was behind this instinct I'll never understand), I drew back into a shadowy crease between two buildings and waited.

Easing my face around the corner after a moment, I caught her moving away from me up the street. I was committed now, as awkward or stupid or ashamed as that made me feel. I would follow her. The woman had disappeared on me once, in the rain in the middle or the night at the harbor. She would not, I vowed to no one in particular, disappear on me again.

I kept a safe distance as she took turn after turn, stopping only long enough to check out the door she'd locked: DELFINOS EXCURSIONS/SCOOTER RENTAL, a decal said in English on the window. Hmm. But I pushed on because I didn't want to lose her, hanging back on straight stretches but almost sprinting to catch up when she went around a corner.

This we did once, twice, and finally a third time, each turn carrying me farther away from wherever the square happened to be. It didn't seem to matter. I heard the clinking of plates and tableware in houses behind curtains, people talking and laughing, a TV or two, no doubt delivering the latest news of austerity measures being imposed on Greece. There was no other news.

Following and watching, I fell into rhythm with the woman's swaying hips. There was the slightest irregularity, a limp, but then I remembered she'd had knee surgery, which was why she said she needed my help in the first place. The rest was all smooth, all sinewy, all swirling beneath the folds of her loose-fitting skirt, her billowing peasant top and the long scarf she wore around her forehead. The more I watched, the more I told myself I should stop watching. And the less I felt willing or able to.

As she took the third corner, disappearing beneath a streetlight that hadn't lit, I was torn between making one final sprint and counting to twenty for fear of stumbling over her. Then, at all kinds of levels, I would have had some explaining to do. But as it was, no explanation was necessary. When I finally did order myself to turn the corner, I saw the woman fifteen yards in front of me but paying no attention to me, melting into a long-haired man's frenzied embrace. I yanked my body back into the darkness, my breath ragged, almost strangled.

II

The *trisagion*—the visitation part of it anyway, conducted around my father's coffin in my mother's living room—was everything Father Michael had promised, and less. To say Friday evening was quiet would be an understatement, as my mother and I passed what felt like weeks sitting with neighbors who'd had no chance to know either of my parents well. There was the language barrier, along with the fact that no alcohol was served, to guarantee that the observance tended toward silence. A livelier reception, I was promised, would take place after the burial, now less than twenty-four hours away. Alcohol would be served for that one, lots of it, as though the gods of all things death realized they had one more chance to convince me this was a happy occasion.

"Thank you for coming," I heard my mother say over and over, her voice little more than a tired whisper. Typically she said this in English after attempting it in Greek, hoping it might help with any misunderstanding. Looking at the blank faces of these Greek neighbors, I saw no reason to hope that either language helped at all.

I hadn't really gotten my head around what it would feel like to share this living room with an occupied casket. The vessel was no more than a plain wooden box, and I found myself wondering if this had been my father's wish too. Something had clearly happened to him when he'd returned to this island—but what?—something that made him different from before, something about his roots. Happily for my peace of mind, my mother (or, once again, my father) had opted for the casket to be closed.

There were only a few pastries from the corner bakery for the five or six neighbors who stopped by to sit with my mother by candlelight, and since they spoke no English, there wasn't much by way of conversation. No stories, no laughter, no tears. They simply sat with her and, only by association with her, sat with me—paying their respects to my father, to his death or to his life, in some manner that made sense within their culture and their theology.

I kept waiting for death to reveal itself as that moment of fulfillment, victory and joy. Obviously from these neighbors with deep creases in their faces and downcast eyes, who sipped the thick coffee my mother brewed for them and finally whispered impenetrably on their way out, I would have to keep on waiting.

Nick called my mother about halfway through the visitation, and she politely escaped to her bedroom to speak with him at some length on her cellphone. When she returned and took her place beside me, she was wearing as close to a smile as I'd seen since I arrived on the island.

"He's close," my mother said.

"To Delfinos?"

Before replying, she glanced at each of the faces in the living room, as though asking their forgiveness for holding a conversation they couldn't follow or join. "To Greece anyway. He's in London."

"That's not so close," I said, with a lack of emotion that surprised even me.

"London, waiting for his flight to Athens. There's been a delay. Weather over the English Channel."

"I see." I wasn't sure if I should ask. "So is he making it in time for the funeral or not?"

My mother's glance around at her neighbors was different now. She was apologizing for me. Or maybe I just imagined that. Maybe I simply felt like the kind of oldest son who needed to be apologized for. "Steve, he's on his way, all right? Your brother's heart is in the right place, even if you're not willing to recognize that. And it breaks my heart, if you have to know."

It was my turn to scan faces. Nothing. No one understood a word we were saying, though I couldn't escape the feeling that the words we were saying were all wrong anyway, probably that we should stop. I wasn't sure I knew how. "I mean, he still has to catch that damn ferry."

"Your brother has some things in place, Steve."

"Things? *What* things?"

"Really, we can talk about all this later." One more glance, this time with a nod to an old woman sitting straight up in her hard chair in the corner. Sons, the nod seemed to say, what are you going to do? The woman nodded back. "Nick says he'll be here. And I have to trust him."

"Funerals don't wait, Mom. They're kind of like death that way."

"I know, Steve. Your brother knows it too."

Thus ended the only significant break in the silence from the first neighbor's arrival to the last neighbor's departure. Each told my mother something intended to be comforting—you could tell by the tone and the hand placed lightly on her shoulder. I had no clue what they were telling her, but I was quite sure it was every bit as lame as anything I'd ever heard in English. "Thank you for coming," I heard my mother say one final time, and we were alone.

"*Whew*," she said, forcing a grin. "Now that was definitely not easy."

"No, I'm sure not."

"You'd think your father might have shown up to help."

I was staring at my hands when she uttered these words, and it took an extended moment for them to register. Suddenly I was afraid for her, at least for her sanity, but when I gazed into her eyes they were laughing.

"Thoughtless of the old man, yes?"

"Yes indeed," my mother replied. "I will give him a serious talking to as soon as I see him."

As I watched, expecting nothing and understanding nothing, I saw the laughter drain from her eyes like a physical thing, and the life from her face and the strength from her shoulders, and I saw her head dip forward at the very moment her eyes were clamping shut. Her head moved side to side even as deep, painful sobs took over her chest, violent shivers that pressed upward even as the cascade of unrestrained tears pressed down. My mother was gasping for breath. Yet when I stood to go to her, she stopped me with an outstretched hand.

"No, please, Steve," she pleaded.

"Mom, I'm here to help you."

"I know. But it's me, you understand. I'm the one who has to deal with this. With everything I'm feeling."

"But you're not alone, Mom."

She looked at me. "I'm sorry, Steve," she said, letting each word sink in. "But actually, *yes I am*."

I didn't like what that said about my mother in this circumstance. And though it sounded correct by all the evidence I'd seen in my life, I especially didn't like what it said about me. I'd always been afraid of being alone—afraid I'd live alone and, yes, afraid I'd die alone. It's one of the reasons, other than the path of least resistance, I'd let myself be drawn into a business that always kept you surrounded. Surrounded by people. Surrounded by problems. Surrounded by noise. My mother had spent her adult life with my father surrounded. But now, here he was alone inside a plain wooden box. And here she was alone too.

Partly to cover my awkward standing, I made my way into my mother's kitchen and fixed a small cup of Greek coffee. I knew how, and it was certainly as easy as boiling water. In fact, it mostly *was* boiling water—then pouring it carefully into the cup with ground coffee at the bottom. Most Greeks, in my experience, drank their coffee sweet enough to be dessert. I never did. And considering my mood, I sure as hell wasn't about to start doing it now.

"Mom," I said gently, approaching behind her, unable to see her face. "Mom, are you all right?"

There was a long pause, but then the muffled sound of her voice. "I'll be okay, Steve."

"You sure?"

"It'll take some time, that's all. You understand?" She lifted her eyes to hold mine. "Or maybe you have no reason to understand. It's about family. He *was* my family."

I struggled with that a moment. "You very much have a family, Mom. You have me and Nick. Whatever has happened between us, we're still your sons. And we always will be. And you have your grandchildren."

"Like Chloe."

"Of course," I said, pouring on a reassurance I couldn't begin to feel. "She loves you, Mom. You're her *yiayia*, after all. Not every all-American kid at the mall even knows what that is—and she's lucky enough to *have* one."

I returned to the place my seat was, but in the empty room, it seemed too distant, too impersonal. Holding the coffee on its saucer in my right hand, I used my left to pull my chair next to hers. It felt good, at first, when I sat. I even let my hand brush across the top of hers where it clutched the furniture with a tightness that surprised me. The touch felt right and loving. Thanks to my mother, wherever her head and heart were taking her only feet from my father's body, it didn't feel right or loving for long.

"Steve," she began, "I have to tell you. I mean, what good is a mother who can't say what's on her heart, yes? And what's on my heart is that I don't like what's going on with you and Bev."

"Mom, please." I nodded toward the coffin, as though it could make some defining sense of everything. "This isn't the time or the place or—"

"Yes, it is, Steve. It simply is. This is all about family. Our family. And how—" I saw her searching for a word, but I couldn't help her find it—"-about how *lost* we are without the people who love us."

"Well," I answered. I had no clue where to begin. No clue was required.

"How's Bev dealing with all this? And Chloe? I hope you called them before you left to come here. Did you?

"Voicemail, Mom. The blessing and the curse. It was the best I could do."

"You can call them from here, if you want. You father had a land line put in."

"I know. But even Dad can't keep it from being the middle of the night in Houston. Yes, of course, I'll call them. Tomorrow. Okay? Except, you know, there's this whole funeral thing I have to do."

"No, Steve. The funeral is what *I* have to do. Don't you understand that? Your father was my husband, for all of his faults, all of his weaknesses. And now he's gone. Do you have any idea how that feels? Or are you so caught up in all your own little dramas, all your own sad little dreams that never came true?"

All I could say was: "They're not little dramas, Mom. You're not giving me or Bev enough credit. We have a lot of big things to think about. Maybe we have options that you and Dad never thought you had."

"There were no options, Steve. We had you and Nick. And that was all."

"True. But it's different now. Maybe not better. Just different, Mom. Some days, it's way more complicated than I think I can deal with. And Dad didn't do me any damn favors, I'll tell you that. I mean, for Christ's sake, you can't pull a man's whole life out from under him and think, oh well, it'll all be okay. It *hasn't* been okay, Mom. Not with Bev. Not with Chloe. And not for one damn minute since he did that to me."

"Steve, you're wrong. I told him you would be about this, but you know your father. The man could probably count on one hand the number of times he listened to anybody in his life. Least of all to me. I told him you'd take it this way."

"Mom, what the hell, he did this to me!"

"I really can't talk about this right now, Steve."

"Gee, thanks."

"I can't. But let me correct one thing, son. And I promise that you will come to understand. Your father didn't do this *to* you. He did it *for* you. And you'd better start figuring out if you can be as grateful as you should be. Because I'm going to be really disappointed in you if it turns out I was right." My mother's gaze was as stern as that of the Savior looking down from the dome in an Orthodox church. "This time, Steve, I want your father to be right about you."

She shook her head sadly, pushing one set of thoughts to the side for later and letting the other set rush back in. "It's—" she gazed directly at me, her eyes on the verge of filling with tears—"it's just a *shame* you two can't settle your differences."

"Mom, please. We have enough going on without that."

"I know. But don't you think your father and I had differences? It's not like he never went to a hotel for a night. But he never went out and got an *apartment*."

"Bev told me to do that."

"Now you know she didn't mean that."

"She meant it. You don't know Bev."

"Of course I do. We've talked. I know she cares about you. And she cares about Chloe and wants her to have her father in the house."

"That isn't what she told me."

"Steve, please." My mother was being my mother again. "People go through bad times is all. Everybody does. Couples, I mean. But you need to be home. With your family. A man needs to take care of his family."

"You sound like Dad."

"He always took care of us."

"Yes," I said. "He always did. Until he *didn't*."

It was a wildly insensitive thing to say this close to my father's coffin. Happily for me, neither he nor my mother was listening. "After this, when you get home, you need to *be* home. Not in some empty apartment."

"I'll see, Mom. And besides." I looked at her. "It's not really an apartment. It's just a place we've set up for vendors. Look on the bright side. I only have to commute to the office from down the hall."

"It's not right," my mother said with awe-inspiring finality.

"I'll do my best, Mom. When I get home. I'm sure things will work out fine." I wasn't sure of that or anything else. "Besides, the way things are looking here, I'm beginning to wonder when that will even be."

12

I woke up early and went for a swim in the sea on the day we buried my father. As always in Greece, this single, simple act turned out to be a multi-step process. Since I'd changed into my new shorts that also functioned as a swimsuit before going to sleep, I needed no change of clothes in the morning. But I did need to close the front door quietly so my mother wouldn't wake (Fotis said he'd swing by to get her later) and walked to the square to catch the early bus. In the winter season, in fact, there was only *one* early bus and one late bus, neither really going to the beach but to a farming village a mile past it. The driver, as usual, would know where to drop me off. As it turned out, there was a sign on the main road, pointing downward with the notation "2.8 km" and an icon of waves and a swimmer cutting sharply through them. If I was lucky, maybe I could pull off something that looked like that.

Ever since straggling my way back to the square after following the woman, all through the sad, silent *trisagion*, I hadn't felt right about anything. I didn't want to eat. And once I remembered it would require a trip to the ATM—which was approximately 25 feet from the café I chose—I decided against even having a beer and simply went home to sleep.

For one thing, I couldn't remember doing anything like it. Who stalked a woman like that? I asked myself, and honestly, only one name came back: Jack the Ripper. Did it mean I'd never made it past high school emotionally, something I wouldn't offer Bev as free ammunition, or did it mean I was perverse, verging on evil? As much as I tried to make light of the whole thing, it had me shaken. Maybe that was behind my desire for a swim in cool, clear waters. Or maybe it was that and a couple million other things.

I had just stepped off the bus and stood watching it lumber on dustily toward the village when my cellphone buzzed in my pocket. I pulled it out and rolled my eyes. It was Bev.

"Hi baby!" My wife's voice was bright. There was considerable glassware making a racket in the background, along with people talking and music playing.

"Where are you, Bev?"

"With the girls. You know, Sophie. And Nicole. And Ashley."

"On a school night?"

"It's Friday, honey. Don't be such a downer."

Bev was right. It was Saturday morning in Greece, which meant it was Friday night in Houston.

"Hey Bev," I said, "I can't really talk now." I gazed around me at the juncture of the two roads, the one I planned to take leading down to the sea. "We'll be burying my Dad in a little bit."

There was a pause. "Oh geez, baby. Oh geez." I could hear her drawing troubled breaths. "I didn't know. Honestly. I talked to your brother, but he must not have mentioned that it was today."

Nick was trying to make it to the funeral. I bet he would have mentioned it.

"How's your mom, Steve? It must be awful for her. Will you tell her I'm so sorry? From me and Chloe?"

"Of course."

"I mean it, Steve. Promise me you'll tell her."

"I promise." My feet were longing to leave the wide highway and start the walk down to the place where swimming arms cut their way through waves, 2.8 kilometers from here. The sun was getting hot.

I could, of course, talk to my wife as I walked. I realized I didn't want to. "Bev, I need to go. I'm sorry."

"Steve, wait. This isn't why I called you. I didn't want you to be upset. You know, like worried, if you couldn't reach me."

"What's going on?"

"The girls and I, well, Maria's coming to stay with Chloe in the morning." Maria was our maid. Everybody who could afford one in Houston had one. We could afford one. "We're going for a couple days at a spa in Austin. Outside Austin. The girls set it up."

"Which one?"

"I don't know. Tra-something, maybe? It's a yoga word, I think. They have lots of yoga. Like I said, they set it up. I'm just going. It should be great. I wanted you to know, in case you call and I don't have service. I mean, the place is in the *woods*."

Bev paused, letting the sounds of the bar ring through uninterrupted, across an ocean from half a world away. And I couldn't shake the feeling there was more to her weekend than a spa getaway with the girls. Sometimes, though, there were things you just couldn't think about. We told each other good night and, in the day, I started walking.

The cicadas—for that's what I'd been told on the island they were, after asking if some kind of electrical generator was behind a clump of olive trees—were buzzing louder than I'd ever heard them. I followed the road down and around, occasionally grabbing views of the bright blue sea, ever closer, each time I saw an opening through the trees.

Was it Bev's tone that had shaken me—too happy, almost chirpy? I mean, she'd had what I calculated was three martinis, and a lot of people sound odd after that. But there was a tension under the shiny roller coaster of her voice, a tension I may or may not have recognized. Bev had been married to Jim at the club when we'd met and started dating. I simply couldn't remember if that's how she'd sounded, other than the alcohol. And why, damn it, did those of us who've been the new man ever, as long as we live, stop wondering if we've become the old one.

And really? Wasn't she the one who was probably giggling right now with Sophie, Nicole and Ashley, all three happily married—well, except for Nicole, who spent a lot of time in limbo on that? She was sitting and giggling and getting fired up over a weekend of yoga. I was the one chasing a woman through the shadows because—because why? Because I'd met her for less than five minutes and didn't know her name?

I wanted to call Bev back and tell her I was sorry, but that would have meant telling her what I was sorry for. I got as far as pulling the phone from my pocket. The beach, as several locals who brought food to my mother's yesterday had promised during conversation in bits of several languages, was magnificent. There was a concrete block wall along the left as I emerged from the trees, plus steps leading up to three houses painted white with blue accents. On the right was a tavern, which of course wasn't open this early in the morning. A boy who looked to be about nine hosed down the concrete veranda beneath an awning and then used a brush to push the water off into the sand.

It was a cove—Delfinos had hundreds of them—with calm clear waters that shimmered in the climbing sun. No one else was at the beach, yet I presumed, since it was a beautiful Saturday on a Greek island, that eventually someone would be. By lunchtime, I figured, the tavern's outside tables would be full.

I took off my father's hat and set it on the wall where it dipped into shade, then took off and rolled up my shirt. My shoes, socks and cell phone joined them, along with the white towel I'd brought from my mother's house. Last off were my glasses, and as it had been forever since I started wearing glasses at sixteen, it took a minute for my eyes to adjust. Seeing less, much less, my eyes took a moment to draw any conclusions from what they could see.

Man, the water was cold—colder than I'd been thinking. It was February, even on a Greek island. It quickly rose halfway to my knees, chilling to the point of burning, and for a cowardly second I considered turning around and only *telling* anyone who asked that I'd had a nice swim where they'd sent me. But no. With a gentle wave, the sea crept up to grab my shorts and then another wave encircled my waist. I shivered and then, some decision made without thinking, I peeled my body forward into the next wave.

Especially without glasses, the world beneath the sea was blurry and shiny and sun-swept, a million tiny bubbles floating and following the slightest movement of my hands or feet. I kicked my way down to the bottom, which alternated smooth rocks with abstract-art patches of sand, then pressed out deeper, coming up for air at intervals, till

I was roughly in line with the entrance to the cove. Not knowing why, I started to pull and kick and breathe as smoothly as I could, making my way almost to the rocks on the left before swimming toward the rocks on the right. My muscles screamed obscenities. But I didn't allow myself to stop. The water didn't feel cold anymore.

This I kept up, with a few rest stops treading water, for maybe forty-five minutes, only vaguely aware there were pleasure boats coming and going from the cove and people throwing down and stretching out on towels along the beach. There were children now, splashing and playing with red and yellow sand buckets and pails. To me, it was all so much Impressionist blur, and I remembered that Monet's eyesight pretty much sucked too. At one point I laughed enough to swallow saltwater, realizing I was gazing back at a beach becoming the postcard I'd seen in a thousand shops.

Finally, my muscles trembling, even treading water in the deep took too much effort. I dog-paddled my way in to where I could touch bottom, and after that figured out that I'd had enough. I felt better, though. I felt, as my father used to say, good as new. Or at least some midlife, mid-point, middle-aged approximation thereof. Stumbling twice on rocks, I made my way up onto the beach's warming sand, past the laughing children, to the invisible line where the bodies on towels began.

Looking back, I'm happy my eyes blinked away enough stinging saltwater and found something like perception when they did. Otherwise, I would have walked right over her.

"Hello," she said.

She sat beneath a broad, floppy-brimmed hat on one towel spread across the sand, with another partially unrolled beside her and two more neatly folded teetering out of a fabric beach bag. Her swimsuit was a black one-piece, neither young nor old, neither brazen nor shy. She was wearing sunglasses, leaning back on one extended arm with fingers touching the sand, the other hand covering her straightened right knee atop her bent left leg. Without trying, I noticed a slight bruising—maybe the hint of a recent scar - underneath her hand.

"Hello," I managed to say. Then, "I'm glad I didn't—" Losing track of the words, I pantomimed tumbling on top of her. She understood and, to my relief, laughed.

"Me also," she said. "Happy."

I shifted my weight from one leg to the other, then back again. Standing shirtless in front of her, I wished I could go on a diet starting six weeks ago. That and sat out in the sun more, even though the pool at our house back home didn't do much for me in the wintertime.

"Swimming," she said. "Did you have a nice swimming?"

"Yes. Very nice. Cold water." I folded my arms across my chest and pretended to shiver. She seemed amused. "But nice."

"Yes. Is good."

I watched as a thought crossed her mind, almost bringing on a frown. "So tell me. Did I *thank* you? The other night? When you help?" She took off the sunglasses, so I could see her deep amber eyes. "Or was I—*terrible*?"

I tried to remember. I remembered. But at the same time, it didn't matter.

"No, no, you were fine. Yes, you thanked me."

"Well, is good, yes?"

"Yes."

I never found a way to ask what I wanted to ask her next, but she answered anyway.

"My—my—*boyfriend*? Yes, boyfriend. Was waiting in his car. He pick me up at ship. And raining. And—later—I think of you and wonder. If I thank nice man who help me."

"Ah," I offered eloquently. "It's okay. You thanked me. And then—" I dared myself to say it. "Then you called me *sir*?"

That certainly made her laugh. She pulled up from the sand enough she could bury her face in both hands and twist her head right and left several times. "I did not. Did I?"

"Why yes."

She seemed to be thinking. "I wished to call you by name. I thought I know name. And then I see that no, I do not. I'm sorry. My English—"

"Is perfectly fine."

"Yes, but," she looked up. "I still don't know your name."

"Um, Steve. My parents named me Stelios. But no, Steve is better."

"You are Greek?"

"American, mostly."

She smiled, the smile a bit of a taunt. "I never would have guessed."

"And you?"

"Yes, I am Greek."

"No, please. What is your name?"

She slapped a hand to her forehead, then reached up to shake my hand. "I am called Elena. No, not E-LAY-na, the way you Americans say always. EL-en-ah."

"EL-en-ah," I repeated. "Like, Helen? Of Troy?"

"Exactly," she said.

I dug desperately for something to say after that. There are conversations in this life that simply end, and there are others we find a way to keep going. I was slowly moving, in my heart at least, from wanting the former to seriously wanting the latter.

"Do you enjoy the beach?" I asked. Hell, who doesn't? But it was something.

"Yes, very much. And my boyfriend says the sunshining—sunshine?—is good for my knee."

"Ah, your surgery?"

"*Bravo*, Steve. You remembered."

She looked at her knee beneath her hand, then slowly let me have a look. There was some bruising plus a ragged purple-black line at the center of it all, climbing over the joint from the bottom of her thigh to the top of her calf. It wasn't ugly, really. But when you thought about it, it looked a lot like pain.

"Accident, maybe?"

"Maybe," Elena said. "But not in car or *moto*—um, motorbike, you say. No, I am—" She stopped, letting out a breath. "I *was*—*dancing*? A dancer?"

"For real?"

"Yes, ballet. Can you believe?"

"Of course I can."

"In Athens at the end, before injury. But in Brussels and Bruge—that's in Belgium." I nodded. Obviously she had spoken with my fellow Americans before. "And in the UK, in Bristol. That's where I learned my *perfect* English." She looked at me, lifted her shoulders to summarize all things and then let them glide back down. "Not exactly dancing in Paris, eh?"

"No. I mean, yes. I mean, that's still amazing."

"But over, yes? *Finish*?"

"Are you sad?"

"Maybe. I was. But now, not too much. It is happening to me, yes? We can do nothing."

"Sometimes, I suppose. Yes."

Her eyes were clear, her gaze uncluttered, seemingly unafraid. "And now you, Steve, who is actually Stelios, why are *you* here on Delfinos? *How* are you here?" She tilted her head, like an artist studying me before committing me to her canvas. "Or maybe you are, I think, a little bit injured too?"

This time, I was the one who had to laugh. "Oh waiter," I said in the vaguest direction of the taverna. "Check please!"

Eventually, I lowered myself to one knee, making sure to plant it on the sand, not on her towel. Then I met her directness with a little of my own. "A family matter, I am afraid. My father has died here. And I have come to help bury him."

"Oh my. I am sorry, Steve. Yes, very sorry."

"It happens," I said. "It is sad. But there is much to—much to *figure out* here, what my father wanted, what I should do—"

"*You* should do?"

"Yes. But, maybe you know the phrase—*long story*."

"Indeed," Elena said. "I do know the phrase."

Following a whim I wished I didn't have, I pretended to glance at my wristwatch—I never wore a wristwatch—and popped the question before I could chicken out. "Hey, might you enjoy a coffee right now? An espresso? I think the place is opening." I grinned. "Or a glass of wine? Or maybe a double vodka?"

Elena looked down at the towel, and I couldn't help noticing as her hand found its way back to cover her scar.

"Oh my sweet friend Steve." She formed her words with care. "I will not ever call you *sir* again, okay? When I see you, maybe in the town? But no, thank you, please. I am waiting." She brushed some sand from her calf, then returned her hand to its official resting place. "My boyfriend, he is diving. Out there, on reef. I just sit here on beach, trying to look pretty." She laughed. "He will be back soon, I think. Is *all*, yes? Is the way it is?"

"What can we do?"

"Exactly," Elena said.

At three that afternoon, I managed to bury my father. He had, according to my mother and Father Michael, wanted a traditional Greek Orthodox funeral and burial in the church cemetery on the outskirts of town, and together we managed, as best we could, to give my father what he wanted. Some things about sons and fathers never change.

Maybe some things about brothers never change either. Nick showed up about halfway through the service, looking perfect in his custom-made Italian suit despite what I'm sure was at least two planes and a final flourish of island boat. He walked up the aisle to sit with Mom and me, forcing Father Michael to concentrate on reading the prayers for the dead.

"Wow," Nick said, smiling as he kissed our mother on the cheek and reaching across behind her to pat me on the shoulder. "What a nightmare that was."

"Ssssh," our mother said, nodding to the casket and the priest.

There was a half-hour liturgy in Greek at the church, followed by a time for locals who knew Dad at least a little to process up to the front and pay their respects. This they did directly to him, bowing before his open casket and then planting a kiss on the gold cross that rested on his chest. My mother and I sat on folding chairs beside the casket, receiving sympathies and other best wishes that Fotis translated in my ear, such as "May you have abundant life" or "May his memory be eternal." Fotis sometimes whispered the speaker's name to me, perhaps with his or her specific association with Dad or his family or his work on Delfinos, and even suggested the proper, traditional response.

With only thirty or so in attendance, this visitation did not last long. While my mother and I thanked people for coming at the door, a small motorized cart carried the now-closed casket to the gravesite. Anything resembling an American hearse wouldn't have fit through the town's narrow, twisting streets.

Yes, there was a grave already dug, with my father's casket on a draped platform beside it. Father Michael was there, as was Fotis, with a frail-looking, white-haired man standing beside him. It had been a while since I'd laid eyes on anybody so pale, with hair and beard looking as though it might crumbled into dust if touched. The old man had sad but affectionate eyes, nodding to my mother and then acknowledging me. This time, Father Michael spoke English.

"Lord in heaven," he began, taking the time to engage each of us. "We deliver unto you this day your beloved son, George Laros. He has labored long and hard in your vineyard in this, his life, and we pray that you will grant him the eternal rest he has earned as his wages." Fotis was standing beside the old man on the other side of the grave, both their hands folded in front of them, and I couldn't help catching his eye when the priest said the word "vineyard." "It is harvest time, dear Lord, God our Father, and our brother George has brought in a good harvest. Help us, Lord, even as we mourn our loss of him, to celebrate his love, his faithfulness and his journey home to you. With time and gentle care, dear Lord, the grapes that grew from old, withered vines have become the finest wine."

My mother and I watched as Father Michael reached down to the pile of dirt created by digging and spread a handful in the sign of the cross atop the casket's wood. Fotis stepped over to us then and handed my mother and me a rose. My mother first, we placed these atop that cross. Fotis and the old man did the same. We slowly walked away from my father's grave and followed Father Michael in silence back to the square.

The priest promised to stop by my mother's apartment in perhaps an hour, once he had cleaned up and closed up the church. When we did get home, there were a couple dozen people from the funeral service who'd prepared a light meal—called a *makaria*, I was told—of baked fish, roasted potatoes, boiled wild greens from the mountainside. We talked among ourselves in English, and the Greeks talked among themselves in Greek during the savory portion, warming enough to each other by pastries and coffee to try crossing over the linguistic DMZ. This happened with the usual starts and stops, the usual misunderstandings and narrative dead ends. There were bottles of local wine, so at least all parties to the meal could smile, nod and clink glasses.

I felt a certain relief when Nick sidled up beside where I was sitting between two old, toothless Greek men, each telling a separate story about our father at the same time and me understanding neither, thinking that at least his arrival would usher in some English. But all my brother said to me, with the merest brush of a hand on my shoulder, was: "Bro, we need to talk." I started to make room for him. He said coldly, "Not here."

My mother nodded approvingly as we walked out, no doubt believing that anytime two brothers talk it's got to be a good thing. I wish I could have been so sure. Talking, in fact, is exactly what we *didn't* do, making our way wordlessly through the town's tangled streets, me leading without intending to, until we stopped at one of the points where the ground simply fell away over a low wall, dropping to sharp rocks and the sea.

"We need to get a couple things straight, you and me," Nick announced.

"Which you and me, Nick? Which one?"

"Huh?"

"Two brothers on the day of their father's funeral? Or a boss and his employee?"

"Shit, Steve. Don't bust my balls over this. It's gotta be done."

"Then don't bust mine either, Nick. I mean it. Not today, for Christ's sake.

"I'm only here today."

Nick seemed to be chewing something, but I'd hardly seem him eat back at the house. His gaze kept shifting from the blue distance where the sky met the sea and the dust that covered the rocks at our feet.

"Mom told you about the airport meeting, yeah? Or was that just Mom, being old and crazy?"

"She *told* me. And no, I don't think she's crazy."

"Okay. You know what I mean. So it was scheduled—what the hell *day* is it—like, tomorrow. I managed to squeeze three extra days out of them. But that's it. There's a lot of other guys in this business they could play ball with."

"Not as good as us."

"You know that, and I know that. But do *they* know that?"

"They came to *us,* Nick. They obviously know something."

"Steve." My brother looked tired, understandably, and he had only two hours before he headed back from Delfinos to Santorini to Athens to Houston. But he also looked angry. His eyes reminded me of our father's, and I didn't like that one bit. "You're just not taking this seriously enough."

"You're being the boss now?"

"Damn right I'm the boss now. I'm what Pop *made* me, Steve. And now I'm doing what Pop wanted—growing this company. You grow or you die, right? Like he always said. Think about it. Twelve to fifteen airports, each store three-thousand square feet, doing $5 million to $6 million a year. With a limited menu, labor costs next to nothing. I mean, a goddamn monkey could make this food once it shows up from the commissary. And monkeys aren't expensive. You hearin' me, bro?"

"You say Pop wanted this?"

"Of course he did."

"Did *he* meet with these people? Did *he* ever hear their pitch?"

"You know he didn't, Steve, but don't be a shit. He was over here, or he was dead. One of those two things after he retired. But he taught us how to grow this thing, how to be ready when an opportunity walked in the door, how to know the next step when we saw it. *This* is that next step, Steve. And when I meet with these guys in D.C. in three days, to sign a letter of intent—"

"A contract?"

"No, a letter of intent. And you damn well know the difference."

"But they can announce it if we sign."

"Sure, and that's good for us. Our competitors will really be scrambling after that."

"That what, we'll be in *airports*?"

"No, asshole. That we'll be taking in $60 million to maybe $90 million a year, on top of everything else." Nick was glaring at me. "I'm gonna be right there grabbin' it for all I'm worth. And you know Pop wudda been there right beside me. Didn't you learn *anything* from the old man, Steve?"

I decided I'd heard enough.

My words came in rasping bursts, and no matter how hard I breathed, I didn't feel like I was getting any air. "Our Dad didn't *do that*. He wasn't like that, Nick. He did what he felt was best for this family, for sure, for this company. But where the hell did you get the idea he was just standing around grabbing money? He understood it was more than that, Nick. He taught us this *business* was more than that. Every goddamn day of his life."

My brother only shook his head with resignation, with sad dismissal, struggling to say what he was thinking, or maybe struggling not to say it. "Shit, Steve, I can see it now. It all makes sense, you know?"

"What the hell are you talking about?"

"Why Pop gave *me* the company to run."

"Then maybe, for Christ sakes, you can explain it to *me*. I've been thinking about it for the last nine months. And it never has made any sense."

"*Really?* You're kidding me, right?"

"No, I'm not. And he only told me that morning, a couple hours before the meeting."

"Well, you know—"

"When did he tell you, Nick? When did he tell you you'd be CEO, and I'd be just the wine guy."

"Pop cared about wine. There's good money in wine."

"Oh Christ. Can you ever get past the goddamn money? It's about our father. And who he trusted with everything he had built."

"You know what, Steve? You're right. It's exactly about who he trusted. Pop always reminded me you're the oldest, like I didn't know that. Like you didn't find some way to tell me that every three minutes since I was born."

"I took *care* of you, Nick. When you were a baby. Pop was working at one restaurant, and Mom was usually working at another. And eventually three cousins plus a one-legged dog were running all the other ones. And what was I doing, this great and favored son of theirs? I was home watching a goddamn baby."

"And that matters *why* exactly?"

"Because now you're my boss. Because that *baby* is my boss. And I hate it, Nick."

None of that seemed to register at all. "And why do you think Pop made me that, huh? At that meeting with our board? You got blindsided, well yeah, sure. But not me, bro. He talked to me about it first, days before, told me what he was gonna do. And he told me why."

"Yeah, why?"

"He told me you could do the wines for us. Cuz maybe that was something you wouldn't screw up. He said you were a loser, bro. You were his oldest son, but you were a *goddamn loser!*"

"That's a lie, you son of a bitch!"

Nick must have felt the punch coming before I knew I was throwing it, and he flung his head to one side. What should have flattened his nose glanced off his cheek, and I felt my weight—every unwanted pound—flying past him with its force. He caught me with a left to the stomach, and I locked my remaining arm around the back of his neck, throwing him to the ground. His face hit rock and exploded into a hundred cuts. Nick ignored them as he grabbed my arm and yanked me down beside him, the knee of my pants tearing right along with my skin.

"A goddamn baby?" he shouted, lifting my head with my shoulders and slamming it down as I angled upward for a knockout punch. "I'm not a *baby*. I never *was* a baby. Cuz Pop wouldn't let me be one. Who the hell can *ever* be a baby when all the old man really needed was a *fuckin' dishwasher!*"

I'd never seen, this side of a Saturday morning cartoon, a punch actually stop in midair. I hadn't known it was even possible. But that's what happened with the punch I was throwing, which for all I knew might have been the perfect thing to knock my brother out. He was straddling me and heaving loudly and spitting blood, some of it landing on his Italian suit and some on my Chinese knockoffs from the island van. All I knew was he wasn't banging my head against the rock anymore. For which I was duly grateful.

Nick looked up at the clear blue sky above us and shook his head several times. "Shit, Steve," he said. "What the hell are we doin' here, bro? And what the hell is this even *about*?"

I blinked at him, a painful smile grabbing the corners of my mouth.

"Happy Hippo," I said. "*What?*"

"You had one, when you were little. And I hated that goddamn thing, you pulling it all over the living room and its mouth opening every two feet to make this weird-ass awful sound."

Nick was looking at me like I was insane. But I knew I wasn't. And that, for the moment, was self-knowledge enough. At last he caught on, opening his own mouth and emitting some cross between a belch and a sexual groan. I took up the challenge and made the dreaded sound a bit better. Nick laughed and tried again, producing a different tone but a solid effort.

"*Jesus,*" he said, trying to find balance and get to his feet. "If any of these Greeks see us like this, what the hell are they gonna think, huh?"

"Lovers' quarrel, maybe?"

"Shit on that, bro."

"Two brothers?"

"I don't know, man." He was standing now, offering me his hand to get up. "Looks pretty weird, is all."

"Hell, Nick. When it comes to killing people you're related to, Greeks wrote the whole damn book."

I was standing beside my brother now. We didn't touch, both of our pairs of hands busy trying to brush ourselves off and straighten our oh-so-different fashion statements. We were hurting, we were exhausted, we were definitely embarrassed. But even as the truth that Nick was my boss sank in for something like the twelve-millionth time in nine months, I knew we were also brothers on the day of our father's funeral.

"Really, Nick," I said, breaking some strange new version of ice. There was always some version of ice, I decided. The Ice Age never went away entirely, not from everywhere in our lives, just from here and there, for a while. "What was I supposed to *think*, at that meeting? Here's Pop, telling the board *you'll* be running LRG? The old man doesn't even dare to look at me, you know? Not once. Cuz he can't, maybe? What the hell am I supposed to think?"

"You're supposed to think—" Nick looked at me, then raised his hand to gently massage the bleeding right side of his face. "You're supposed to think—"

"*Tell* me, Nick."

He grinned, theatrically stamping each of his feet on the ground of Delfinos. "You're supposed to think, bro—this shit is *hard.*"

I was grinning too. I draped my arm lightly around my brother's shoulder. "The next time we build an island, Nick, we are *so* puttin' in carpet."

15

It was nearly six by the time the reception ran its course, and by that time Nick had brushed off and straightened his suit, hugged our mother, shaken hands with me and gotten Fotis to drive him down to the port, where his boat to Santorini was waiting. Father Michael did make it in time for a few pastries, a cup of thick, silty Greek coffee and a sip or two of the wine, a white that tended toward sweet but, I observed, had excellent acidity for balance. After the last guest departed my mother excused herself, no doubt for a rendezvous with her sleeping pills, and Fotis, the old man and I were left sitting in the parlor with nothing to do and seemingly, by that point, nothing to talk about.

Amazingly, after several hours in his presence, all I'd picked up was that the old man's name was Avery. That and the fact, even though he looked like an Orthodox cleric out of his official attire, he spoke with a soft British accent.

Avery's threadbare light blue shirt was tucked into a pair of jeans, but then again all the guests had looked somewhat the worse for wear. That's what you get, I suppose, from buying clothes most of your life from the back of a van. He stood up and stepped over to the table, picked up the open bottle of wine and refilled glasses for Fotis and me before doing the honors for himself.

"You seem to enjoy my wine," he said.

And then, of course, I knew.

In the course of my days on Delfinos, I had heard bits and pieces about a man from England who grew his own grapes here and made his own wine, and had been doing so for many years. It was obviously enough years that the young people weren't around and the old people couldn't remember. The wine was good, even after spending my career visiting *chateaux* in France, *fincas* in Spain and *castelli* in Italy, always being offered their best—with an eye toward my buying it in large amounts for our restaurants. Something told me there were no large amounts of wine to buy from Avery, even had I wanted to.

"It's muscat," said Avery. I'd thought so, though I was keeping my options open, this being a country whose wines were numberless and not regularly poured. Yet it was different from any muscat I'd ever tasted. There was a sweetness to it, but also a floral quality that reminded me of viognier in Provence. I wasn't sure what I would "do" with this wine in any of our restaurants, other than drink it with a reasonable amount of happiness, which I then proceeded to do.

"I like it," I said.

Avery nodded his gratitude, first at me, then at Fotis, presumably for bringing him to meet me. But if I felt that was some smalltime version of the typical "taste and sell" moment, the kind I endured with wine salesmen every working day of my life, the next thing Avery said stopped that train of thought nowhere near the station.

"I was working with your father, you know," he said.

Avery, as he explained with affection tinged with sadness, had indeed been trying to help my father with the abandoned vineyards he had a acquired with the house, as well as with turning the long, low building on the water into something resembling a winery. It was not at all clear if Avery had been paid for any of his work or his local expertise, acquired through 37 years of living fulltime on the island. Indeed, from his stories, I concluded he grew up in a midsize town south of London but never truly felt alive until he came here. The fact that he lost a wife and a son in the process of "feeling alive" seemed a price he was prepared to live with.

He owned what seemed like an acre stretching downhill from his home, which he had built, expanded or improved on his own, one wall, one ceiling, one floor at a time. Outside his door, he grew rows of muscat, famous when produced by the French village of Beaume de Venise—which he vinified in what, when he moved into the house after its original owner had died, had once been the garage. Avery did not own a car. I had visited large wineries that had started out in their owners' garages, in California especially, going back to the 1960s—but I'd only visited them after everybody had a lot more space, a lot more help and, naturally, a whole lot more money.

Avery seemed pleased that I wanted to come visit his garage sometime, though no one (least of all me) had any clue how long I'd be visiting Delfinos. He was carefully tipping the last drops from the last bottle into our glasses when he told me in his ever-gentle and undeniably bookish British accent, "Yes, I would like that. I would like that quite a lot." He gazed at me intently. "But what I really want to show you is your father's property."

"Well, I've actually seen it," I answered. "Fotis took me there yesterday."

Avery laughed heartily, and so did Fotis. I figured I may as well laugh too.

"Oh," Avery said, still chuckling, "that's just looking at dirt, actually. I want to show you everything your father really had in mind."

16

It was dark by the time the three of us left my mother's apartment. We hadn't heard a noise from her bedroom in at least two hours, so no one felt any need to tell her good night. Happily, I'd managed to locate a handyman in the town who could, at long last, install a lock on the front door. I understood the dynamic, having heard people boast much of my life about this or that wonderful place, where everybody sleeps with their doors unlocked. It was not the way I felt comfortable leaving my mother all by herself.

I was definitely feeling the wine. I had forced down grappa with the owners at many a winery in Tuscany, so I knew a thing or two about this heavy drinking drill. But I actually knew nothing about having *tsipouro* in what had to function as a distillery, inside or outside the prevailing laws. Increasingly I had come to suspect that outside was where more activities took place on Delfinos than inside.

It was a long way between street lights. Perhaps the gauze over my eyes was the result of Avery's muscat, or perhaps it merely reflected a life lived more comfortably in the dark than was common in my Houston life. Every three to five steps, it seems, a cat was roused from some silent slumber and scrambled over left-out wooden crates and shimmied over a stucco wall. Sometimes I saw them, sometimes I only heard them racing away, knocking over whatever was in their path.

At the end of one especially shadowy alley Avery and Fotis led me down, there was a kind of open barn door streaming with yellow light. As we approached, I caught sight of men who were loud and more than a little drunk, sitting at a weathered wooden table piled with sausages and bread, and refilling small shot glasses by passing around what had once been a liter bottle for drinking water. The stuff inside now looked like water, but it certainly wasn't.

"These are my friends," Avery said. Instead of introducing them to me, and knowing I'd never catch or remember their names, he simply introduced me to them as "Stelios." At almost the same time, Fotis gathered his face into a wide grin, spread his arms out wide and launched into a long story or joke, using my name several times to increasingly raucous laughter. Avery added his own comments along the way, clearly comfortable speaking, thinking and living in Greek.

When the jokes, seemingly all at my expense but without the slightest hint of why, calmed down, Avery put his hand softly behind my arm and steered me away from the table up three metal steps to a platform.

"This is something you have to see," he said.

The two of us stepped onto the platform, which featured a copper cauldron that appeared to be connected to itself by numberless copper tubes. The air itself was warm, almost, hot the result of our now being suspended above a flame that got regular applications of wood. I, naturally, was reminded of a thousand Texas barbecue joints in towns so small you marveled that they even had one, but here the mission was anything but "low and slow." Inside the cauldron, I saw a foam-topped purple-brown liquid kept at a rolling boil. Whenever it wasn't, it was time for more wood.

"It's the *must*," Avery said, looking to make sure I knew that already. I nodded. "It's what's left over after." He glanced back around the table. "And all these guys here, probably the only thing they all have in common is that they all make wine."

"Here?"

"No, of course not. In their garages, of course." He grinned, his eyes shining in alcoholic glee. "That is why, on this island, there are so very few cars."

Avery led me down the three metal steps on the other side of the platform and out along a piece of pipe that ran from somewhere within cauldron to a spigot similar to the kind that's on a garden hose. He stopped at the spigot, handed me a clean glass and motioned for me to hold it underneath. By then, the room had gone silent and all eyes were on me. Avery opened the valve and—nothing happened.

"Patience, Stelios," was all the man said. And enough of the men at the table understood that they murmured their admonitions and encouragements as well. Being a winemaker, as indeed being Greek, was all about patience.

Finally, with only the slightest dripping sound, a single drop of clear liquid came out of the pipe and into my glass. A moment later another did, followed shortly by another. My hand felt the heat of the liquid rising through the glass. Avery brushed my hand away and replaced it with a plastic liter bottle which reached upward from the concrete floor.

"Now," he said, "you must taste."

I toasted the men at the table with a lift of my glass and then, mustering all the theatricality I could, dragged all the liquid into my mouth, swirled it around my cheeks and tongue, and then swallowed. There was no taste to speak of. This spirit was, essentially, a newborn. But it was anything but nice.

First along the back of my throat and, almost simultaneously, from what felt like the bottom of my stomach, a conflagration erupted. Like a volcano. And everything inside me became the lava. As Avery, Fotis and the men of the town enjoyed the visual, I made it a special point of not erupting myself in any more public way. Avery slapped me on the back and pointed me back to the table, where I was welcomed with bear hugs and a passed plate of sausage. Somebody handed me a full glass of *tsipouro*. I had, apparently, passed the test.

I'm not sure how long we drank together that night, or even how many plates of sausage I grabbed pieces from, downing large chunks of ground, seasoned pork and pressing it down with torn-off pieces of crusty bread. At some point, I realized that all my life I'd been about the taste of wine, rather than the alcohol it delivered. The alcohol, I'd always believed, was an almost-undesirable side effect of indulging in so many flavors. Here, taking my place among the men of Delfinos at the height of a financial meltdown, it wasn't about flavor at all. It was 100% about the alcohol.

I do remember, as the last *tsipouro* bottled was corked somewhere after midnight and the group started to thin, Fotis raising a toast to my father. I joined in, naturally, along with everybody else. I felt it was my turn to say something eloquent or maybe profound, but I couldn't. We all simply clinked glasses one final time around the table, muttered unintelligible Greek good nights and started to disband. It wasn't clear who would handle the cleanup, but it was clear that wouldn't be happening tonight.

Avery headed home, while Fotis accepted steering me to my bed in my mother's apartment through the darkened streets as yet another component of his entirely undefined duties. Most of the street cats seemed asleep by now, so there was far less scrambling and climbing and disasters from just inside the encroaching shadows.

We passed through the main square at some point, my mind groggily revisiting all the things that had taken place at the church and, sure, even at the police station. I had come here to do a job, as I'd always gone places in my life, first for my father and finally for my brother. Each time the job was clear, and each time it could be finished, and each time I could leave, knowing that another job awaited me somewhere else as close as the next meeting in our boardroom. Not so now, not so here. There was, it seemed to me in that moment, no beginning or middle or end to anything on Delfinos, simply a kind of onrushing *now* that demanded something from me but refused, for all my best efforts, to let me in on the secret of what it was.

The air above me in the square, I suddenly realized, was filled with music—rustic, Greek music, its simple beat made more pronounced by the stomping of what must have been a dozen pairs of peasant boots. The second floor of a building I hadn't noticed before was alive with leaping, swaying and spinning shadows cast upon curtains that shielded the outside world from light.

"Fotis," I slurred, unable to take another step, unwilling to ever leave this moment of shimmering golden glow. "What is that? Can we go inside?"

The man smiled indulgently, once again the parent addressing a selfish, impulsive child. "Please to follow. I must get you home, my friend." He placed a firm hand on my shoulder to press me forward at the same time he glanced upward toward the glowing windows. "They are the dancers," he said. "And they are dancing."

17

"Despite more than 300 grape varieties that no one can probably recognize or pronounce," Avery was saying as he spooned another dollop of yogurt into the space between his mustache and his beard, "I see the future of Greek wines as bright. It isn't just about some glorious past, you know."

"Aren't most things in Greece?"

"Often, yes. But this time, no."

It had taken more than a week to get our schedules together, which is funny considering how little actually gets done on any given day on Delfinos. Fotis, the matchmaker—not to mention the guy with the car and the boat—was busy with actual tourists some days, and Avery was busy other days, doing hard-to-define things around his vineyard that nonetheless were urgently in need of getting done. And then there was me, working on both sides of the Atlantic by phone, email and FAX to get George Laros' final affairs in order. I wondered, more often than not, why my father had chosen me to handle this unforgiving job—when he'd chosen Nick to handle everything else.

This had, to the surprise of no one, required three more trips to the police station to discuss and sign documents with Colonel Petrakis, each time for another hundred euros—that ATM and I were practically on a first-name basis. And that meant dealing with banks and several attorneys in Athens and back home in Houston on quantifying my father's personal wealth. Not the corporation's value or earnings or revenues, thank God. Just his personal net worth. That was net worth enough, I decided after going over the papers the first time.

I had not seen Elena, despite what I realized were my best efforts. I'd gone swimming at the beach a couple more times. I had mixed emotions about her office, the place behind the door I'd seen her lock that evening. While pretending to be strolling by, I glanced in casually a once or twice, but a different young woman was working the desk—was that even her job, I wondered, or was she more behind the scenes? The worst times were when I walked past the door on purpose and then refused to look in, afraid that she would be there and that I would think of nothing to say. She'd suggested we would encounter each other around the town, since Chora *was* a very small town. But for whatever reason, we had not.

I don't think I would have followed her through the streets again anyway. The memory of her with her boyfriend remained too vivid and too painful somewhere deep inside me.

The night before this breakfast with Avery and Fotis, Beverly had called me again, which meant it was late morning in Houston. Chloe was at school, and she had hoped we could talk—but once she had me she had changed her mind. She really wanted to talk in person, she said, and when would I get finished with all this and come home anyway? I couldn't tell if my wife was more disappointed or more angry when I told her I didn't have a clue. Did I not *have* a clue, I wondered after telling her "I love you," hearing the mandatory "I love you too" and ending the call? Or did I simply not *want* a clue?

We met early at Irini's just off the square, the first place I'd eaten so memorably after getting off the ferry that night. I actually inquired, through Fotis, whether she had that meatloaf baked in chicken skin for breakfast, but she did not. I had to settle for a selection of spicy local sausages and scrambled eggs. Being some version of vegetarian, Avery opted for yogurt—yes, of course, it was "Greek yogurt"—and a small plate of sliced fruit. No wonder he kept his boyish figure at an age that had to start with a 7, maybe even with an 8. Breakfast for Fotis was thick black coffee and five cigarettes.

Everything bad that could ever happen to any wine-producing country, from wars civil and otherwise to having illiterate immigrants as its first sales team in America, had destroyed the foundations of an industry going back to, well, Greece. The ancient one. The real one. Yes, the glorious one.

"If the ancient Greeks didn't invent wine," Avery explained, "they certainly invented wine enjoyment as we know it. And then, just when Greek's wine's future looked plenty dark enough, they were overrun by the Turks, which meant alcohol was forbidden. It was forbidden, in fact, for nearly four hundred years, and never quite recovered from the shock."

As a result of all this unrest and suppression, the Greek wines that existed at all were, in Avery's eloquent turn phrase, "pure crap." Making things worse was poor people's attempts to cover up by adding pine resin, a demented idea. To this day, I knew from the occasional "Greek wine dinner" at one of our restaurants, many customers stayed away because they mistakenly feared we'd be pouring this tar-tasting *retsina.*

"Everything changed in the 1980s," Avery explained. "And it was, much to their chagrin, the damned Italians who taught the Greeks what to do. You remember 'dago red,' right? Little Italy was never a safe place for decent wine."

"People love Italian wines. We sell tons of fine Chiantis. And man, super Tuscans —"

"Now, sure. But it took a wakeup call in Italy. They saw that quality was improving around the world and prices, in general, were dropping—meaning that, at some point, nobody would buy their immigrant rotgut anymore. They *invested*, Steve."

"Sounds like the Mondavis in California."

"Precisely. There were visionaries in Italy too, charismatic people who showed a vision of the future. Better grapes got grown, and better wines got made. And it wasn't just 'Greek wine' anymore. It was *agiokitiko* from Nemea or *assyrtiko* from Santorini. See? They hired winemakers from California, from Bordeaux and Burgundy. They sent winemakers to UC-Davis. And suddenly, surprise, they were making wines the world wanted to drink, not just Nikos and his three-legged donkey."

"The crisis?" I asked. Nothing in Greece seemed to happen anymore without some reference to financial woes.

"Slowed things down, certainly. Being broke does that to countries. Probably stopped some people. But it's not the end of the story." Avery grinned. "And it's certainly not the end of *my* story."

Fotis heard his mobile ring in his pocket, held up a hand to excuse himself and moved outside to answer. I certainly hoped nothing had come up—not with his taxi, not with his two boats, not with his TURIST INFOS kiosk, and not with his family.

"So Avery," I said, "you're saying that's what my father wanted to do here?"

"Yes, of course. But that is already being done, in virtually every Greek wine region. What he really wanted to do was organize the growers of this island into a force that created and then became a brand. DELFINOS, the business would be called. A Laros Family Winery."

"Our family brand?"

"No," Avery corrected, "the *island* would be the brand. Your old man never got tired of lecturing me about that."

"He was something of a master," I had to admit. "Ahead of his time, to boot."

Avery snickered affectionately. "On Delfinos, any time you bother to get out of your bed in the morning, you're considered ahead of your time."

Fotis was smoking a fresh cigarette by the time he returned to our table. He didn't bother to take a seat. He nodded in the direction of Irinei who as on my first visit seemed to be napping in her chair. "Perhaps, Stelios, you should pay this nice lady. I think we should be on our way now."

"Is everything okay?'

"Why not?"

"The call?"

"Business, my friend. It goes, yes?"

That seemed to be that. I roused Irini long enough to write the final bill on a slip of paper—I would never, I suppose, be able to understand a long string of Greek numbers—and handed her enough euros, rounding up. Fortis gave us a lift in his taxi down to the port and then let us help him drag the smaller of his boats across the sand till it floated on the water.

Avery climbed in shakily and Fotis had me stand holding the boat in knee-deep water so he could run up to his "beach house" and grab the gas can. For me, even with all the water and sand and sunlight, a certain intense seriousness pervaded today's trip. It was not like the first time, not a trip for idle curiosity mixed a sense of filial duty. What we saw today might make me have to actually do something.

"My father," I said, gripping to hold the boat steady in the gentle waves pushing in from sea. "He really wanted to do this?"

"It was his dream."

I let that single word roll around my brain for one moment, and then another, finding its way into corners I hadn't even known existed.

"You know what they say, right, Avery—what the wine guys always say?"

"No, what?"

"They ask me, 'How do you make a small fortune in the wine business?'"

"How?"

"You start," I said, "with a large fortune."

Avery stood beside me on the patio where my father had died. Happily, Fotis had removed the wheelbarrow, the shovel and even the pile of dried concrete in my absence. It made things like this easier, to be sure.

"George talked about Robert Mondavi a lot, actually,"

"Dad did?"

"Yes, absolutely."

I glanced around to find Fotis, but he had already disappeared down the steps to the beach, pressing his mobile tightly against his ear to hear in the roaring wind. In the boat on the way here, he had explained it was his wife calling incessantly about their granddaughter, who had caught something of a cold. His wife, Fotis explained, had gone to the same doctor on this island for years—and had gone to that doctor's father before that. But let the grandbaby sneeze twice and no doctor here was good enough. A trip to Santorini might be in his future, he said, shaking his head, and that meant a three-hour ferry trip each way starting this afternoon. He jokingly said he'd welcome a faith healing right about now, and Avery and I had both laughed.

"Because everybody thought Mondavi was crazy?"

"Partly that, I think."

"Everybody thought Mondavi was crazy, when all California knew how to make was bloody *plonk*."

"Everybody but Mondavi."

"Of course."

"But also no," Avery said. "It had to do with his family, more than that. With what they did to him when he was young."

I know I had heard the story, something like a million times, but I had to force myself to not be angry that my father had shared it with this—this man who wasn't his son. It was the story of why conversation with my grandfather had never been comfortable, whether it was with my father or with me. And it was especially the story of why my Uncle Elias, his wife and my cousins had never been to our house for any holiday.

"Twenty bucks and a handshake," I repeated. "Did he tell you about that?"

"Yes, that's what *his* father gave him."

"When the old man kicked him out of the business and out of the door."

"Robert Mondavi," Avery said, nodding. "Same basic story. Except maybe without the twenty bucks."

Shielding his eyes from the sun, Avery gazed up at the terraced rows along the mountain beneath Agios Nikolaios. I had the impression he had hiked up and across the rows many times, presumably deep in conversation with my father, working over the plans and particulars of this "dream" I knew nothing about. I kept smashing up against that. Was it resentment? Disbelief? Some weird kind of jealousy? I was feeling weird kinds of just about everything on this island, so I could hardly rule out jealousy. Still, just when I thought we were heading up to look at old, abandoned grape vines, Avery started down.

"I've never seen the winery," he said.

"Really? I'm surprised."

"I suspect there's nothing there." He kept climbing briskly down toward the beach, where we could still see Fotis on the dock on his phone. He was holding it with his left hand and swatting excitedly at the air with his right. "Come along, *Stelios*," Avery said, emphasizing my Greek name. "Let's see exactly what your father left us to play with."

At the bottom of the stone steps, we climbed awkwardly onto the concrete slab that supported the long, low building, making our way along the missing windows till we reached the single door. This was made of wood, very old wood, with a rusty knob and even rustier hinges. Not knowing if it was locked—there was a hole for a key we'd never hope to find—Avery turned the knob and pushed inward gently, then with greater force. He shook the door knob vigorously once, in case paint might be sticking it in place, then pushed one more time, until the hinges tore out of rotten wood.

"We'll need to fix this," he deadpanned, letting the door lean against the wall.

Even with every window broken, the interior was more darkness than light. There were glints no matter which way you looked, and the first few I moved to check out were simply broken glass. The floor of the building was simply the concrete, ever ready to trip you in the dark with one or more wooden pallets broken in sections, each entangled with lengths of rubber hose. There were wooden crates in the shadows too, and I pushed them carefully to the side as needed to pass from one apparent zone, one apparent work station, to another.

"Hey," Avery called from the opposite side of the space. "Are you thirsty?"

I turned and he was holding up a wine bottle with no label and, as best I could see, no cork. It did seem to hold some wine, however, until I moved closer. Avery tipped up the bottle as though to drain the black material filling its lower third, but nothing came out into his mouth.

"I'll pass," I said.

He tossed the bottle over his shoulder onto a mound of straw beneath a low rear window. I half-expected a donkey to poke his head in, and that probably wasn't the dumbest expectation I'd ever had in my life. I kept digging around, uncovering things that had no meaning until I could examine them in more light. One area was full of bound ledgers, most of their pages filled with columns of Greek that even a local might have trouble reading. I thought they might contain something that would help us, but it was likely they did not.

"Oh my," Avery shouted from the front corner, a place more drenched in shadow by virtue of being farthest from any window. "Come see what I think we have here."

I hustled over in that direction, responding to the excitement in his voice and banging my knee into the side of a small shelf buried in a substance from above best not studied too carefully. Wincing and limping slightly, I made my way to where Avery stood before a ghostly form beneath a stained bed sheet. He let me stare at the form for a moment, his grin becoming wider all the while.

"Would you do the honors?" he asked.

Finding a piece of fabric that seemed loose, I gave the whole thing an upward tug. Nothing jumped out to tear off my arm, so I applied stronger and steadier pressure, lifting the sheet past any place it caught. With one final effort, I yanked it free, letting it fall to floor beside a contraption made of ancient wood and rusted metal.

"As I said, Steve, *oh my*."

Even I, with my nose buried in the high-tech, computer-controlled, stainless-steel corporate investments of today's wine business, recognized what I was looking at. It was a large wooden barrel with space between each of its slats, topped by a screw that turned to press down a piece of flattened stone, with a wooden box underneath that narrowed on one side to form a channel. We were looking at the machine, the entirely manual machine, which had long ago pressed grapes to produce the juice that would become the wine of Delfinos.

"Wow" was all I could force myself to say.

For perhaps ten minutes more, we poked around the old wine press—I resolved to bring a flashlight the next time I came to visit. Who knew what I'd find? Eventually the dust and airlessness of the close quarters got to us and we moved back outside onto the slab beside the sea. Fotis was waiting for us.

"Yes," he said, somewhat bitterly. "My wife manage to locate the only doctor to be trusted with *her* baby in these entire islands. And that doctor is, as I feared, on Santorini, where of course he can make more money with the tourists. We must get back to town soon, I am sorry to say. I have a ferry to catch."

We commiserated with Fotis as best we could. This felt strange, I realized with slightly warped humor, when I was a few thousand miles from my wife and Avery seemed almost as many years from his.

Avery suggested that Fotis and I accompany him up into the vineyards—briefly, he promised. He said he wanted to make sure I knew what we were dealing with here. I'd seen the vineyards, had climbed the goat trail almost all the way to the church. I told him I knew what we were dealing with, but he wouldn't take no for an answer.

All the way up, about half way before we stopped, Avery talked about grapes—about the way they had to be pruned every year, not too little because they carried too much weight but also not too much, because the yields were too low. He talked about muscat, the grape he and several others on the island grew with some success, and also about assyrtico, which made a crisp and delicious white wine associated with Santorini.

"I think we can do that here, I really do," he said. "Your father brought in a chemist from the polytechnical college in Athens, to evaluate the soil. It was as he suspected. The same soil. The same sun. The same winds. What we have here, my good fellows, is Santorini without the tourists and sunscreen. What we have here is our chance to do something *wonderful* for this island."

It was an intoxicating vision, I had to admit, even if it also seemed a crazy one. As it turned out, what Avery said was only the start of the crazy. When I dared ask how he intended to find vines and, most of all, how he expected to get them to this mountain, the man merely nodded. He knew then he'd been right to insist I come up here. And he'd been especially right about how little I actually knew about making wine. Avery picked up a dried gray stick from around his feet—one of hundreds here, maybe one of thousands—and swiftly cut a deep slice into it with a knife he pulled from his pocket.

Grinning, he held the vine out to me, pulling gently at the dozen connections that still bound it to this piece of parched earth. The slice was green inside the wrinkled gray. It was wet.

It was alive.

I had taunted myself long enough. I'd dragged, since our board meeting, everything that was mine through enough self-obsessive mud to last me a lifetime. As soon as Fotis dropped us off at the square and Avery started walking home, I set off along the street with no name. It's true: none of the streets of Chora had any names, but this had become the only one that mattered.

It was pleasant among the tight, white plaster buildings, with small splashes of sunshine finding their way into shadows. Cats slept on window sills and on woven chairs in doorways anywhere there was an inch of shade. I located the door I knew all too well by now, already open to let in the breeze, and I stepped inside to face an instantly smiling young woman at the booking desk.

"May I help you, please, sir?" she asked in precise, uncomfortable English.

"Is Elena in the office today?"

I have to say, my question confused her completely. Her expression betrayed that she knew who I was asking for but did not understand why. That was a mystery that waited at the heart of whatever Elena actually *did* here. But I had asked. There was no taking the words back. And even the temptation to run away when the young woman disappeared through a closed door seemed unworthy of whatever impulse had gotten me this far.

"May I—" Elena said, the door opening. She stopped. "Steve. Why are—" She sensed the young woman's presence behind her. "Oh, Melina. Everything is fine. I will be back. In two minutes only."

I felt my elbow gripped by an eagle's claw. After scanning the narrow street in both directions—no one was there—Elena moved us twelve or fifteen feet from the door and glared at me.

"Do you know anybody," I said lightly, "who can make me a deal on a used *moto*?"

More than a week to think about it, and *that* was the best I could do?

"Steve, please," Elena said. "You cannot come here to see me. You must not. It is—" I felt the word *dangerous* coming on, but all I heard was "not good."

"I understand." I was all too aware of the sun, the breeze, the plaster, the sky. Everything was starker, more dramatically inked in than it had been up till now. "I'm sorry, Elena. But—"

"You know you must not come here." She pressed her right hand to my chest. It felt good, until she put her strength behind it, pushing me away. "And you know why."

"Your boyfriend." It was not a question.

"Yes."

"I don't see why—"

"No, Steve. My boyfriend *owns* this business."

I caught her turning to glance at the door, as though the sound of our voices might carry for miles, to other islands, as though at any moment Melina or somebody a lot less forgiving might burst out, perhaps armed and dangerous. I felt awful, really. Awful for coming here like this, awful for walking in with a brainless joke on my lips and causing this woman so much concern or heartache that she hadn't asked for, didn't in the least deserve.

"Of course," I said, all resignation.

"I cannot see you here. Is not possible."

Something in her voice must have gifted me with what I said next, because it had seemed, for several eternal seconds, the farthest thing from my mind.

"Then *where*?"

Elena raised her hands to cover her mouth and shut her eyes tight.

"We cannot," she said.

"Yes, Elena. We absolutely can."

Sometimes in this life, thinking is a visible thing, a painful labor you see in the eyes and across the gathering forehead. This, for Elena, was one of those times.

"Tomorrow night," she said quietly. "On the square. Ten o'clock." She turned and made it half way to the door before stopping to face me one last time. "Up the stairs."

And a lot of things that hadn't made any sense to me suddenly did.

20

When you wake up like clockwork at six every morning, which is my blessing and my curse, it's a long, long wait until ten at night. Leave it to my ancestral countrymen to do everything that matters after my bedtime.

To make the hands turn on the non-digital clock in my mother's guest room, I went to work on my father's not-at-all-new desktop Dell computer, which naturally he had brought here from the place of its construction. I suspect that, by now, it was slow on its own, but it was made all the slower by the island's snail's–pace internet. I worked on my father's estate—logging in bank statements and answering questions from seven banks in Houston and three in Athens—for what had to be seventeen hours. By the time I ran out of things to do, it was nine–thirty. In the morning.

The clothes van came to my rescue, and this time I was ready. I kept the man parked in front of my mother's apartment for a solid hour, engaging him in a conversation neither of us could understand though I peppered it with every Greek word I could think of—and buy a decent chunk of his men's stock. I got shirts, dress pants and cargo shorts, plus a couple pairs of tennis shoes, socks and underwear. I even found a pair of jeans, the thing I missed most from my life in Texas, that didn't fall around my ankles if I hitched them with a thatched belt.

Nothing was of any particular quality, of course, and nothing I bought or even looked at was produced in Greece. Everything hailed from the latest Asian country renamed by some coup, or by the popular revolution that toppled the last coup. By this point, I didn't care. By the time I got my new wardrobe sorted, drawered, hung up or folded, my mother emerged from her bedroom.

"Good morning, Steve. How are you?" she asked brightly, moving, speaking and no doubt thinking more slowly than she realized, a clear result of the doctor's pills.

"Fine, Mom. And you?"

"Well, I'm fine too."

She came into the kitchen, where I was drinking black coffee that I'd dripped and crunching on a couple slices of toast I'd made from whole–wheat bread from a tiny market along the town's cliff face above the sea. She was wearing a white print dress with colorful flowers, tied along her left side with a wide bow. Her white–streaked hair looked carefully brushed and she had put on a little makeup. My mother studied my breakfast disapprovingly, almost moving around it to make sure it was no more and no less than she thought.

"Can I make you," she said, "a real breakfast? I have eggs. And I had Fotis pick up some extra bacon when we knew you were coming."

I gazed up into her eyes. "No, Mom. I'm fine."

"That stuff won't stick to your ribs, Steve. I'm perfectly happy to fix something."

"Mom, really. It's okay." I thought a moment, wondering how much it was safe to say. "This is the way I eat at home now, you know." I wished I could tell her this was how *we* ate at home, but I really wasn't sure. I didn't live at home anymore. "Mom, everybody knows I need to eat healthy things, especially doing what I do for a living."

This was true, as far as it went. But it wasn't exactly about something as delightfully vague as "eating healthy." It was about blood tests with numbers attached, about fat and cholesterol and having arties that actually allowed blood to pass through them once in a while. For Steve Laros of the Laros Restaurant Group based in Houston, Texas, the Days of Foie Gras and Roses were officially over.

"Can I pour you some coffee? I made enough."

She didn't answer, merely settling into the chair across from me. "I need to talk with you, Steve," she said. "About some serious things."

"Of course." I'm not sure why, but I reached around from my chair to set the plate of toast I'd been enjoying on the small kitchen counter. I took two quick sips of my still-hot coffee and waited for her to start.

"I've been talking with Nick, Steve."

"Yes," I said, filling the silence she left there.

"Nick and Sylvia have been very helpful in this, you know, helping me think this through. And yes, giving me some options."

"Options are always good."

"And, well, I've decided it's time for me to go home."

"America?"

"Houston," she said. And for a moment I felt a twinge of pure jealousy, since my mother, without a house in Houston, still felt she had a home.

"Nick says I can stay with them as long as I like, as long as I need to figure things out. I can help Sylvia with the kids a little, like every Greek *yiayia* should, but they're getting big enough they probably only want to do things with their friends. I'm sure I'll get a place of my own, eventually, when I find something." I caught myself wondering exactly who she was trying to convince. "Steve, a lot of my friends are widows now, and there are places that are nice for us in Houston. Really. It will be fun."

I thought what seemed a long time before speaking. I was feeling far too many contradictory emotions to be sure I could talk in complete sentences. "Dad wanted—" I stopped. Wrong idea. "Mom, it's up to you. And I guess I'm not surprised."

"I'm glad, Steve. I didn't want to, well, hurt your feelings."

"Mom, it's okay. This isn't about my feelings. It's about your life, about you being happy. And sure, there are a lot of great reasons for you to go home. Your family, your friends, great doctors and hospitals."

"You'll think about that, Steve, when you're old."

I was thinking about it already.

"The thing is," she said, "I don't know what timing is best, for me, for Nick and Sylvia, for you." She giggled, and somewhere inside that I saw the little girl she'd surely been. "Honestly, I'm ready to go right now. Throw a few things in a suitcase and I am *gone*."

"I know it must be painful for you." I swept my hand around the tiny apartment, as though it were some palace in Monte Carlo. "Being here, I mean."

"Yes. But no. It's not that."

"Okay."

"You see, this thing—this whole thing with the house, the winery—it was your father's dream." That word again. "Not mine. I went along, of course. He'd been a good husband and father. He had his faults, but I have to give him that. I loved him, Steve. I came here because, well, it's what I do. But without him—his dream makes no sense to me, Steve. No sense at all." Her lips struggled to form a smile. "I ought to hang a sign down by the port on my way out: "In Memory of George. This Goddamn Rock."

I almost didn't take time to laugh. There were too many things I wanted to tell her. "But there's so—"

"I have a few dreams of my own, Steve," my mother interrupted me. "You know? I haven't had much time to think about them, with my husband and my children, and of course just putting up with that business. But there *are* dreams, always. I just need some time to figure out what they are."

"I bet you could do that here. On Delfinos." This time, my smile was genuine and lasting. "It's an excellent place for dreaming."

"For me, no. It's not. For some people, yes maybe. For others, it's just a place to wait to die. That would be me, Steve. And I won't settle for waiting to die."

"Yes. I see. So when?"

"We can talk about that, of course," she said. "But may I please have that cup of coffee now?"

As her facts unfolded, she had talked at length with Nick about the timetable. There was, of course, a ferry to Piraeus every day, even in the winter. LRG actually had a preferred hotel in Athens—I couldn't image why, but then again, I hadn't stopped between plane and ship on my way to Delfinos—and a taxi from there could get her to the airport. And a flight from there could get her to Houston. It was all figured out. It was all I could do to look happy for her.

"That's great, Mom. So, in about a week?"

"That's what we're thinking, yes. I would sail out of this horrible place today, if I could. I don't know anybody here, not really, not like home. But that's not best." She saw me looking at her, perhaps sensed some disapproval—though seriously, why I *would* disapprove was a mystery to me. "This isn't my home, Steve. Houston is home, and I guess it always had been. Even my family, if you go back farther than I care about, is from some village in northern Greece. Nothing like here."

"I understand."

My mother seemed to stiffen, becoming some stern memory of herself that my memory had long ago displaced. "That's *me,* Steve. I'll be fine. I promise." She gazed at me, without the forgiveness or acceptance or love or whatever it was I was hoping for. "The only person I'm worried about is *you.*"

I wondered if, in Greek, worry was the same word as love. Maybe I would figure that out someday, when I was old. But not here. Not now.

"I'm doing okay, Mom. I'm organizing Dad's stuff. I know what I'm doing."

It's really not fun to hear your mother laugh at you, though I suspect she hoped I missed it. "Do you, Steve? Really? You come here to help me, and that's fine. I asked you to. I needed the help. But that's *over* now. Everything you do here, you could do in Houston. While being there with your family. While being there with our business, with all this airport stuff. They need you, son."

I'll never forget who I thought her "they" meant.

"Is that what Nick told you? *What?* They couldn't open seventeen more stores in five states this year if I wasn't there to pick wines? Or do the airport deal, for that matter. Nick was telling you that? Well, I'm telling you: *Not.* The goddamn things open themselves by this point, and as for wine—"

"Don't get upset."

"I *am* upset, Mom. And as for the wine, I guess it'll be like the Bible story, Mom. You know, where Nick wanders around telling everybody, 'They have no wine.' Hell, maybe he can just hire Jesus as a consultant and hook him up to the water fountain. They'll *have* wine, Mom. A monkey with a copy of Robert Parker could do what I do."

"But Nick says—"

The hand I raised in front of my face told her to stop, and she was smart enough to do so. I was drawing short breaths and feeling the beginnings of that steel band that loved nothing better than to close around my heart. I waited for it to ease up, let my breathing slow down, before I said another word.

"I'm sorry, Mom."

"I'm a grownup," she said, smiling with sadness in her eyes.

"You're my mother." I smiled too. "You'd better be."

I stood up. Sensing what I wanted, what I needed, my mother rose too and stepped away from the table enough that I could take her in my arms. I'd probably hugged her more in the past two weeks than in the past thirty years. We stood together for a warm, protective minute, though it was unclear to me who was protecting whom, and then she pulled back enough to look me in the eyes.

"Your family needs you," she said. "And more than that, Steve, you need *them*."

"I don't know, Mom." I covered up by staring at my feet for a moment, then at the counter that held my healthy whole-wheat toast, and finally let my eyes make their way back to hers. "I really just don't know."

21

"You are here," was her greeting. She was fiddling with her collection of keys that would open the door to the stairs. The door was not taking it well. I had pulled out what seemed a reasonable amount of euros, left them on my table and sprinted across the square.

"Yes. I am."

I'd been stationed at the table since seven, a small glass of *tsipouro* in front of me. I'd grabbed a quick souvlaki at a café—especially quick since the rest of the island wouldn't be tracking down dinner for hours—then delivered a salad and an *avgolimono* soup to my mother. She set the order on the kitchen counter, thanked me and said she might feel up to eating something later.

Fotis stopped by my table for an hour or so, back at last from Santorini. The baby did indeed have a cold or flu, and the miracle doctor had prescribed a week's worth of Amoxil. For this, Fotis groused, two adults had taken a three-hour ferry trip and paid for one night in a tourist hotel on a beach they had no chance to enjoy.

I offered him a tsipouro, and he had three before he had to get home and help his wife with the baby.

All the while we sat there, the men of the island stopped by, the men from that night at the distillery. These, I understood, were the growers who'd hoped to sell their grapes to my father. They reminded me that this had been his dream—it was obviously their dream too. Dreams die hard, I knew, especially when there's a chance that money might change hands. The men deferred to me in odd ways—ancient ways, I thought—addressing me with a level of respect nobody gave to anybody back in the States. Least of all, around LRG, to me. I felt like some combination of Bill Gates and Don Corleone, and I didn't know how I felt about that.

I was alone again on the square by nine. Though that was still early for Greeks, and indeed a few of the men might be back to drink, smoke and play cards later, it was late for them to get home to the dinner their wives had been cooking. They were older than I was, for the most part, so their children were grown. It was just them and their wives, perhaps with little to talk about and even less to do. But I didn't know. I *couldn't* know. And that made me sad. I'd managed to nurse that single *tsipouro* all night, but the thought made me want another. Happily, that's when Elena arrived, dressed in loose clothes and carrying her heavy-looking black bag over her shoulder, and started to unlock the door.

"You will see," she said. "What I do."

"But you work—at the *moto* place."

She shot me a laugh so quick and so dismissive it sliced right through me. "Okay, yes, maybe, Steve. That is what I do." The lock at last clicked and the door swung open. "But this is what I *love.*"

I took the bag from her to carry upstairs, and yes, it was heavy—like two large suitcases that blocked the escalator on a ferry what seemed a lifetime ago. She'd had no trouble carrying this bag when I spotted her, but it took an effort for me. I found myself thinking of all-day ballet classes starting at age four, followed by a career of practice and performance. I made a mental note to never underestimate Elena's strength again.

I took a seat on one of the benches that covered three sides of the open room, the room with the glowing curtained windows I'd seen from down on the square. She went to her bag where I'd set it and removed first a CD player—the kind of boom box or "ghetto blaster" I hadn't seen around Houston in years—and then a stack of CDs with colorful covers.

"I come to class early," she said.

"Me also." She realized I was mimicking her, but happily found it in her heart to smile.

About fifteen minutes before ten, young men and women made their way up the stairs, sometimes in twos and threes, and began strapping on the shoes they'd brought in bags of their own. The women's shoes were small, the men's more like boots, but more pliable than any boots I'd ever slipped on in Texas. Both styles featured long ribbons or straps, which were crossed and re–crossed till they were tied inches below the knee.

Elena gathered her students around her and spoke to them. I picked out only my name, "Stelios Laros," once and then again, no doubt presented as a stranger from a strange land. Several of the young men glanced over their shoulders in welcome. The young women kept their glances to themselves. Elena picked a CD with slow songs on it and came to sit by me while the dancers warmed up. We watched in silence together as they navigated a kind of square dance in slow motion, each taking turns moving into the other's space.

"It's fascinating," I said finally. "Thank you, Elena. For letting me be here. Letting me see this."

"It is dying, Steve."

"What on earth do you mean?" The word "dying" had so many other contexts for me these days that Elena's got lost among them.

"Dying, you know? Going *away?* All of it? All of *us*?"

I understood but had nothing I could say.

"So when my boyfriend say to me: Come to Delfinos, I say I must teach dance. I must teach the old dances." She smiled. "To the young people. I work, I say to him. I help him. But I must teach the dances. Before they are gone."

"And he said—"

"Of course."

I nodded.

"Yiannis understand what is important to me," she said with more than a little fire. "I am lucky woman, yes?"

"Yes, Elena. I guess you are."

That was all the conversation I got for the next two–plus hours, till after midnight. The men and women looked the right age to have decent jobs, at least the beginnings of decent careers, and I wondered how they'd ever get up and go to work in the morning. Then again, they were Greeks, so presumably it was what they did. Besides, with the crisis, it was a safe bet several had no job and no real prospect of a job. What they could do right now, all they could do, was dance.

It was impressive. I paid particular attention to the way Elena taught them, showed them each new move—and, in the case of the men, each new athletic leap. With her surgery, she couldn't do those things. But she pushed and led and encouraged each dancer to that point she could go no farther and then, using her strong arms, she lifted the man or woman into the precise position that came next. They'd try it once or twice on their own, and then she'd step in and arrange their bodies in correction, turning a hand a few degrees outward, fixing the angle of an errant foot. Even as a lifelong awful dancer, I found myself transfixed.

It was all, I slowly realized, courtship. Fast or slow, restrained or acrobatic, the dances were all about courtship—about shy women circling men, waiting for someone to move, to advance, and about men doing tricks to impress the women. This was courtship that was *courtly*, I knew. Old–fashioned. But I had strange flashes of recognition as well. As so often in my own life, I wondered with confusion and surrender: Who was the hunter and who was the prey?

The dancers glistened by the time Elena let them go. They unwrapped and packed away their shoes and boots, chatting quietly, then flung their floppy bags over their shoulders and headed out by way of the stairs. Elena packed her own bag as I stood at one of the windows, pressing the curtain aside to watch kids share a joke on the square, wave, tell each other *Ciao* (the Italian adopted into Greek, apparently) and set off in different directions. The square was deserted by the time I faced her. The bag was hanging from her shoulder.

"Well," she said, her tone light, "what do you think of my—my—holy crusade?"

"Holy," I repeated.

"And now you know what I do—I mean, what I love. And I think, Steve Laros, maybe now you can leave me in peace." She giggled. "Maybe."

"Is that what you want, Elena?" I suddenly felt miles away from her. I left the window and moved closer. As she figured out what to say next, I moved closer again. I hated being miles away from her. I *couldn't* be miles away from her.

"Yes," she answered. "I think it is."

I barely heard her. I drew her into my arms with such force that her bag fell to the floor. I covered her full lips with mine and kissed her without wanting to ever stop. She shoved me backwards with both hands, then used one to stop me from falling—which proved fortunate when she decided, a half-second later, to pull me back against her. There was an audible collision. "*Now*," she said at last, drawing away. "We stop, yes?"

"No."

"*Yes,*" she said, with the same voice I'd heard her use to correct careless dancers. "We stop this now. We stop *everything*, Steve, okay?"

"I really think I love you, Elena."

"And that, my friend, would be a very bad idea."

"Why?" I felt like such a *guy,* asking the world's dumbest question with the world's straightest face.

"I have a boyfriend, as I tell you," she told me. She held back momentarily. "And you, sir, have a wife and a daughter back in Houston."

That stopped me, but not for any reason Elena or anyone else would think. "But—*how*?"

She let herself smile with satisfaction, not without a bitter, knowing edge.

"The Internet," she said. "Amazing thing, yes?"

"I—I—I was going to tell you. I wanted to tell you, but we never got to talk. I *would* have, maybe tonight."

"Of course," Elena said.

I was telling the truth. But it was equally the truth that Elena didn't believe me.

"Now you must look," she said, with less emotion than I expected, far less than I wished. "You are here and I am here. It is a small island. You will do what you must do, with your father's—"

"Estate."

"With his estate, yes. And someday soon, you will go back to your nice life in Houston. And maybe sometimes you remember your friend on Delfinos. I, on the other, um—"

"Hand?"

"Yes, hand, I will return to my Yiannis, and to his business. His businesses, really. His family has lived on this island forever. They are respected. He asked me to help him build something wonderful. He is *buying*, Steve. New things, new properties. He has so many plans. He want to marry me. And I have been search—is that the word in English, *search–ing*?—for a new life. He has been giving one to me."

"*I* can give you a new life, Elena. I know I *want* to."

She looked at me sadly. "Why, why, why," she asked. Her words became a whisper. "*Why* please does the best thing happen—always at the worst time?"

To that, the most I could do was shrug.

All the way down the stairs to the square, and all the time Elena was struggling to lock the door, I had a question eating away at the back of my mind. It was, I'm sure, the least romantic question in the history of the world. But I thought I had to ask it, because I was beginning to suspect I knew the answer.

"*Elena.*"

She stopped. The street lamps dropped circles of liquid gold on the stones, like pools left from an unexpected rain. "Tell me just one thing, Elena. *Then* you can go. This is Greece. It's the middle of a financial crisis. And nobody I meet acts like they have money to buy an *apple*. So how in the *hell* is your boyfriend—this *Yiannis*—buying up everything in sight?"

She cocked her head, looking at me but not understanding at all. "He has a special gift. For finding—how would you call them?—*investors*."

"Somehow," I said, suddenly studying every detail of every inch of the square, "I'm not surprised."

The next morning, waking up before light in my mother's guest bedroom, I felt as though all the island's donkeys had spent the night aiming their hoofs at my head. Many of them had proven quite accurate. It certainly wasn't the *tsipouro*, as I'd consumed only one in my effort to make the hours pass before seeing Elena. It had lots more to do with beating up on myself. I felt brave yet cowardly. I felt stable but in the middle of a nervous breakdown. I felt as premeditated as a murderer but uncertain even if I would be lucky enough to draw another breath.

I was in love. If there were any words to describe how I felt, those had to be the words. But this was a stupid love, a hopeless love, probably even a dangerous love—I didn't know about Yiannis Mariotis, but I had my suspicions. I felt like one of those desperate guys in the movies who's just been given a month to live. And I was frightened for Elena. Somehow she'd been drawn to this island by her own love, her own passion for a new life when the old one had been taken from her. I was painfully aware of how such an ill-advised, poorly reasoned, profoundly destructive thing could happen. It was happening to me.

Few things show my confusion more clearly than what I did next: I stole Fotis' boat.

To do that, of course, I had to leave my mother's apartment, walk the three kilometers along the mountain road to the port in the dark and drag the boat from its preordained place on the sand. I was just about to push off when a moment of good sense prevailed. I walked to the small house in which Fotis slept, located a pen and paper in the mass of trash, fishing gear and outboard motor parts filling the porch, and left the man a note.

"But your honor," I heard a voice a lot like mine say in some faraway court of law, "I left him a *note*."

There was plenty of gas. It only took a few pulls before the outboard kicked into action and, after a few corrections and overcorrections, I found the right feel for steering around the dark promontory into open sea. The sky was lightening along the horizon in the east, and I could see patches of cloud and then bits of "rosy–fingered dawn" struggling to climb through them. Homer would have been so proud. And as I always told Chloe when she was little, just to see her laugh: I *don't* mean Homer Simpson.

There was peace in the steady thrum of the motor, and the steady foot massage of the waves. I tried my best to let go of everything, to think of nothing—just to feel. But my life had not prepared me just to feel. I was jealous of others who were different, who were better and more, but I didn't know who those people were. A lot of them probably lived here, I decided. But I was sure their lives sucked every bit as much as mine did.

And then, as suddenly as it had started, it was over.

Without asking my own permission, though everything inside me knew I was going to my father's house, I shut off the motor. It was quiet, silent really, except for the occasional call of a seabird. I had been running and doing, doing and running, every moment since I came here. And I understood: all that something I hadn't been feeling was coming up on me from somewhere behind the boat. It made no sound, it carried no wind or wave, yet when it struck I doubled over with a pain worse than anything I'd ever begged a doctor to explain. I threw my head into my hands without caring, my tears flooding out through my open fingers. The thought crossed my mind that I might never be able to stop.

Tears always stop, of course, if you can afford to wait long enough. And I saw no reason to wipe them from my face and hands or wring them from my shirt when I carefully slipped over the side and disappeared beneath the waves in the blinding morning sunlight. It was a baptism, as Father Michael would have been happy to explain to me. Except that for just this once, I already knew.

Within half an hour, I was dragging the vessel up onto the beach and trying to remember, to the smallest detail, how it had been placed when I stole it (only borrowed it, I would insist) to make my run. I hadn't run terribly far, but it had been far enough. Satisfied, I walked up to the house, listened till I gathered no one was up and about, and grabbed the note from the place I'd left it. There was a fisherman's café opening for business as I walked past it toward the docks and the road. I crumpled the piece of paper and two-pointed it into a can that smelled like yesterday's catch. In some elemental way, I was free. I knew exactly what I had to do next. In all the time I'd spent with Avery over the past few days, he'd made only the broadest allusions to where he actually lived. I'd seen the street he took from the square, watched as he pointed to someplace called home as part of various stories, even noted that all the men who grew grapes seemed to know where he grew his. But I didn't know, and it struck me as funny that only *that* place made any sense for me to go right now. Walking up a couple blocks from the port, I heard the morning's first bus cough to life after its driver stepped out of a café, drained his coffee and slapped the cup atop the white wooden rail.

Excellent, I thought. A bus back to the town had to be a good start.

From the square, there were only so many streets I could choose that went in the right direction; unfortunately, none of them ever met up with the others along the way. I followed two dead ends, or at least streets that petered out into a few huts in the dry, burnt-over Delfinos countryside. Each time, I had to go back to the square to try another route. The third time was, as often predicted, the charm.

I found myself perched on a rugged outcropping of gray rock, with only a memory of Chora to my left and a small, rustic house to my right—and, oh yes, the dust and smoke and noise of the airfield construction spread before me. If anything, there was more equipment working the site today—an earth mover, a pile driver and some super–sized version of a Texas backhoe. When it came to making the most decibels, there was clearly money on the line. Rubles, I'd come to suspect. Unless the Russians were using euros now, which they most certainly knew how to do.

And in the middle of all this, seemingly unaffected, stood Avery. He was watering a series of rose bushes at the end of each row of winter–dormant grape vines.

"My dear boy," he exuded when he spotted me standing at his gate. "How good of you to find my little piece of paradise."

"I thought I would. I thought I could."

"And you have."

While not wasting a drop of water on the nearest rosebush, Avery planted a swift kick on the gate and it opened outward to let me in. I used a hand to pull it closed, and then followed the old man as he moved deeper his vineyards.

"I wanted to talk to you about something," I said.

"All in good time, Steve. First we need to walk this land."

It sounded huge, profound, almost *biblical*—until I realized that these very feelings, these very passions, were as ancient as the Bible, maybe more ancient. They came from the time humans first poked around this island and started wondering how to call the forces that directed their lives by a name.

"This is muscat, of course," Avery said, as though I surely would have recognized the vine. I didn't. I dealt with wine in my job back home, and wine always came in bottles, and bottles always came with labels—plus printed sheets of "tasting notes" to tell me exactly how it tasted. In Avery's vineyard on the island of Delfinos, there clearly would be no tasting notes.

It was a bit over an acre, he explained, the biggest parcel acquired with the house when he bought it, a few others along the fringe acquired from neighbors as the old timers passed away. Now, Avery laughed, he bet a lot of young people wished they hadn't sold him their grandparents' crappy land on this crappy island. They would have a place to go and live.

"That's what this is for you, isn't it?" I said. It was only grammatically a question. "A place to go and *live*."

"Why, that's putting it too kindly," he laughed.

As we stepped across some low–lying, undeveloped rows on the outer edges of his vineyard, I felt the wind pick up. By time we reached the summit, it was roaring in our ears.

"Cover your eyes, Steve. It can get rather dusty up here."

My hand was already on the way to my face, and we both stood that way for a moment, the blue sea stretching in every direction, watercolor suggestions of other islands in the distance. Avery's mountain dropped directly to the sea, and I could pick out sharp knives of rock pounded by foaming surf below.

"This," Avery said, "is what I really wanted to show you."

At first, seen through my fingers, the hard ground seemed covered with Christmas wreaths—except these were gray and dry and stick–like rather than bright, jolly green. Forcing myself to focus, what the ground held were actually vines, not running along the surface or hanging from wood or wire. These vines were wrapped or woven into tight little rings, some rings no bigger than a foot across, and they seemed almost tossed onto the ground rather than planted there.

"Santorini," Avery said.

"What?"

He smiled at me, lifting his hand as long as he dared so I could meet his eyes. "It's how they grow grapes there, on Santorini. Because of the high winds. Your father asked me to try these. He wanted them for his vineyard."

"What are they?"

"Here, Steve, you are gazing at the first assyrtiko ever cultivated on Delfinos. Here is your fortune, if you happen to be looking for one. And here is our future."

After that, we stood in silence. Not least because we couldn't stand there for long. Eventually, in the wind roar, Avery gestured for me to follow him—down through row after row of his muscat, down to some peace and quiet. Once we dipped beneath the wall of rock, the wind died as though it had a switch, and all I had left was scratchy eyes and a very dry mouth. Before long we were strolling along his hedge of roses.

"Quite civilized, don't you think?" he laughed. "Not a bit like—up *there*."

I nodded my agreement. My mouth wasn't working yet.

Avery led me inside his house. The place was neat and clean, the plaster walls accented by bookcases and shelves of light wood. He said he'd done the work himself, which impressed me. Doing what I do for a living—what I *did?*—I'm never above noting when somebody's good at something. It might turn out to be something I need. The kitchen was spotless, with the uncluttered, no–gadget countertops any serious cook learns to value.

Avery sat me down at the kitchen table, which I noticed was covered with diagrams of parcels of land. The writing on the sheets was all in Greek, which had the effect of making what I took to be Delfinos feel more like *terra incognita* than ever. I had to laugh at myself. There I was using Latin, when a tiny amount of Greek would do me a hell of a lot more good.

Partly on a whim, partly because of the stacks of papers and partly because it's why I'd tracked him down in the first place, I said, "Avery, tell me everything you know about the Russians."

"And that," he answered, his eyes both sad and shining, "may require a nice cup of tea."

The Russians had started coming to Delfinos, Avery explained after finally giving up on making me add milk to mine, in the early 1990s. Since he'd already established himself on the island by then, this was a vivid, personal memory, not some history from the library. But then again, he said with a smirk, they were mostly criminals.

Mafiya, and bigtime crooks to boot. The people who owned things that politicians wanted. The people who *had* people killed, rather than actually killed them. And for better or worse, he insisted, they didn't ruin the island all that much, since they mostly stayed on their yachts. Their occasional underling came ashore, buying the fresh meats, fruits and vegetables that few on the island could afford anyway. And then of course the vodka.

"The shops started carrying it, taking up valuable ouzo space," Avery chuckled. "The way of the world, I should say."

I nodded. It was.

"But then, about the time of the financial crisis—the beginning anyway, before we knew how bad it would be or how we were going to live through it—they came here in a different way. The fur connection was made, via Poland, and the resorts were built for the masses. And plans for the airport—or airfield, or whatever the hell that monstrosity I have to look at from my vineyard every day is going to be—were drawn up. That's when I started paying close attention, you know. And I've been paying close attention ever since."

"Avery, there are things here I don't understand."

"It *is* Greece, after all."

"Yes, I know. Fotis talks about the goddamn Russians, and so does everybody else on this island. How did they get here, then? What happened? Who let them? And can't we, in that famous American phrase, 'Just say no'?"

Avery gave me a tired and bitter laugh, lifting his right hand to run his fingertips together. "There's always this stuff, Steve. Always. I know we ought to be able to stop them. And I know we need to stop them. That's what all these papers are about. Every minute I'm not working with my grapes, I'm working with records from the municipality."

"Municipality? The local government?"

"The island government, actually—the entire island, and also the region, which includes most of the Cyclades. But what I've found is that the trouble is here. Far be it from me, a Brit, to explain how Greek government works—or doesn't, mostly—but I've managed to satisfy myself that the trouble is here."

"The municipality?"

"Indeed."

"So where is this place, these people, this thing? I haven't got a clue."

Again, the old man chuckled. "According to Fotis, you've already been there." Far greater bitterness than I was used to found its way into Avery's voice. "For all intents and purposes, here on Delfinos, the 'municipality' is your good friend Colonel Petrakis."

"Oh shit," was all I could say.

For the next ninety minutes, Avery talked to me about the Russians. Seen from his vantage point—even seen from his house looking west to the resorts beyond the mountains—it wasn't pretty.

At some point, paging through his stacks of documents as I listened, looking for some way all things on Delfinos might fit together, I asked my friend idly, "Do you happen to know anybody named Yiannis?"

"Only about half the men who live here."

"Crap, Avery," I said. "Come on. It's a start."

Barely. In time I came to see the history of Russian tourism here as a matter of "cover counts" and "check averages." In my business, the first is how many people you serve at any specific breakfast, lunch or dinner—any "meal part." And the second is the average of how much money each person brings in, whether one guy is treating a hundred or a dozen girlfriends are going Dutch. How many chef–artists had I encountered over the years, all of them wanting to open a restaurant with only ten seats and a check average of $300. As Rocky used to say to Bullwinkle: That trick never works. No, our family stayed in business because we average four–hundred covers per meal part and maybe, depending on the concept, an average check of $25, plus alcohol. Do the math.

On Delfinos, once word got back to Russia from Mafiya kingpins, the oligarchs arrived next—and they were merely the Mafiya kingpins who, as we say in Texas, cleaned up real nice. Or maybe the sons (and sometimes daughters) of Mafiya kingpins, though these tended to be spoiled, crude, careless and stupid.

Eventually, after the crisis and the departure of the foreign banks from Cyprus, popular tourism came calling. Thus the bargains on furs. Thus the strips of beach resorts, shops, restaurants and bars. And ultimately, thus the airfield. This would be an air*port* eventually, with three flights a week from Athens and Moscow, courtesy of Aegean, Olympic or Aeroflot. Before long, flights would arrive and depart every day.

There would be wear and tear on the island, the terrible kind that comes with too many tourists who spend too little money. It was cover counts and check averages, Greek island–style. Like upholstery in our restaurants, Delfinos would start looking faded and torn after too many Russians. By then, though, it might not matter. By then, there'd be no real Delfinos left. And by then, the Russians would have moved on to another playground.

"We've got to stop them," Avery said, nearing the end of his narrative.

Whatever document I was perusing at that moment, I answered, "I know."

If I, after watching too many detective films, imagined the truth jumping off the page in my direction—that all real estate transactions would be marked "Purchased by Yiannis for Boris"—I was due for a major letdown. But as I perused the stack of deed registrations organized by year over the past eight, I picked out not a single Russian name.

Lissaiou, Giamniadakis, Angelou, Korovesis...

There was, in the purest sense, nothing out of the ordinary. It did seem the number of transactions had increased during the past three years, a period coinciding with the greatest expansion of Russian activity on Delfinos. But—these were also the years of the financial crisis, when every Greek suffered but some managed to suffer a lot more happily than others.

Finally, in frustration verging on despair, I constructed a single stack of all the deed registrations, twisting each year sideways from the one before out of respect for Avery's obsessive labors. I let out a long breath and flopped hard against the back of my chair, my chin settling almost to my chest.

"Nothing?" he asked.

"Nothing."

"Surely you think *something*, after all you seen?"

"I think," I said, "that Greeks still use a lot of lovely stamps whenever property changes hands."

"It's true."

"And I think some Greeks still have beautiful penmanship—at least the people who sign shit like this for a living."

Avery understood. We were nearing the end of a long road. My eyes were burning. As I rubbed them, shooting sparks through the center of my brain, I pictured again the transactions I'd seen, over and over and over, each time a property changed hands. There was no theme, no recurrence, not clue—

Except.

I picked up the top, most recent batch of papers, double-checked what I remembered and pointed to the bottom left of the top page.

"Avery, what's this right here?"

"Hmm." The old man looked, slowly raising his hand to his beard and stroking gently. "I actually believe that's the *agent*. The person or company who handled the sale, you know, between the buyer and the seller."

"And I personally believe, Avery, that nearly all the real estate sales on Delfinos over the past five years have the exact same agent."

"*Mariotis*," he read, giving each syllable its own space. "Very, very old family on this island. And very respected."

All I said was, "Bingo!"

24

Having made plans for our next step, Avery and I were talking at his garden gate when my mobile vibrated in my pocket. If anything, the few calls I received these days had become even fewer, not least because I'd shunted the banks and attorneys onto email to maintain a paper trail. That left only the one attorney in Athens who kept suggesting we have coffee. An Old World touch, to be sure.

I retrieved the phone from my jeans pocket, saw one of those numbers that seemed to run on forever and ruled out Fotis. I was starting to recognize his number that ran on forever. The voice on the other end of the call was probably the absolute last I expected to hear.

"Hello, this is Steve Laros."

"Yes," the voice said. "It's Elena."

If you could draw a spectrum of emotions, from ecstatic to suicidal, I think I suddenly felt every one. I waved to Avery, who understood about the phone call, and walked quickly along the path to the road back into town. I stopped exactly where I'd stopped before spotting Avery among his roses, on that rock outcropping over the sea.

"Elena. I'm sorry."

"It's okay."

"No, I mean, I'm *sorry*. I've been thinking. I had no right to expect so much of you, to ask so much of you, no right at all. You're a good person, Elena, and I guess I needed a good person in my life. Make that: I *need*. But that doesn't mean you have to do anything or change anything or—guess what? I don't know what I'm saying."

"I know what you're saying," Elena said.

"Well, good. That makes one of us."

I was happy to hear her laugh. But I also heard a lot else, a lot of noise close by. There was loud talking and loud music and loud cars or motorcycles, maybe both. The music may well have been bouzoukia. But hell, for all I knew, it was bailalika. That's what it sounded like. But the way my brain was racing, Beethoven would probably sound like balalaika.

"Where are you, Elena?"

"You know, those resorts. Yiannis had a meeting."

"Oh," I said. "Yes, of course."

"Don't be mad at me."

"Mad?"

"I mean it, Steve. I called you, didn't I?"

My tone eased up. The grip on my heart did not. "Yes, you did call me." I thought a moment, and then the words started tumbling out. "I've been there. There are hotels and restaurants, very lively places, and I imagine discos late at night, and then—"

"Please," Elena said, and the feverish tone of her voice shut me down. "Stop talking."

I did.

"Steve, I've been thinking too." I didn't know if the breaths filling my ears were hers or mine. "I may be foolish—you now, being a fool? But I would like to *see* you again."

I swallowed. Then, since the first time didn't work, I swallowed again.

"Of course, I said. "There is always lunch."

"Yes, Steve. But no. There is something I would like to do, if you are willing."

"Of course."

I heard the muffled sounds of movement, perhaps Elena moving into a quieter place away from the crowd.

"*Eh la*," I said, using the Greek for "tell me," and surprising myself for doing so.

"I have been, Steve, you know, listening about you. You know, listening? Not asking, for that would be bad, yes? But hearing what the people are saying. And they are very happy you are here."

"I'll bet."

"No, really. They talk much about your father's house. Much about the winery they say you will build here."

"Boy, no secrets on this island."

She laughed. "Maybe not." Which was cruelly funny, all things considered. "I want to tell you, even though I know it is wrong to say. Do you understand?"

"Oh yes. I have a master's degree in wrong, apparently."

"*Please.* Hear me. Yiannis must go to Athens for several days, for meetings. They are sending the seaplane for him on Friday. In the morning."

"Seaplane—" I had nothing to add, apparently.

"I would like very much if you would show me, Steve. The house, the winery. Tell me about it all, please. Honestly, and no, I don't know why. But I think it would be good—a good thing, maybe. For us."

"Yes. I'm sure we can do that."

A whirring, popping sound had begun strangling the phone line, the line that wasn't a real line, the secret that wasn't a real secret. And I knew the call was about to be dropped. The last thing I heard Elena say before the silence was, "I want to go and see—" The universe was crashing down around our connection, but I'm sure I heard Elena say "—your dream."

25

"Good morning," I said with a smile to the young woman at the desk pressed against the inside of the window. "May I please speak with Mr. Mariotis?"

The headquarters of Mariotis Real Estate were in the high–rent district of Chora, which therefore made it the high–rent district of Delfinos: Old Town along the cliff to the sea and its pirates, an area originally developed by the Venetians. The Venetians who ruled the world. No matter where you looked in Old Town, there were perfect white houses with perfect blue or purple shutters, perfect flower boxes in windows with perfect cascades of explosively red flowers. It looked like a postcard. In fact, it *was* one. I'd seen the street I was walking along in several tourist shops opening for business along the way.

"May I ask to you?" the young woman said, the traditional notification that English would be a problem. "Are you wishing the older Mr. Mariotis or the—or the—more young?"

I smiled forgivingly. "Younger."

"Yes." She smiled too. "Younger."

"The son, I believe. If he is in."

"Please," she said, rising from her desk by the window. "I will inquire. Of him."

"And yes." I handed her my LRG business card. "Please tell Mr. Mariotis I will take only a few minutes of his time."

I found the only other chair in the outer office and took it, which was good since my wait lasted a while. Long enough for Mariotis and the young woman to have a solid chat about me. Long enough for Mariotis to make one or more phone calls. Finally, the woman came out, followed by a man in his mid–to–late thirties, trim but strongly built, with a mid–to–late thirties stubble of a beard and long, wavy jet–black locks. I had definitely seen him before.

"Mr. Laros," he said, extending his hand. "How are you this morning?"

"Lovely day."

"Indeed it is. Before we go into my private office, may I offer you some coffee? I am just about to order some for myself."

"Of course."

"Greek or filter?"

"This *is* Greece, no?"

He laughed and spoke rapidly to the young woman in Greek, then motioned for me to follow. Along the white hall beneath three sunny skylights, I slowed to study four framed portraits. Mariotis seemed to appreciate my interest.

"These are my ancestors, who started this business," he said, then corrected himself a bit. "Of course, this business didn't *exist*, exactly. Except as something the Turks used to do to steal from us. My family has been here on Delfinos since before the War of Independence."

"1826?"

"Bravo, Mr. Laros."

"We still learn a few things in America."

In my own life, I'd seen such halls, with portraits and other photos of my grandfather and even my great–grandfather. Except *these* men all looked like mustachioed bandits and revolutionaries on their way to becoming wealthy, suit–wearing merchants. In the earliest photos we have of my ancestors, they all look like busboys.

I actually *was* interested in the photographs, but I also wanted to stall a bit in hopes Mariotis—Yiannis—would feel the need to push our conversation along. This was Greece, where a conversation can take a generation just to get to some point. Our coffee arrived, delivered by a boy who looked about ten and carried the two cups on a silver tray. We took a few ceremonial sips before getting down to business.

"I knew your father," Mariotos said, setting his drained cup on his desk and facing me in one of his two visitor chairs. Clearly, *couples* tended to buy real estate, here or anywhere. It made me ache a little. Mariotis gave his head a quick bow. "May his memory be eternal."

"Thank you," I said warmly, scanning the room for a place to set my cup. Mariotis was rising to take it from me when I spotted a small side table. He nodded that it would be okay and I placed my cup atop several glossy magazines.

"Yes," he said. "He came to me when he and your mother arrived. He asked my—assistance?—in viewing some properties. And of course I helped him with the purchase of the house. Quite impressive, I think?"

It was a question, so I answered, "Quite."

By now, Yiannis Mariotis was leaning his chair back against the wall—which held a giant map of Delfinos, with a smaller, closer–in map of Chora's streets cut into the lower right–hand corner. His fingers were laced together across his chest. His long hair was covering the port at which I'd landed.

"Mr. Mariotis," I said. "I notice that you say my father bought a *house* from you—"

"With my help. Not *from* me."

"Of course. Did he speak with you perhaps about a winery? About building one?"

"At the beginning, no. In fact, he never spoke directly with me, or with my father who was involved, about any winery on Delfinos. I have heard things, though." Mariotis smiled in a way that edged toward the sinister. Or was I only imagining that? "People *do* tell me many things."

"I see." I wasn't sure where I was going, but I understood that I had to go there. "It is good that you still have your father with you. *Fortunate*, may I say?"

"Yes, very. He comes to this office many days. He is a great man. He built many things. He taught me many things. About business."

"And so—I think you will understand the special *burdens*—of being a son—to a man like that."

"Of course."

"I am considering—" I stopped. This was more than I'd told anyone so far, yet with Elena's words still in my ears and our visit to the house and winery in my future, it was sounding more natural by the second. "I am considering some *completion* of my father's dream."

"I see."

"*Some* completion, I say." I smiled. "I do not know yet what kind. And I thought you might help me, as you helped my father.""

He paused, then brightened into business formality. "I am at your service, Mr. Laros, as is my—*this* company."

I stood up. Mariotis tipped forward, confused by my doing so.

"I'm sorry," I reassured him. "I have some things—some places—in mind as part of a business plan here, and I want to ask you about them. Our family, as you know, has certain resources." I nodded to the map behind his desk. "If I may—"

He stepped to the side as I moved behind his desk. Tracing my finger around the map of the entire island and then the Chora inset, I located the main square and then inched west along streets that were becoming strangely familiar. My finger moved into the broad plain before the line of mountains, then started back again, reaching the edge of town below Avery's house.

"There will be an airport, yes?"

He laughed. "Well, like Delfinos—very small. But yes. The work goes on, even with the crisis. Mostly private planes, corporate, charters perhaps. Why not?"

"Big runway, it looks to me."

"Build for the future," Mariotis said, as though that would always explain everything.

"Of course." I nodded, considering said future, then turned back to the map. "So along this street right here, there are small buildings that are connected in an interesting way. Am I correct?" I was. "Some occupied, some abandoned—quite rundown, really—and a few are listed for sale. With *your* sign on the wall."

I turned to see Mariotis studying me. He did not look happy. His jaw was working as he tried to determine the next best thing, his options presumably ranging from handing me a brochure to having me killed as I walked back to my mother's.

"Oh *that*." He made light of the real estate, lighter than I felt he should. "We have only a few properties there, as you say. And, if you must know, those properties have recently been taken off the market. A buyer has been located. We are waiting for the contracts to arrive from Athens." "

"What a shame," I said. "The buildings, if I might acquire all of them together, would fit nicely into our family's plans." Pausing, I looked back at the inset near the bottom of the map, visibly refusing to let the idea go. "If I may ask, what are their plans for these properties?"

"Hmm. Commercial development, surely."

"Like mine."

"Yes. But frankly, as with your father and his winery, I am not told everything, as I'm sure you understand."

"Of course."

"I am happy you stopped in, Mr. Laros." He reached to open his office door inward. "If you don't at all mind, I will keep your card. If I find something that might be of interest, may I reach you at this number? Your mobile?" His eyes locked on mine. "Or perhaps at your mother's apartment? She seems, as I'm sure you know, a very sweet woman."

I wasn't certain how to escape his eyes, or escape the meaning of what he was telling me. Yiannis Mariotis knew where my mother lived.

"Thank you," I said. "I'm happy that someone in Greece has the money to do some good things."

He shook my hand, released it and nodded me toward the outside world. "Please remember, Mr. Laros," Mariotis said, his voice lowering. "Someone *always* has the money."

My brother Nick called me on his cellphone from Birmingham, Alabama, that afternoon. He was there recruiting a management team for our latest seafood concept, and he tried to sound chatty about that and everything else, but Nick was never very good at sounding chatty. He asked how I was doing and how Mom was doing and then admitted, somewhat illogically, that he'd just gotten off the phone with her. She was worried about me, Nick reported.

"That I know," I replied, and left it at that.

"So, hey bro." As a younger brother, Nick had always needed to out–American me, just as I had to out–American our father. "When *can* we expect you back? I signed the letter of intent on the airport thing, but the shit's piling up here, bro."

"I'm sure it is, Nick."

"So maybe you should just fly back with Mom. I got the travel people on that right now. Maybe just make it a double."

"I don't think so, Nick."

I heard him breathing. "So, you can tell *me*. What's goin' on over there? Mom says Dad's estate is coming right along. And except for that crazy house, most of it's right here in Houston anyway. Am I right?"

"Mostly right, yes."

"Then come home with Mom. This is serious, Steve. Good stuff—for the family, I mean. She'll be staying with us for a while. Maybe then you can finish with the whole estate business. Hey, from what I hear, the Internet's a lot faster here."

He laughed. I didn't.

"You need to listen to me, Nick. And at least this time, you need to *do* what I tell you."

"Okay. What do you mean?"

"It's about Mom. I can help but I think she's listening better to you right now. And you need to get her out of here. Off the island, I mean."

"I don't understand. I'm working on—"

"I can't talk about it. You need to get her on the ferry tomorrow, even if she has to spend a night or two in Athens before flying out. There are places she can stay that are—safe."

"You're kinda scarin' me, man. You're also not making any sense."

"I am. You just don't know."

"You can try me."

"No, I actually can't. Just know there are people here, Nick. Bad people. And I don't want our mother where they can get to her."

"Why would they? I don't understand. This sounds nuts to me. Paranoid, bro."

"Do it, Nick. I'll explain later."

"I sure as hell hope so." He breathed in exasperation. "Jesus."

I wanted to tell him what I could, about the winery, about Fotis and Avery, about Mariotis, and yes, even about Elena. But there really was nothing to say. So I told him: "I'm not sure what I can tell you, Nick. Except there's a lot more here than I expected."

"Dad's assets?"

"Maybe. But probably not. It isn't *all* about assets. It's about trying to do what our Dad wanted. I mean, doesn't any of that make sense to you? It isn't only about what money he can leave us in some bank. It's about—it's about—"

"What the hell are you *talking* about, Steve?"

"It's about what he can leave us for our *lives*."

"Jesus Christ." I knew the tone. Nick always got it when he had to yell at somebody when that somebody was a relative. "We need you here in Houston, Steve. Bev and Chloe need you too, by the way, whatever the hell crazy shit you've got goin' on with that. And yeah, I have been pretty damn patient, right? Letting you guys work this out. But come on, man. Pop didn't just leave you some winery fantasy on some no–account Greek island—"

"Nick—"

"*No*. You know what he left you? And me? And all the rest of us? He left us a serious business to run. And you, bro, are not exactly doin' your damn part." He was rolling now, way past stopping. "If I could, I really think I'd—"

"You *can*, Nick. You surely *can*."

That actually did stop him. We stayed on the line without speaking for one minute, then two minutes. I was sitting at an outside table in the square, staring at a beer I'd ordered but couldn't bring myself to start drinking. The sun was shaking its way down through the leaves. There was a breeze.

"Come on, *bro*," I said, using his word on purpose. "Do you want to fire me, or what? If you do, then we can talk about it. You know we can. Or our lawyers can. Or whatever."

"I *don't* want to fire you. I just want you here. Here is where you belong, Steve. I don't like what that place is doing to you. Not one goddamn bit."

"Nick," I said, drawing a deep breath full of leaves and the sea. "Would it ever cross your mind in a million years that I *do*."

We gathered that night at 11 at the distillery—Avery, Fotis and me, plus as many of the grape growers of Delfinos as we could round up in a hurry. The fire was burning wildly under the antique still, and tsipouro dripped from the spigot into a series of plastic bottles.

With an effort, working between our two time zones, Nick and I had managed to book tickets getting my mother off the island the next day. The head of LRG's travel department worked from home in Houston, instead of sleeping, to arrange her flight from Athens after only one night at the Grande Bretagne. I'd never stayed there, of course, but Nick had a couple times. Accustomed to welcoming heads of state, the old hotel knew a thing or two about security.

We even convinced our mother, Nick on the phone and me going "home" for a couple hours in person, not to mention to anyone she was leaving. We assured her that anything she forgot to pack or couldn't fit in her luggage I would deliver when I returned to Houston "very soon." Even in the moment, I suspected all three of us knew that was a lie.

"My friends," Avery began once all the men had sat at a tight constellation of small tables he'd set up. I know that's how he began because Fotis sat close to me at one of the tables, whispering his quirky efforts at translation of the old man's Greek in my ear. By this point, I was pretty good at translating his translations.

"We have asked you here tonight to talk about serious things," Avery said. "For a very long time—you know this is true—we have suspected that our island is under attack. Just as it was when pirates roamed these seas and fired their cannons up at this town, our lives are at stake, I now believe. Our lives and even the life of our island." I heard murmuring, along with the almost simultaneous effort of others to shut up and listen. "Do we want," Avery asked, "to lose the life of our island?"

"*Oxi*," virtually every man in the distillery said, a few close to shouting the Greek word for "no." It was what the Greeks had told Mussolini's Italians and then Hitler's Germans, and it was what some of my relatives in Houston commemorate each anniversary with a holiday. How many countries on this earth celebrate "No Day"?

Avery let the men quiet down on their own, studying the oversized unlined notebook he had managed to secure to the table beside him. I didn't know what he was going to write or draw with the marker in his hand. At the moment, there were only two squares drawn on the sheet just below the midpoint, the one on the left marked SELLER, the one on the right marked BUYER. I'd filled Avery in by phone on what I knew from meeting with Yiannis Mariotis—or what I thought I knew. He and the Internet had taken it from there.

"The problem," he explained, "was that we didn't know what was really happening. Most of all, we didn't know what it meant to us, because we couldn't see the pattern. And that wasn't simply because we were dumb people, but because someone was going to great lengths to keep us from knowing the truth." Avery pointed his marker at each of the two squares. "See this? This is all we knew, all they *let* us know. It was eternal: one man sells to another man, one family to another family. Man and property, changing hands, as always. And then we wake up—and there's a resort, there's a boutique selling furs we can't even wear here, there's an airport ruining my view."

Avery laughed at his own joke, and I tried to join him. But by now, most of the men in the distillery were miles beyond thinking anything was funny.

"Until now, there was always something missing, beyond what was typical. But tonight, thanks to our friend from America—" he nodded to me. "—we can start to see what is happening to our island and who is doing these things to us." Again, he nodded to the squares. "This is where it starts, but not where it ends. There are people who buy these houses and land, and they are all Greek people. *Good*, we say. But there is something about these Greek people we have not known. They are paid a fee for one job, one job only. They make the purchase and then immediately transfer the ownership."

Avery drew a line upward and then another square. "To a holding company called DELOS VENTURES, chartered in Athens. That, my friends, is the last these buyers have to do with this real estate. And as it turns out, DELOS VENTURES doesn't have much to do with it either." He drew a line sideways, followed by another square. "For it immediately becomes an asset of PETRO DEUTSCH, headquartered in Switzerland but with its principals in Frankfurt."

"Goddamn Germans," one of the men uttered.

Yes, in Greece, people remembered World War II. Even people not born till *later* remembered World War II. Most of all, though, Germany these days was the source of "fiscal responsibility." Read: austerity measures imposed upon Greece. Read: joblessness and misery.

"No," Fotis spoke up. "Goddamn Russians."

Confused, the men turned to Fotis and then back to Avery.

"You see, my friends, while PETRO DEUTSCH is based in Switzerland and Germany, its mission is to sell oil to Europeans. To countries, cities, maybe private power companies, for all I can tell. What matters here is that it's all *Russian* oil. What matters is that it's, in truth, a Russian *company*, lock, stock and babushka." Fotis had trouble translating that, but I heard enough to catch the drift. "And what matters most to us here tonight is that, one way or the other, PETRO DEUTSCH is looking to be your next–door neighbor."

The men seemed to be transfixed by Avery's diagram, and I could see them staring at it, struggling to figure out what was missing, what kept the whole entirely sensible idea from quite making sense. One man, a grower named Alexis, finally chatted with the men at his table long enough to distill what was missing into a question.

"How can such a thing happen on an island like this, with only little banks, little businesses and little properties—most of them like my place, tied up in court since my grandparents died? I'm just living there, man, not owning *shit.*" The last word was in English. The men laughed roughly. "I just don't see how anybody is able to pull any of this off here."

Avery nodded, leaning to reach with his marker beneath the two original squares. He drew slanting lines toward the center from the bottom of each square, then wrote in bold capital letters: MARIOTIS.

"Holy God," one of the men uttered. He looked like he was about the start crossing himself.

"How in the hell," another man growled, "are we ever gonna stop *them*?"

Avery glanced at me. I stood up, ever the friend from America. "I have a few ideas about that," I said.

The next Friday, with my mother safely ensconced with Nick and his family back in Houston and me moved out of her apartment into a simple side-street B&B, I picked up Elena from the second cove on the left. At least that's what I took to calling it when she suggested we meet there—or more specifically, that we not leave from the port in the boat together. Greeks are nothing if not busybodies, she insisted, and Yiannis could be very cruel sometimes.

Truth be told, this upset me to no end. Yes, I actually *did* wish to save all the women on earth from cruel men in their lives. Except I couldn't. Except they didn't want me to. Except they had *chosen* those men. More often than I care to remember, they'd chosen them over *me*. Still, there was the cove, the second one after I steered around the promontory and headed north along the eastern side of the island. Elena would be waiting for me there.

And then she wasn't.

I was glad I'd worn a white, long–sleeved oxford shirt with my jeans, since it provided protection from the burning noonday sun.

After forty–five minutes of standing on the rock–strewn beach, I started looking for shade. I'd just located a rock that provided some when Elena, dance bag flung over her shoulder, arrived at the bottom of the trail.

"I am sorry," she said as I took the bag from her. "The seaplane was late. I was with him."

Preferring not to ponder that, I pondered the dance bag instead. It was full but much lighter than it had been at her class. I stowed the bag beneath the bench seat across the middle of the boat, helped Elena onto the seat and then waded out pushing and pulling till I could start the outboard motor.

It was, as always, hard to talk over the roar. I'd borrowed two glasses from the B&B and poured us each some white from the cooler at my feet. Elena, on the other hand, seemed to lighten and loosen with each foot we moved away from the shore. She started out wearing yet another of her colorful scarves and the floppy black hat I remembered so well from the beach. But within fifteen minutes she'd removed both and faced me from her seat, her hair free to toss and tangle around her face in the wind. I half–expected her to tie it back. Beverly would have before she even climbed into the boat. Elena tied nothing back. She was smiling.

The sea route to my father's house was simple and familiar by now, but I found myself looking at all things in new ways because Elena would spot something I hadn't seen before—a cave high above the sea that housed a gathering of baby goats, a flourish of color from water or vegetation on the rock as lovely as the world's greatest painting—and point it out to me without saying a word. After a while, it became a game, with me nodding and grinning whenever I finally figured out what she was trying to make me see.

"This is it," I was able to announce dramatically at last.

"The place," she picked up, "that Steve Laros plans to live."

"The place I plan to *camp*," I intoned with pseudo–solemnity as I turned the boat toward shore after rounding the final formation of jagged rock.

I steered toward the concrete dock as the land rose up around us, the mountaintop church of Agios Nikolaos slowly dipping from our view as the winery building on the left and the half–finished house on the right rose into reality. Perhaps, after all the work I'd done here over the past few days, the house was a little more than half–finished. I tied us up at the dock, lifted out cooler and dance bag, then offered Elena my hand. She took it and stepped up.

Truth is, within a matter of days, Elena's plans to visit and my desire to make my father's house livable had ceased to be independent things. They'd moved from simple pragmatism—the sooner I got something done at the house, the quicker I could move out of my B&B—to more like cause and effect. Each time I'd made a trip to the cove from the harbor, the boat loaded with tools, lumber, fabric or furniture that hung out over the sides and back, I pictured telling Elena this or showing Elena that. I knew it was dangerous to look at life this way, and especially dangerous to look at Elena this way.

There was still no power on the property, and I didn't know how long it would take someone to run some sort of cable down the cliff face from whatever kept the handful of lights burning at the church each night. But I was okay with the days being bright and the nights being dark, the meals being cold and the bath water being salty. For the first time in a long time, I had the perfect home.

Elena let me grab up our stuff, preferring to move slowly and silently along the winery's front wall and gaze in through the missing windows. I stayed a couple steps behind, enjoying the view. When she reached the end of the concrete, she lowered herself onto the sand and started with her uneven step across the beach to the stone steps. She'd heard me talk about my father's death, about my initial reluctance to spend time outside on the patio he'd been building with tile. She was surprised, therefore, to see that I had boated in and set up the table and two chairs that waited for us there beneath a bright yellow umbrella.

She nodded her approval of where we'd have lunch. I dropped off the cooler and followed her around the back and inside.

Actually, there was no back wall and only a partial roof—a blue tarp I'd tied with rope between us and open sky. You could still see the rafters and the way they sat so comfortably in the top of the plaster walls. The kitchen and bathroom remained largely unchanged, which meant largely nonexistent. But beneath the tarp I'd managed to build a plywood platform, a box and nothing more, and wrestled a full-sized mattress from the harbor and up the hill to toss onto the platform.

"You have done many things," Elena said, smiling in the indoor-outdoor life I'd created, without a single other human being helping, hindering or picking out the tablecloth color and pattern, though mostly because there was no tablecloth. During one early trip to the general store in Chora, Fotis had happened upon me staring at a shelf full of choices and said, "Hell, my friend, just get the one you want."

"I don't know what I want."

"Of course. You are a husband."

"Exactly," I said, and we both had laughed more insanely than we probably wished we would have.

I found myself thinking, looking at Elena looking at what I'd done with the house, that not knowing what I wanted was not an issue anymore.

Having run out of touring opportunities, since it was only a two-bedroom house, we headed down to the beach. I had packed a couple towels that I'd swiped from my mother's apartment as she was moving out, so all Elena had to do was peel off her loose-fitting top and unwrap the skirt that covered her black, one-piece swimsuit. Wearing my all-weather, all-purpose khaki cargo shorts, all I had to do was step out of the new deck shoes I'd picked up in town and toss my shirt up among the rocks.

The water was cold, bracing, terrific. Several times Elena dived under the surface and swam toward my legs, only to yank herself up with a mildly embarrassed grin. At least once I sneaked up behind her as she swam and started to push her under, only to realize that, considering her strength, I'd have to grab her body all kinds of ways to succeed. We were good-natured about it, though. I suspect we both understood.

Lunch at the table beneath the umbrella was penne I'd cooked at my B&B that morning, once both the official B's were out of the way. I'd tossed the pasta with slices of grilled chicken breast in extra-virgin olive oil mixed with fresh oregano and a squeeze of lemon, then tossed it again with chopped tomatoes and Kalamata olives. At the table at the beach, I sprinkled feta cheese over the top, then poured us each a glass of Santorini assyrtiko.

We called it lunch, but it was winter and the sun was dropping quickly on the western side of the mountains. In the end, we almost had to race to finish eating before the lights up at Agios Nikolaos would be our only illumination. I opened another bottle.

"So this is your wine," Elena said, swirling the golden liquid in the early twilight.

"No, it's our *grape*. Our wine will be from Delfinos." I smiled. "And therefore it will be better."

"Of course," she giggled.

Elena didn't say she had to get back to town, when or if she felt she ever had to. And I wasn't about to ask her about that.

Dark came on quickly, pushed against and then over the mountains by dark clouds that swept in from the sea. I lit a gas lantern and strung it from the underside of the umbrella, but after a while too much rain blew in anyway. We left the dishes to wash themselves and carried our lantern and our wine into the house.

For a long time, without having any sense of time, we talked. We sat on my sheetless mattress, cross-legged with our knees touching lightly, atop the platform I'd built, sipping wine and stopping now and again to watch the rain creating a solid wall in the darkness along each of the tarp's four sides. We talked about my life—my childhood bussing tables in my father's restaurants, my first heartbreaks, and about meeting and marrying Beverly. And we talked about her life, her dancing and her boyfriends in cities where she settled to dance for a while, all collapsing around her in Brussels at age 36 during Act II of *Les Sylphides,* leaving her crippled and crying on the stage as some kind soul brought the curtain down. We walked about other things too. Too many things, maybe. Except there was no stopping us. Until *she* stopped us.

"Are you always," Elena asked, teasing me gently, "so open with strangers?"

"No, not really. There are too many strangers." I smiled. "But you have never, for one moment, felt like one of them to me."

"Then, Steve, may I—what?—may I *suggest*? Yes." She handed me her glass. "May I suggest you put down our wine, please stop talking and kiss me right now?"

For what felt like forever, we stretched to kiss across the chasm created by our knees, the kisses soft and affectionate and teasing and comfortable, until they weren't anymore. She moved first, sliding against my hip and slipping back across my chest into my arms, her hands reaching up and drawing my face down. Catching her eyes, I placed one hand on the strap of her swimsuit, and her hand joined mine, tugging the suit off her shoulders. She lifted herself off the bed to let me finish the job. By the time I paid any attention, my cargo shorts and oxford shirt felt like they'd been gone for decades. It was touching and stroking and moving together, teaching and learning, discovering new places that suddenly weren't new anymore. I tried to say "I love you," but I don't think they got out before she covered my mouth with her own.

"Please," she said, "*please* you do to me—"

"What, Elena? I'll do *anything*."

"Do to me, Steve—what you do to your —"

My eyes questioned. "No, not her. I want—"

"*Anything*."

"I want—more."

"Yes," she said, her voice low, her words more breath than sound. "Then you must *not* do to me what you do." She lowered her eyes as a grin formed, then raised them back to meet mine. "Do to me what you *dream*."

So I did.

"You may ask the priest to bring the holy water," Elena giggled, her cheek moving against my chest, moments before we drifted off to sleep. "But I think we have christened this house nicely already."

The rain had stopped, finally. It had drifted over our mountains and away from our island at the time Elena and I had been least likely to notice. There was only dripping and splashing and flowing, rain-water making rivers over rock till it found its way to the sea. Elena had, at last, stretched from the bed and retrieved her dance bag. Unzipping it, she drew out two pillows and two sheets. We spread these around us without ever climbing free of them. Nothing was tucked into anything else, merely tossed and wrapped, but the sheets covered us against a chill that came in right after the rain.

"Housewarming gift," Elena slurred sleepily. I smiled, not at all sure which one she had in mind.

I slept more deeply than I normally do, perhaps more deeply than I had in years, but not all that much longer. I woke and touched my phone on the floor—it glowed 3:37. I rolled my eyes, snuggled back up against Elena beneath our nest of sheets, and after a few minutes decided it was time to get out of bed. My mouth was dry, dehydrated from all the wine. I gently rose, slung my legs over the side, and tucked in the sheets so Elena would be warm. It seemed too much trouble to locate my clothes, so I stepped outside on the patio naked.

The breeze was chilly, so I only stayed in it a moment, just long enough to dump out one of our wine glasses and fill it full of melted ice from the cooler. I downed it in one gulp, then dunked it into the end of our Ice Age once again. I carried the water back into the bedroom, which was warmer with walls blocking the breeze, and then to the unfinished side of the building facing the sea. I leaned against the wall that seemed most solid, Elena sleeping quietly behind me, the flat sea all around me.

All the clouds were gone. The moon had risen since we went to sleep, turning the dark sky to cotton and painting the sea in silver metallic. The water glinted, it glimmered, it glowed. It was a sheet of ice stretched from our house to the limitless end of everything. It burned my eyes, accustomed as they'd become to the unending darkness. I couldn't take my eyes off it, even as my thoughts careened from light to dark and, with a pleasurable nudge or three, back again.

Everything was different now—that much was clear. I had found a new life in a new place. These facts demanded something of me, something I was certain would be new, even as I wasn't certain what that something was. I had done much that was wrong, but I'd done it in order to do something right. I wondered how God, sitting in the church at Agios Nikolaos on the mountaintop, spent his days and nights parceling out things like that. Weighing things. Slicing and dicing our hopes and dreams and failures.

In my time on Delfinos, I'd felt my body changing. It was tanned, naturally, to a degree that no corporate warrior gets other than returning from two weeks in the Caymans. But this tan was different, as I didn't remember one moment of *seeking* the sun. My shape and physical condition had changed too, as each day of walking and climbing and hauling and hammering made my chest and shoulders broader, my stomach flatter, more *engaged* in everything I carried and every move I made. I looked down at myself, something I'd long ago taught myself never to do. I could see a difference.

And still, for all this rampant good health, there was that other thing. It won't go away, I lectured myself. There are tough decisions ahead, I reminded myself. And there are things you need to tell the people you love—or at least the people who love you. Who are *supposed*, by everything your world back home is betting its life on, to love you. On what timetable of the gods would Elena ever feel like one of those? Could I dare to let her feel like one? Gazing out at the silver platter of the sea, I wasn't sure I could make it through such thoughts without crying.

"Steve."

I heard the whisper at the same I moment I felt Elena's hand touch the center of my back, moving upward to rest on my shoulder. I didn't turn entirely, but I could see that she'd slipped on my white oxford shirt. Her cheek settled beside her hand on my shoulder and I reached up to stroke her hair. We stood that way for several minutes, not saying a word, feeling each other's warmth in the chill of night, sensing our closeness. Then there was something else warmer still, alighting on my shoulder, one after another, and running like heated rainwater down my back. With each tear, Elena seemed to surrender more, shuddering once or twice against me, then heaving with deep, painful breaths that became groans.

I turned. She looked up at me. I waited for her to say something, but she shook her head and, without warning, threw herself against me, shaking in the arms I used to encircle her, drawing her closer still till I hoped she could find peace and safety and tiny flecks of something like joy inside me.

She spoke a single word against my chest, but the sound was muffled. And when I asked her to say it again, she dissolved into almost violent tears. Slowly, she took control of herself and finally pulled back from me. I wouldn't let her go far, my arms draped over my shirt covering her shoulders.

"Yiannis," she said, her eyes filling for about the twentieth time.

I felt terrible. For all my self-convicting and self-justifying thoughts about my condition, my marriage, my life, I hadn't spent any time thinking about *hers*.

"I know," I said, halving the distance between us. "I'm—sorry."

"No, Steve. Please, *no*."

I stopped. She formed her lips deliberately, to pronounce the words, as though they came to her from very far away, only one at a time.

"Yiannis—told—me—to—do this."

I didn't understand. All I could say was "What?" and the way I said it, with so little knowledge of anything or anybody, made her tears flow all the more.

"He make me. He tell me to ask—to come here—with you."

I didn't mean for my arms to drop from her shoulders, almost to make a noise hitting against my body as though falling from a great height. It was all I could do not to fall right along with them.

"Why?" I stumbled, heading somewhere that ended up nowhere then grabbing the next road I spotted. "Elena, how did this—happen?"

"Yiannis, he wants you to leave here. He wants you to stop."

"Okay." Buying time. "Okay. Yes. But this is not Yiannis, Elena. Here and now. This is *you*. I don't understand."

"He said—"

"What?"

"He said you would be bad for our island. That you would try to stop things from happening."

"If I can, I sure as hell will. I love this island, Elena. And now I know I love you."

She shut her eyes tight. I couldn't tell if my words made her want to kiss me or kill me. She shuddered again and stiffened before my eyes.

"He had someone," she said. "Someone come here, to this house."

"Here?" Ah, the eternal feeling of violation. Even in a house missing several walls.

"Yes. The man. Come here with *camera*."

"Why the hell?"

"A video camera," she said, nodding back toward the bed, then turning her eyes to meet mine, as though pleading. "*For us.*" I couldn't believe it, didn't allow myself to believe it. But I was beginning to understand. Every word Elena said next shocked me to my core. Yet, by this point, every word Elena said next—I already knew. "For your wife, to show her. To—what?—*threaten?*" I nodded like an insane man, approving vocabulary words when my entire life was crumbling around me. "Yiannis said it would make you stop."

I thought about that. Until I told her.

"It won't."

Was that the slightest smile? It was gone before I could be sure. "I know that," Elena said. "I know that about you. Now."

"Are—" something was shifting inside me, something that hurt to shift because it had been in the same place so long. Something so heavy it held me down, until it couldn't and didn't anymore. "Are you okay, Elena?"

She was looking at the floor. Then at me. I held her gaze, and she held mine.

"There is no video, Steve."

"What do you mean?"

My breath did strange, dizzying cartwheels in my chest and in my throat. I watched as she reached into the pocket of my oxford shirt and pulled out something small. In the moonlight, the thing barely hung off the edges of her hand as she lifted it to me, the light of the universe glinting off two silver connectors at each end of the wire.

"I changed my mind," Elena said.

The storm of uncertainty, of betrayal, of fear inside me raged on. The best I could do was force it into a corner where I could try to deal with it later. I wasn't sure I could deal with it at all. After a while, she cried some more, less violently than before. And we finally sat side by side on the bed looking out to sea, my arms around her, waiting for the dawn.

30

I sat nursing a coffee at the port, watching in the late afternoon sun as an old woman in black swung octopus after octopus from a wicker basket against the rocks. It was messy work, with no shortage of blood and ink, but it was necessary for turning a tough sea creature into something tender enough to eat. It was enough, if barely, to take my mind off what I had to do as soon as Fotis came to pick me up.

It had been nearly a week since I returned Elena to the second cove on the left, and I'd sat in the boat with the motor turned off for the longest time, afraid she might come back down out of the rocks to be with me, at the same time hoping she would. But she didn't come back to me then, or that afternoon, or the next day.

Our briefest of phone conversations made it clear that she had returned to her life and her job—meaning to Yiannis, who had re-turned from meetings in Athens. I tried to ask how he'd reacted to the failed videotape, but she'd brushed my question aside. After our one phone call went so poorly, I limited myself to a few all-business texts, about what her dancers could and couldn't do, about exactly how they could fit into our plan. She said she couldn't attend tonight's meeting. That didn't surprise me at all.

After one more glance at the time on my phone, followed by one more look out at the rocks—the old woman was gone, making me wonder how long I'd been thinking—the phone in my hand reminded me to call Beverly. As I suspected it would, it rang ten times before her message kicked in, all about how much she regretted missing my call and how much she hoped I'd leave my name, number and reason for calling. I listened. It was the same message she'd had for two, maybe three years, so it was insane of me to think I heard something different in her voice. But I thought so anyway.

And then, it was my turn.

"Hi Bev, it's me. I'm sorry I missed you. Or, wow—I mean, it's the middle of the night, so I guess you're asleep so I probably shouldn't be calling you, huh? But it's me anyway, and at least I can leave you a voicemail. I hope you'll give me a call. I've talked to Nick, and he says you two came over for dinner with Mom. Um, that's great. Anyway, please call so we can talk." The orange sun was starting to flame out behind the rocks, and I had to shut my eyes and look away. "There's a lot going on over here. So, we can talk. Okay?"

I clicked off, feeling empty, feeling like an idiot. It was the third such message I'd left for Beverly in as many days.

"Hello, my friend."

I was just lifting the coffee to my lips and realizing the last thing in the universe I wanted was coffee when Fotis appeared beside the table. He looked me over quickly, then more slowly—my tan especially gave away that I'd spent every day since Elena left working at the house. I'd even started dividing my time between there and the vineyard, following Avery's instructions to cut away weeds and anything else that might suck the life out of the wines. Then again, he quoted the old maxim that "the vines must suffer." I wasn't having any trouble making sure they did that.

For his part, Fotis hadn't been around at all, having finally given up on sending his computer genius son out fishing by himself. Fotis had, for all practical purposes, become a fisherman himself, heading out in his larger boat before dawn and not returning till dusk. From what I'd heard around town, father and son were doing well—several restaurants around the square told me proudly they were buying all their fresh fish from them. Fotis was deeply tanned as well, with all the creases around his eyes glowing white, and when he took my hand between both of his, the skin was rough and hard.

"No wonder those guys were so happy to follow Jesus," he laughed, half-lifting me from my chair and hustling me off toward his taxi. It was all I could do to drop a few euros on the table before the two of us were on our way.

It was dark by the time we made it up to the town and found what might have been the last parking place three blocks away. The steps outside the church were already filling with men and women, standing in small groups smoking and talking, often separated by gender even though many were married. They gathered too beneath the street lamps of the square, and still others emerged from the darkened streets carrying flashlights. We spotted Avery almost as soon as we arrived, standing with the group of grape growers I'd met when we first talked about this, excerpt that even their numbers had grown. Avery introduced to the men, then turned to me. He was grinning.

"Amazing, isn't it?" he said. "So many are here."

"Yes. Thank you,"

He laughed through his white beard. "Don't thank me. Thank the man of the cloth, who practically threatened them with eternal damnation if they didn't show up."

As though that was his cue, the door to the church swung open and Father Michael appeared. He pressed the door shut behind him, looked once or twice around the square, then locked it with a key from a very large ring. Spotting our small group of instigators, he headed our way down the stone steps.

"The room is ready, my brothers," the priest said. "If you will follow me—" He led us to an alley along the left side of the church. "Reminds me a bit of Chicago in the old days."

"And you, Father," cracked Avery, "are too young to have any old days."

In the moment before we were to enter the alley, a hulking figure stepped out of the shadows, and I mentally kicked myself for not noticing him earlier from the glow of his cigarette. The people from the square had gathered behind us, and together we all laid eyes on Colonel Petrakis, his legs spread for balance, his large arms folded across his chest.

"Good evening, Father Michael," Petrakis said in Greek. I could understand up to a point. Fotis filled in a few blanks later. "Is there going to be a problem here?"

"Certainly not," the priest replied.

"Do I have your personal guarantee of that, Father?"

Father Michael stopped moving. The two men faced each other, less than a foot separating them.

"The question, Colonel, is: Do I have *your* personal guarantee?" He glared at the police chief just enough that his eyes caught what little light there was in the shadows. "It seems to me that Scripture study is an appropriate activity for a church such as this one. The people must be fed."

The colonel's jaws were working, turning his mouth into something cruel, his thick mustache and eyebrows into dark things that closed to cover vulnerable targets in a fight he knew was unavoidable. But then they relaxed. The man stepped slightly to the slide, letting the entrance to the alley remain a tight squeeze.

"Of course," Petrakis said. "Feed the people, Father." He looked at the ground then let his eyes slowly rise to meet the priest's. "But I will remain stationed here. In case you come to need my assistance."

The priest nodded, and before too many could give the passage much though, started into the alley, with Avery, Fotis and me directly behind him and the rest of the island people behind them. He looked each in the eye as he or she passed. He nodded without warmth to those he recognized. He stopped little short of writing each name in a notebook.

Father Michael unlocked a door when the alley reached a dead end, and bright light poured out from a kind of community meeting room. A simply draped table on one side was set with pastries and coffee, and there was a small platform with Avery's original display pad on an easel. He had kept the original diagram that began with the simplest transaction, the one between BUYER and SELLER. It still read MARIOTIS at the bottom, but I knew he'd get to that in the course of all we'd discussed, debated and decided over the past three days.

The priest thanked the people for coming, and I looked from face to face around the room. The growers were there, ones I knew, ones I'd never seen. At my special request, Irine was also there, looking just after dark no less sleepy than that first night Fotis has imposed upon her to feed me. And though Elena was not in attendance—I'd never given up that hope entirely—two of her older male dancers arrived just as introductions were being made. They would, I knew, report to her, without so directly risking the wrath of Yiannis Mariotis.

Avery gave the crowd, especially the newcomers, an outline of our findings in Greek. I didn't even make Fotis translate for me this time. I knew what he was saying well enough that the words took on the correct meaning all by themselves. He outlined the chain of ownership that kicked in on the island each time a struggling Greek sold real estate to a Greek who appeared to have more money, moving by way of Switzerland to Germany, into control by a Russian company more involved in Greek real estate than in selling Russian oil to European buyers. By now, that must be the sideline, I thought, not the other way around. It's all a bit of a shell game. And it was, the darkest and most dangerous sense, brilliant.

I stirred from my thoughts when I heard my name. I understood enough. Avery was telling them about me, about my "important" job in America, about my newfound commitment to Delfinos—which apparently came as no surprise in the gossipy world of a small Greek island. He told them too about my family, my great-grandfather sailing away from the island to find his fortune in America. And now, I think understood him to say, the great-grandson was sailing back. That was my introduction, but no one applauded. Indeed, I'm sure I didn't want anyone to. There was only silence, a cough and a couple clearing throats as I walked up to the display pad and turned to the next page.

It featured a column of words I'd organized, just as I would have in another lifetime, just as had been organized for me perhaps a hundred times. The list read:

Concept
Personnel
Transport
Decoration
Food
Beverage
Entertainment
Lodging
Result

I glanced at the list one more time, thinking of a couple things I forgot to add but vowing to cover them at some point anyway.

"In this least likely of places," I began, "at this least likely of times, there is something we can all do to help ourselves and save our island." I looked around the room. "And it just might turn out to be magnificent."

31

"What I see here as a newcomer," I said, forming ideas into brief, logical blocks for Avery to translate, "and I certainly apologize for the many things I don't understand—what I see here are two things. The first is that laws are being broken—regional laws, national laws, probably even European Union laws, because as we all know, everything we Greeks *do* these days is against the law in the EU." I waited for Avery to translate. I knew he had when the people laughed bitterly. Most of the men nodded as they laughed. "But, my friends, it is clear that nothing will be done. For one thing there is corruption." Starting with the police chief right outside in the alley, I thought. "But most of all, prosecutors' offices have been decimated by the austerity. The only prosecutors who still have jobs are hiding beneath their desks, hoping nobody notices them except on payday."

Avery translated. It was information, but hardly a new idea to the people in this room. The television news commentators, I knew, spoke of little else. They always sounded angry to me.

"I believe we should look at this another way, should work at this another way." I waited for Avery, but instead he waited for me. "The cause of our troubles—the root cause, the original cause—is that we on this island have no work, no jobs, no money. We are hurting here. And because we hurt, we feel we must sell. For a long time, we thought we were selling to our neighbors. We were sad, we were worried. But in the short term, there was some relief, and we could think about starting some new life. But we were, as Avery has shown—" I pondered: Misled? Betrayed? Completely screwed?

"*Mistaken.*"

Avery translated, and the final word, however he managed to convey it, had the desired effect. People grumbled, whined, threatened, shouted, all at the same time. Now this, I thought, from the people who gave us *democracy*. Messy and angry and loud though it was, I supposed I was actually looking at it.

"Now I propose," I started over the din, and by the time things calmed down, I had to repeat myself.

"I propose—we address the root problem and let the prosecutors keep hiding beneath their desks in Athens or Brussels or wherever the—" I saw the old women around the edges of the room, and my sense of propriety caught me in time. "*Wherever* they are. I propose that we create something together here on Delfinos that will *be* our job. It will be our paycheck. And it will be our salvation."

This *did* get some applause. I was glad, since applause only lasts so long when you give people hard work to do. You might as well start out with some cheering.

For the next forty-five minutes, I used the chart to outline a tourism-based enterprise that would draw together all major (well, okay, less minor) industries and assets on Delfinos into one piece of what might be called performance art. It would respect the old ways, it would celebrate them, and it would serve them in a way that forced the world to take notice. The story we told would be our story. The food and drink we served would be our food and drink. The products we sold would be our products. And the places people would stay, if and when we convinced them to do so, would be our places.

It was a new day and a new time, I said. And the only ways for the old ways to remain here was if we protect them. Others never would.

Not others from Athens. Not others from Switzerland or Germany. And sure as hell not others from Moscow.

My talk left ashes in my mouth and emptiness in my soul. It was so easy to talk about doing such things, and so very hard to actually do them. I promised that in the coming days I would meet with individual members of the community and small groups to talk about their investment—obviously, sweat equity would be the only equity, with me tossing in limited amounts of money as required. I wanted Irini to do the food, though she would need help and, though it broke my culinary heart to know it, instruction. Her processes would have to be streamlined to serve large numbers of people, her ingredients and techniques standardized. I wanted the growers to supply wine and, of course, tsipouro. Hell, I even wanted Fotis to organize transportation, but not in his falling-apart taxi but in a collection of decorated donkey carts that could carry people up to Chora from the port.

Most of all, I wanted Elena. Yes, of course. But I also wanted her fire, as I'd learned from her that of all things Greek, it was the dances that transported past into present most profoundly. As I remembered from a movie I saw on a date with Beverly years earlier, *there will be dancing*.

Colonel Petrakis was still there watching when our Scripture study let out. In wondered as I passed him if he'd has a spy or two in the community room, and just as quickly I guessed the answer was Yes.

Avery, Fotis and the growers dragged me up the street for a quick tsipouro at the distillery, though I knew it wouldn't be quick at all. I had one, then another, forking down hunks of spicy sausage with chunks of chewy island bread. Somebody brought out a platter of tiny fish from a grill behind the building, and I ate those too—head, tail, bones and all. I knew it was how it was done here, and even as my view of things grew hazier from the tsipouro—in fact, *because* my view of things grew hazier from the tsipouro—I wanted it to be done that way forever. For my children. For my children's children. For *me.*

The party was still going strong when I excused myself, feeling ever the lightweight from America. I needed sleep. I needed time to think. I, in fact, needed a whole lot of things, most of which were highly unlikely to ever come my way. We were in this now, in my idea, my crazy dream perhaps, and I understood that the men and women of Delfinos would work till they dropped to make it happen—as long as I was there to remind them, to—the word rang through my mind, a new word unaccustomed to dwelling there—as long as I was there to *lead* them.

I found my B&B after a couple of wrong turns in the dark—blame it on the tsipouro. With each step through the streets, however, I felt more inklings of danger, all imaginary, I promised myself, till every dripping faucet and every squealing cat sounded like evil closing in around me. Blame *that* on the tsipouro too. I used my key to open and carefully close the outside door, then awkwardly made my way upstairs to my room. Plugging my phone into its charger, I fired off one more effort to reach Beverly.

It was morning in Houston, so much better than calling in the middle of her night. But when her phone kicked over to voicemail, I hung up. The last thing I needed was to slur my way through some message. In any husband-wife conversation, from the beginning until the end of time, that would *become* the conversation.

I slept deeply and drunkenly for something between a minute and a year—about three hours, it turned out—dreaming all the while of a storm that pounded Delfinos with an artillery barrage of thunder. The eruptions shook and rolled over my head, until they woke me and forced me to understand that they were real.

Locating my glasses on the night table, my vision still blurry, I clung tight to the railing as I took the steps slowly downward, where, if anything, the pounding was getting worse. Two thirds of the way, one of my feet slipped and I was left dangling, both hands grasping the rail, until I managed to right the ship. At the bottom, I saw a large form through the smoked glass and, half-knowing I would live to regret it, pulled open the outside door.

"There has been death," Colonel Petrakis said, displaying as much emotion as a granite marker. "We think he kill himself. You will come with me."

"Did you know of his problems?" Colonel Petrakis asked, once I'd taken two sips of the coffee on a tray of his desk and had him refill my water glass three times. "Did he speak with you about?"

"Problems? No. I mean, never. *What* problems?"

"Financial."

"No," I said. "It never came up. It just seemed he had enough money."

"*Seemed*," Petrakis repeated with more than a little scorn.

"What are you talking about, Colonel?"

He pulled a stack of papers—some folded from the mail, others flat like recent computer printouts—toward the center of his desk. He looked at them. He let his hand settle upon them, as though a breeze was likely to carry them away inside his office. The one thing he didn't do was show the papers to me.

"Yes, Mr. Laros. There were problems. He was—what are you Americans so very fond of saying?—*depressed*."

"No, he never seemed depressed at all. He seemed, um, happy. Excited, even."

"And why would a man like that be excited, Mr. Laros?"

Col. Petrakis was an interrogator, ever ready with a question about one man that might get another man into trouble, might lull another man into telling him too much. I thought back over the past eight hours, about our meeting at the church, and realized there were too many dangerous places that I might topple into.

"Just happy. Good things, you know?"

"So, your friend was not depressed, you say."

"Not to me," I said thoughtfully. "Not ever. It would not have been his—his *nature*."

"I see."

In the room at the back of police headquarters, on a stainless steel rolling table, Avery Graham had not looked much like Avery Graham—and I'd been brought there, at least on the surface, to officially identify his body. He was shorter than I recalled, but that had everything to do with parts of his legs lost in the fire—as Colonel Petrakis pointed out. He had no clothes over his skin and, in places, no skin over his bones. Yet his teeth had frozen somehow into a gruesome smile, one whose friendlier next-of-kin I did recognize. And while I have no idea how or why, the flames had spared several fistfuls of his soft, snow-white hair and beard. They seemed utterly impossible with all the rest of him burned black and hard. Yet there they were.

"Ye—" I said, but the word crumbled and my mouth filled with something that tasted awful. I gagged it back, once and then again, looking at my hands to avoid looking at the body. None of which helped at all with the smell.

"Mr. Laros," Petrakis said, focusing me. "Is this the body of Avery Graham?"

I moved my head side to side but forced the motion to go up and down. "Yes. Yes it is."

"Thank you" was all he said, leading me back to his office.

Where we sat now. Talking about Avery's financial life.

"It would appear," the Colonel said, "that your friend was another victim of the crisis. My information states that he moved the bulk of his assets from Great Britain to Greece five years ago, wanting it closer at hand. Wanting access, I assume."

"Okay."

"He invested his money in a financial place in Athens—"

"Like a bank?"

"Yes, *like* a bank. But not a bank. A financial place."

"Brokerage?"

"Yes, that could be the word in English. And as these papers show, his investments had not done well since the crisis began. In fact, the place itself—the, brokerage?—is, at this moment, on the verge of collapse. We believe your friend feared losing everything."

"My friend, sir, did not *fear*."

Petrakis only laughed at the very notion, waiting for me to say or ask something else.

"And may I presume, Colonel, these investments were not guaranteed in any way, not insured?"

That got me a derisive snort. "Mr. Laros, no. This is not your America. Here there are not such niceties." He looked at me, his look moving from good cop to bad cop without warning. "Perhaps you have seen enough here, I think, Mr. Laros? Perhaps you should go back to a place you can understand."

I said nothing. But *no*. He wasn't about to get that out of me, not even with the gentlest man I suspect I'd ever known lying dead only steps away. Not yet. Not *ever*.

"So, Colonel, what exactly do you think happened?"

"I questioned several who saw him at the distillery. Who said you were with them as well?"

Of course I was with them. Why did everything sound like a capital crime when Col. Petrakis happened to mention it?

"Yes. I left about 1."

"So they said. Around half-past two, the others decided to leave also, and apparently Avery Graham offered to stay and clean up. There was much trash, I'm told. Much food and drink."

"All right."

"So they left him alone at the distillery and headed home. He had his own key to lock up. According to what we think, it was then than the man became depressed, seriously. And whatever he did in what order, it involved starting a fire at the distillery. You know, with the flames from the tsipouro? The still? He started a fire, which damaged the building quite a lot before we got there and located some water."

"Are you telling me that Avery Graham killed himself by setting the distillery on fire and then letting himself burn up inside it?"

"No, I'm telling you the fire was a cover up, a trick. To hide his suicide."

"What?"

"Many men have done similar things, I'm afraid, so their beneficiaries could collect the full insurance money. Or for many other reasons, of course. Suicide being the shameful thing it is."

"I'm not understanding you."

Really? Was what I saw and heard on the Colonel's lips a contemptuous laugh? "The fire did what you saw to his body, Mr. Laros. The fire did its *job*. But what turned your friend into the corpse on that table was a single bullet to the brain."

After leaving the police station, I managed to grab two hours of not-so-restful sleep before Fotis picked me up to go to Avery's house on the edge of town. It was a good idea, we decided, to dig through his things to make sure that whatever mattered was secure—and whatever wasn't secure didn't matter. We were not the first to have this good idea.

"Jesus Christ," Fotis exhaled, feeling Avery's front door push inward as he grabbed the knob to insert the key.

There was clothing strewn about the floor of the front hall, and matters only got worse as we ventured deeper inside. In the office, Avery's computer was gone—the CPU unit anyway, giving the monitor and keyboard the eerie look of being left behind after the Rapture. All the desk drawers were pulled out, papers and files and even pencils divided between being inside and being out. Someone had made quick work of their search, much quicker than we had envisioned making ours. In the instant debate, titled To-Take-or Not-to-Take, take had clearly won out.

"God," I said. "It's 9:30 in the morning. I'm not sure who the police even told by now."

"My guess is that the police told the police."

Having made the trip, we figured we should try to find what we could, but the whole processed seemed disoriented, if not downright doomed, by everything being such a mess. The very nature of such a search implied you were digging through things the way the person left the in death, the way he'd kept them in life. Their very positioning in Avery's life seemed the ultimate clue, and now we'd have no idea.

I kept thinking back to the stack of papers on the police chief's desk, the papers he never let me see. Avery had been dead only two or three hours by then, and yet there the papers were. Had Petrakis visited the house already, or had somebody else? At some points, thoughts such as these became paranoia. But I was beginning to doubt that paranoia was the biggest danger on this island.

"Stelios," Fotis called from another part of the house as I was taking papers from the floor and arranging them in stacks that meant absolutely nothing. "You might want to come see this."

I found him in Avery's bathroom. The medicine chest on the wall was open—in fact, the mirrored door was hanging by one hinge, as though the last guy looking for a few pills in there was named Mr. Hyde. The sink directly beneath it was filled with bottles of prescription pills, many apparently ordered over the Internet from pharmacies in the UK. Fotis held out one bottle to me, the one with instructions: Take Once Daily for Depression. I had told Fotis of the depression-suicide theory, and he didn't give it much credence either.

"What do you think?" he asked.

"I don't know."

"It says what it says."

"Yes, but only—" I hated myself for even thinking this, "only if it isn't a lie."

Fotis glared at the prescription for a moment, then slipped the small plastic bottle into his shirt pocket.

I made my way into Avery's bedroom. This made me as uncomfortable as would just about anybody's bedroom, especially when they'd just died unexpectedly. The bed wasn't made but it wasn't tossed and turned either, just a little bit bad everywhere except on the right side where a single person had crawled in and out alone, probably for several nights in a row. It was a look that was becoming all too familiar to me. There was one pillow where presumably Avery had laid his head, plus three others piled to the side. Part of a paperback novel protruded. I looked at the bed without touching. I didn't feel the least bit okay about touching.

It was a small, simple bedroom, one not intended to impress anyone. There was, however, an armoire shoved into one plaster corner, and when I opened it I discovered we were the second guys to search. There was a personal safe inside the armoire, and the combination lock had been cut out, perhaps with some kind of welding torch. What remained was rough and tangled from the heat, and I grabbed carefully in order to open the door. The safe, the kind of thing it made total sense for an unmarried old man to keep for his few remaining valuables, whatever those might be, was empty.

I stopped in the doorway on the way out, turned and tried to think of what I'd seen. I gave it a moment, then another, then I gave up. I was most of the way to the kitchen when I turned abruptly and raced back to Avery's bed, to what appeared to be his side, and reached carefully for the paperback under the pillows. It pulled out easily, clearing my path to whatever else my friend had been perusing night after night as he drifted off to sleep.

And that's what was there, when I pressed my hand deeper, the stiff edge of a file folder. It had nothing so official as a label, merely a marker's quick notations at the center: LAROS WINERY. That's what I'd been hoping to find, in one of the few places it wouldn't have been found already.

Before I located Fotis outside, I located the water he'd boiled on the stove to make tea, so I helped myself to water and a bag of Earl Gray. The whole morning seemed unreal enough already—toasting a dead guy from England with a cup of tea didn't make it seem any more so. Fotis was hanging up his mobile phone as I approached.

"My son," he said, as though that explained everything.

"Baby sick again?" I don't know where that came from, but I didn't like it. I attempted to cover with a smile.

"No, my friend. Not sick today." We met at the edge of Avery's vineyards, where each row came with its own well-kept rose bush. We clinked our mugs. "Actually, I was speaking to my son. The computer genius."

"As opposed to your son the fisherman?"

"Exactly." He smiled a bit sadly. "I gave him all the information from the pill bottle. I figured he could find out more than you and I could."

"I'm sure that's true."

"He said he would try."

"You have Internet at your house?"

He chuckled. "We do now."

We walked slowly along the line of roses, doing a half-stop at each row of grapes—or at least at the pruned vines that would give them up by late summer or early fall. It was heartbreaking for me to picture any of this, to think about it, the grapes looking for the wrinkled hands that would pick them. I wondered how long it might take, how many weeks or months or years, before Avery's vineyard looked like, well, like mine.

"What do you think, Stelios? What do we do now?"

My feet kicked at the rough, dry dirt as I struggled for what I wanted to say, what I needed to say. Surely the word was getting out from the police by now. More and more of the people who'd heard Avery speak at our meeting were learning he was dead. A decent number of them would be guessing his death was no coincidence, no accident, and surely no suicide. Hell, by nightfall, we might end up with nobody on Delfinos willing to do what we planned.

"We can't stop," I said. "What would that tell them?"

"Exactly what they want to hear. What they've always heard."

"Yes. So we can't tell them that, can we?"

He shrugged. And we walked on.

"Look, Fotis. First off, do I still have *you*?"

"Three generations, my friend. That's what I've got at my house now. Under my roof. I don't want to lose them. And they had better not lose me. You hear what I'm saying?"

"Of course. But really—"

"Really *what*, Stelios? What else does a man have? His life, his family, his work, his—"

"His island."

"Sure. But when have I *ever* had this island? It was the Turks forever. And then rich guys in Athens. And then, maybe, rich guys here. I say 'my island,' but isn't that just many bullshits? Really, when this ever been *my* island?"

"It's just a goddamned rock, yes?"

"What?"

"My father didn't tell you?"

"No."

"My whole life, he called Delfinos 'that goddamn rock.' And he always thanked God that his grandfather had been smart enough to get the hell off it. But you know what, Fotis? In the end, my father came *here*. Nobody knows why, not even my mother. He came here to do something, to build something. And now, this same goddamn rock is mine. I want, no, I *need*, to build something here too."

Fotis and I had had stopped walking. He casually draped his right arm over my shoulder. It felt fatherly, it felt brotherly—it felt, maybe, simply right. "I need you to understand something, my friend," he said. "There is no way in hell our friend ever killed himself. You know what that means, yes?"

"Yes," I said. "It means that whatever we decide to do had better not remain our little secret very long."

"Hey baby," said the husky, remembered voice over my mobile phone. "You rang?"

"Yeah Rox, how are you?"

"Let me see. What's it been? Twelve years? You don't call, you don't write. It's worse than being a Jewish mother around here. And now, here you are. Calling me at my desk, no less."

"So, um," I said, duly chastised, "how *have* you been?"

Roxanne Dupre, from the exotic section of New Orleans called Treme, had been my last serious girlfriend between college and Beverly. Self-described as *café au lait*—which she defined for anyone who asked as being "black, French, Spanish, Sicilian, Irish and probably Choctaw Indian"—Roxie played at being black whenever it suited her career needs. That included when her hometown *Times-Picayune* was hiring only black reporters after getting beaten up in federal court, and it included coming to Houston to write an "urban affairs" column with her picture on it for the *Chronicle*. It probably didn't hurt at the *International Herald-Tribune* in Paris either; her byline appeared regularly over hard news and features from every corner of Europe. Quite often, though, Roxie felt no need to play at being black at all.

"We'll get to that," she answered, with a tone that worried me. "Tell me, Steve, how are *you*? Still in Houston? Still opening or taking over all the restaurants in the world?"

"Sort of. But no, not really."

"So, *dites-moi, mon amour*."

"I'm on Delfinos."

"Sounds Greek to me."

"It's an island."

"Man, you Laros boys get around, don't you? Some *souvlaki* joint? Coals to Newcastle and all that?"

"Not so much, Rox. Look, I'm on my own." I stopped as though to ponder the phrase, but quickly realized I didn't really want to. "My father died here. I came to help my Mom. But now she's back in Houston. And I'm not."

Roxanne laughed. I always loved her laugh. "Getting in touch with our inner Greek, are we?"

"Yes. I mean, no. I mean, I don't know."

"Now there's the Steve Laros I loved so well."

And it was. It was our story. Roxanne was older, and apparently had known what she wanted every day of her life. I was younger, and knew practically nothing I wanted ever. Yet she *was* an intriguing chapter, before she grew weary of writing the whole damn book herself. One night in her bed, our antics somehow uncovered a poet in me—a really bad poet, I'm sure. And I went all moon and June, all hearts and flowers, professing my undying love till it must have seemed I'd never shut up. Roxie squinted at me in amused disbelief, more and more, until I finally noticed, in the middle of some sonnet or other.

"Man," was all she'd told me then. "You really *did* need to get laid."

How can you not be in love forever with a woman like that?

I was smiling so much at one of my life's favorite memories that I almost forgot it was my turn to talk. "I'm on this island, Rox, where my family came from. You know, way back. And where my father retired, except then he decided to die instead. And it turns out, once I get here, that all he really ever wanted to do was start a freakin' *winery*. Can you believe that? I feel like I'm supposed to do that now. Start the winery, I mean, not die. I hope."

"Well, Steve, you always did really like to drink."

We had met at an iconic Houston bar that masqueraded as a Mexican restaurant, a place known to all (but especially to late-arriving restaurant workers) as CLUB NO MINOR. The sign on the door was semi-literate, but the bar served strong margaritas and kept the lights mostly off. Rox and I were dating within a week. We never actually moved in together but camped out almost nightly in each other's beds. Like any authentic Houston activity, it involved lots of driving.

"What about you, Roxie? You keep making me talk about *me*. And quite possibly, it's starting to scare the shit out of me a little bit."

"So, do you really want to hear this?"

"Hear what, Rox?"

In what was becoming silent but full-scale panic, what I heard was Roxanne Dupre drawing a very deep breath, for none of the reasons I liked to remember. "It was ovarian, Steve. You know? I guess I never really needed the damn things anyway, as it turned out." She and I had talked about having children, always someday, so that stung more than a little, intended or not. "Here today, gone tomorrow, right?"

"But—but—you're okay now?"

"It turned out to be nothing that a worse-than-death, out-of-body experience of radiation and chemo couldn't take care of. That was last year, Steve. Last spring. I'm looking and feeling a lot better now. I come to the office almost every day."

"They promise you're okay, though, right?"

"Steve, they're doctors. They don't promise *shit*."

In that moment, it was all I could do not to break down and tell her everything about the past six months—about my physician getting worried, about *him* sending me to a urologist, and about *him* sending me to the Medical Center for a biopsy. I wanted to tell her everything, and how horrible it felt every step of the way. But I hadn't said a word to Beverly and Chloe. I hadn't said a word to Nick, the CEO who, at least in some small way, depended on my actually being alive. And worst of all, although this made no sense to me now, I hadn't said a word to Elena. There had been, for all we'd done, no moment in which to actually tell her.

"God, Rox, I'm sorry."

"Marcel's been wonderful about it, though."

"Marcel?"

"He's French, you know," she giggled.

"*Sacre bleu*!"

"He's French, but he's nice anyway." She paused, thinking. "He's 37 and I'm 56, and you know the worst part, Steve? I mean, really? He deals in *antiques*. Which I guess explains a lot, doesn't it?"

"You will never be an antique, Roxie." I felt a swell of burning emotion from my chest all the way up into my throat. "Not you. Not ever."

"Thank you for that, babes. I mean it. Call me in another twelve years to make sure you're right, okay?"

"I'm writing it on my calendar. There, it's a date."

I no longer had a calendar. There was an awkward silence. But as always with Roxanne Dupre, it didn't last for long. "Hey, you called me. So what can I do you for?"

I laughed. "It's something for that newspaper that pays you—"

"At least *this* week."

"Yeah, that one."

"I'm breathlessly reaching for my notebook, as we speak."

"That's good," I said. "It's kind of a story thing."

Delfinos is hardly the most media-crazed of places, but the following Wednesday all news vendors on the island made sure to carry extra copies of the *International Herald-Tribune*. This, I suspected, meant ordering more than two. By the time I picked up mine and tracked down Roxanne's story over coffee on the square, four other tables were turned to the same page.

"Greek Island Seeking a 'Fair Fight,'" proclaimed the headline. Roxie, I felt, had nailed the story, calling me three more times to check facts as she assembled it. She even broke a cardinal rule of journalism by making my quotes better than they actually were.

> *By ROXANNE DUPRE*
> *This Saturday, as the sun dips beneath the Aegean Sea, the people of the tiny Greek island of Delfinos will welcome a small group of intrepid odyssey-makers to experience their food and their wine, their music and their dance. According to veteran American*

restaurateur Steve Laros, the main dish on the menu will be authentic "Greek Island Life."

As founder of the "experience" of that name (he refuses to call the evening a "show"), Laros is betting a great deal of the island's future and an undisclosed amount of his own money on the public's interest in digging deeper than "folklore" on more visited, nearby islands like Mykonos and Santorini. Eventually, he says, he'd like Delfinos and its dinner experience to draw guests from those islands and even renovate rustic houses for them to spend one or two nights off the beaten path.

"When I came to Delfinos, I found something of value," says Laros, 52, who serves as a vice-president of his family's Houston-based LRG Holdings, with eateries in 19 states. He came to the island to help settle his father's estate. "At the same time, I found a situation in which those essential things were under attack—sometimes simply by modernity itself, by the onrush of travel options the world prefers now, and other times by the current fiscal crisis. Lastly, I saw danger from certain foreign powers who are buying up the island one square foot at a time, developing foreign-owned resorts and other businesses that manage, wonder of wonders, to pay little in local taxes while hiring virtually no local employees."

Asked to elaborate, Laros describes a complex and allegedly corrupt system of real estate transactions, beginning with compensated Greek "straw buyers" and ending several holding companies later with a petroleum concern chartered in Germany but owned entirely by Russians.

Greek Island Life was born of this situation. The evening, Laros said, will begin at the picturesque Delfinos harbor, with a torchlit procession of donkey carts up to the main town of Chora. Awaiting visitors on the decorated square will be a feast of local food specialties, toasts with local wines and the local distilled spirit known as tsipouro, and live music with a demonstration of traditional dancing by the local young people.. After the "experience," visitors will be taken back down to the harbor the same way, serenaded by bouzoukia.

"I think Greek islanders can convince our guests they're, well, Greek islanders," Laros laughs. "And remember: in Greek, the word for stranger is the same as the word for guest."

The Houston-born restaurateur hopes to market Greek Island Life through all aspects of the travel industry as well as promote it to everyone planning visits to the island; but he has arranged the debut as a booking for passengers aboard the MV Adonis, the high-end 50-cabin "yacht-ship" of the Shimmering Seas cruise line. By no means is this a private performance, however—in fact, Laros stresses, the more public it is the better.

"I guess this is where my American and my Texan roots kick in, maybe more than my family's Greek roots," he says thoughtfully. "Where I come from, we hate bullies, and we always root for the underdog, for the little guy. No matter how you look at it here on Delfinos, that's what we're dealing with."

My goal in speaking with Roxanne had not been so much to challenge the bad guys as to put them on notice that the world, as much of it as we could reach anyway, was watching—with the desirable side effect of keeping me alive. The distance between alive and dead seemed very short on Delfinos these days. It was enormously painful that I hadn't been smart enough to do any such thing before Avery was killed, especially since it was Avery who uncovered nearly all of the information in the story. The villagers assured me and Fotis they wanted to help, but from the fear I saw flickering across their eyes at times, I couldn't be confident who, if anyone, would show up to do the work.

The business with the MV Adonis was a late-breaking, happy development, one that had everything to do with how the foodservice business operates. Miguel Benavides had been one of our company's very first chefs, working his way up from washing dishes in our original Houston fried seafood place. When we could offer him no greater opportunity, Miguel applied to Westin Hotels, and I wrote him a glowing recommendation. Eight years later, when Shimmering Seas was born—right before the recession must have made them wonder what they'd been thinking, or drinking—Miguel emerged from a large field to become the cruise line's corporate chef. He showed up for his interview with a written endorsement from me. When I called and it turned out the ship could drop in for dinner during an overnight sail from Mykonos to Santorini, Miguel had no reason on earth to tell me no.

A box at the bottom of the article was boring but important. It gave an international phone number for our enterprise, set up by Fotis' son to ring through to my mobile, where a special code would show me the call was about Greek Island Life. And it also pointed to our first effort at a website, complete with a credit card payment function for buying tickets. Something inside me wanted to offer T-shirts announcing "I Survived GREEK ISLAND LIFE," but I kept telling myself to worry about first things first. Like surviving all this myself.

That was how and why I ended up at Irini's restaurant the next afternoon, talking with her via Fotis about our menu. Yes, I told her, there had to be a Greek salad—which she refused to recognize by that name. *Horiatiki* was what she called it, and while I couldn't get a straight answer on whether that meant "country," "farmer," "shepherd" or something like "redneck," having it was all that mattered to me. For an entrée, guests could certainly opt for moussaka or pastitzio, the dynamic duo of Pop Greek Cooking, but I lobbied hard and finally won the right to serve Irini's meatloaf-cooked-in-chicken-skin from my first hour on the island. Yes, it was my sentimental favorite, plus a dish undeniably local. But it was also one of the most magnificent creations I'd ever put in my mouth. A second argument concerned how it ought to be cooked, Irini sticking by small individual loaves but me carrying the day for large hotel pans with chicken skin draped across the top. I was nothing if not a guy who knew how to feed lots of people.

I called Roxie twice in Paris with my gratitude, but both times had to leave a message. Would I ever again leave her a voicemail without worrying that something had gone wrong? She phoned me back, bright and cheery, just as my meeting with Irini was breaking up and

I was heading for the house and winery. I waved for Fotis to wait at the water's edge when I saw who was calling.

"Was it good for you?" Roxie asked, and even if I hadn't recognized her number, I would have recognized the attitude.

"Thanks, Rox. You might have saved my life."

"That was the general idea. So, your people like all this on the island?"

"You bet. It kind of galvanized them, in fact." To my surprise, most has pushed—or been pushed by the reality facing them—beyond being afraid. "It's the hardest these people have worked since the Turkish occupation. And we've even gotten phone calls, quite a few, in fact."

"Happy to service you." She giggled deep in her throat. "I mean, *be* of service."

"Of course. So hey," I said. "You and Marcel are going to be here, right? You need to see what hath Roxie Wrought."

"Not sure, babes."

"I told you, I'll get the plane tickets. You and that Frenchman of yours."

"Marcel is all over it," she said. "I mean, here it's still winter in Paris, and you happen to have a Greek island handy."

"So what's the problem?"

"The paper doesn't allow us to accept freebies."

"Even from an old friend?" I laughed. "A *very* old friend?"

"Maybe. But then, you understand, I couldn't write about it."

"Oh," I said. As much as I wanted to lay eyes again on Roxanne Dupre, I needed her to write about what she saw and ate and drank on Delfinos. After I couldn't think of anything else to say, I simply said "Oh" again.

"See? There you have the problem."

"Well, screw it if we have to. You and Marcel get your butts to Delfinos. I promise we'll put on a heck of a—"

"Show?"

"*Experience*," I countered to her delight.

"We'll see, babes. Start the wheels turning. We will just have to wait and see." I heard her voice take on that teasing tone I remembered. "And one more thing, Steve. Our owners really *did* like the story. Now *they're* running it too."

"Of course," I said.

"The *Trib* was yesterday's news. Tomorrow our owners are picking it up."

"Roxie, what are you telling me?"

"We're owned by *The New York Times*."

The air was brisk out on the water, but not as much as it had been—when?—a week ago, a month ago? My entire body soaked up the warmth of the afternoon sun as Fotis steered us toward the cove, and I suddenly realized that, on the Greek island of Delfinos at least, one more winter was past. It was almost Easter. Like so many things in my life, I'd grown up hearing that spring was "in the air." For the very first time, I could feel it. I could breathe it.

"Are you ready, my friend?" Fotis shouted over the guttural roar of his outboard.

I certainly was.

As we rounded the rocky promontory and turned toward shore, I saw the one thing my father had only had time to dream of. Everywhere I looked, from the long, low building on the dock to the house perched above the beach on the mountainside, men were working. We had to pull up on the beach because two large work-boats filled the concrete peer, stacked with studs, drywall, inner and outer doors and rolls of cottony orange insulation. Even before I stepped out on the sand, I heard hammers and table saws cutting through the boat's noisy propulsion.

"Amazing!" I shouted to Fotis, climbing out and struggling with my desire to break into a sprint in all directions at once.

"You bet amazing," he said, "what giving people a paycheck can do."

He was right, of course. Even more than he realized. In fact, the whole truth was still struggling to dawn on me.

I'd finally made contact with that banker in Athens, the guy who'd insisted on meeting me for coffee. After a phone conversation that told me nothing, I'd caught the overnight ferry to Piraeus, then a train to Monastiraki in time for a nine o'clock meeting. My father, said the banker once our coffee and pleasantries were done, had taken out a small life insurance policy and placed it in his keeping. As George Laros had always maintained a $5 million policy in Houston, this news came at me with more than a little shock.

Sitting at the outside café on the small square, I heard the traffic on the street and the barkers revving up at the flea market and the hordes emerging from the Metro station. I looked down at the opened envelope, at the check made out to me as beneficiary for two-hundred-thousand euros, and the typewritten memo attached to the check.

> *To Steve,*
> *DELFINOS*
> *The Laros Family Winery*

There was a second folded page behind the memo, and on it I recognized my father's carelessly efficient handwriting. It took me a moment, seeking and receiving a nod from the banker, before I dared to read the words.

> *Steve, do you know the Greek word* chorio*? Did your mother teach you that one? If not, she really should have.* Chorio *is the place you're from—in our culture, it's always a village, even if you have to dig back for generations. Never a city, and certainly never anyplace in America, no matter how long a Greek family lives there. Or, yes, how*

much money a family has made. Still, chorio *is not only a place, Steve. It's a meaning and a direction. You go back there, if you're lucky enough, because it reminds you who you are and what a person is put on this earth to accomplish. It reminds you even if you never thought you knew in the first place.*

I understand that it hurt you when I gave the company to Nick to run, and it hurt me too; but I gave it to him because he needed a company. I'm sure your brother will do a good job. It's what he does. Just as my father planted what I brought in as our family's harvest, I'm confident Nick will do his best with what I planted. But for you, Steve... For you, I've created something of greater value, my own best shot at that pearl beyond price. If you're reading this note, it means I left more work for you to do than I wish. I'm sorry. I wanted to do more, I wanted to do better, like all fathers. But this place, Steve—it was always my chorio. *I want it to always be yours.*

Love,
Dad
P.S. I told your mother to bring you here.
P.P.S. And yes, it really is a Goddamn Rock. But what are you gonna do, huh?

Those were more words than I could process. And at least one of them near the end, the one I'd never once heard from my father's lips, was worth a lot more to me than two-hundred-thousand euros.

Before heading back to the port, I opened an account with the check at a bank that had an ATM on my island and grabbed a stack of checks. I had one more coffee, unable to forget what a brief moment it had been, really, since I'd first waited in this same port, in this same cafe. That time the skies had been dark and rain had been falling and the world had been nothing but shadows. On this day the skies were blue, the seas glassy calm. And now I had—I'd been handed, one piece at a time, without knowing it—a brand new life to live.

That new life was now taking shape before me, thanks to the best workmen my father's insurance money could buy. I had an hour before I had to head back to Chora and meet Elena on the square—for all my trying, it would be our first face-to-face conversation since I'd dropped her off at the cove. She always had some reason she couldn't see me, some of them quite creative and all reasonable enough, until I noticed the end result:we never saw each other. Even today was about work, checking the stage that had been built to her instructions, which had come into my phone via text and forwarded to Fotis to share with the village workers.

The hour I had was enough to check out the basics of the winery. A roof had been added to the house, replacing the suddenly beloved tarp above the platform I'd built for my bed. All the appliances had been positioned and hooked up to power or water as needed, and best of all, there actually was power, courtesy of a thick cable now running pole-to-pole down the mountainside from the main cable to Agios Georgios. I suspected, having seen the interior illuminated at night, I'd always harbor a preference for the thing that happens when gas lantern meets moonlight.

Walking across the sand toward the winery, I heard a deep-throated growl from above my head and looked up just in time to glimpse a small bulldozer—on Delfinos, we *had* no large bulldozers—making progress on the dirt road over the top and down through the vineyards to the back of the buildings. The winery now had glass windows instead of holes in the front wall, plus a mostly new roof that would keep out the birds and the rain. The trash I'd pushed my way through in the dark with Avery was gone—several boatloads of trash, in fact—leaving only the ancient crusher on its crash pad and a single fermentation tank. A new wooden shelf had been added since I'd been here last, ready for the testing, measuring and other chemistry that helped grapes become wine. I would have to count on the island's other vintners for help with that, which they were happy to give since I'd be paying them for all their grapes.

It was the vineyards themselves that required, and received, our greatest attention. Fotis must have brought in a dozen guys, paying them to follow Avery's instructions set forth in that folder I'd found at his house. Two-thirds of the men were working in the existing terraces rising behind the house, digging with shovels and chopping with machetes, liberating the still-living vines from their prison of neglect. And the rest were clearing a new patch above the winery, leveling a few places as needed, where our "experimental vineyard" of Santorini-style assyrtiko would go in.

Yes, we would follow the old way—Avery's way—wrapping the vines in tight circles to help preserve every drop of moisture and protect them from the winds. I could never look at this work in progress without hoping that Avery was looking down from somewhere.

I left each set of workers with assorted instructions, half-hoping they'd ignore whatever the hell I said and keep doing what they were doing. I saw Fotis offer me a thumbs-up with a question in his eyes, and all I could do was give him a thumbs-up in return. He grinned and led me back down to his boat on the beach.

Elena was waiting at a table on the edge of the square, surrounded by an entirely different kind of construction site. Men worked on ladders above her head, stringing light bulbs and banners across the air, while other men hammered together rows of extra-long picnic tables with benches only on the side facing the stage.

"Good afternoon, Steve," Elena said, rising as soon as she saw me. Her voice was friendly enough but also formal. Or perhaps it only sounded formal in light of all we had done the last time we saw each other. She offered me one cheek for kissing and then the other.

"How is it going?" I asked. We were standing, and I couldn't tell if she wanted us to sit down.

"Good. The stage is good. Your guys do a good job." As at the house and winery, the idea of anyone on Delfinos being "my guys" seemed strange, improbable, perhaps impossible. Yet Elena probably understood what was going on better than I ever could. "Come to see."

She led me across the square and, reaching for my hand for a moment of support, stepped up the twenty inches onto the stage. Feeling the unexpected ways she pressed down as she stepped, I could tell she was protecting her knee. Not letting go of her hand, I partially stepped and partially let her pull me up to her level. What I saw was something I hadn't counted on as recently as a week earlier.

The stage did have a little bounce—as she'd instructed by text, the better for her young dancers' knees to survive into being old dancers' knees. "You never want to dance on concrete," Elena said, and I took her at her word.

Yet what the stage also had was a view: three sections of table rows, straight across the front and angling off from the sides, creating a kind of picnic Greek amphitheater. It wasn't quite the theater on the Acropolis, but I figured it would do nicely. We'd managed to track down the only two "follow spots" within a hundred miles, their wiring drying out in a warehouse on Mykonos, bought them and had them shipped here by ferry. They were now secured on two second-story balconies on the far side of the square.

"This is exciting, isn't it?" I said, meaning it. But when she said nothing, I tried again. "Isn't it, Elena?"

"Yes," she said. She stared at her feet. "Steve, I really need to get back to the office. I—"

"Hey, I mean it, can I talk with you a little?" I glanced around the open space. All the men were busy. No one was listening, no one was interested, only the sun beating down on the town, on the mountains, on the sea. "Can you talk with me? We really need to stop this."

"Stop what, Steve? What do you mean?"

"Stop, well, not talking."

"Okay, of course. What shall we talk about?"

"Follow me. Please. Would you?"

She allowed her eyes to meet mine, perhaps for the first time since I walked up to her table. She nodded. And she followed as I started in through the maze of narrow streets. I knew where I was going. What I didn't know was exactly why.

We stopped where the street stopped, just past the entrance to the old Castro where the town ended in the cliff it presented to those pirates who attacked from the sea. I stopped at the whitewashed plaster wall and Elena stopped beside me. We both looked out, over the edge, to the rocks glinting sharply in the white foam far below.

"Elena, what is going on here?" She didn't answer. I'd hoped she would intuit my every question, my every concern, and simply answer, thus forcing me to say no more. But there was, apparently, so much more I would have to say. "I love you, Elena."

"Please don't *say* things like that."

"Why don't say them, Elena? Why shouldn't I say them, if they're true? Doesn't true count for anything anymore?"

"Of course it does, Steve."

"Then yes, I love you and I want you and I see a *life* with you here, a life so different from the one I had before—the life I've always needed without knowing it. Isn't there something in your life like that, anything at all, maybe with your dancing? Something you were put on this earth to do? Isn't there anything that helps you understand?"

"Of course. You've found what you want. But don't *you* understand? I've lost what I want. It's gone, Steve, in one little moment. And now I've got a very long life with nothing that I want, nothing that I believe in. Is that anything *you* can understand?"

"I thought—" I started but had to stop. Not only was I unsure what I wanted to say, but I was even less sure how to say it. But it had to be said. "I thought, just maybe, what you wanted, what you believed in, Elena, might have a little to do with me."

Before I knew what I'd said, and possibly years before I would truly understand it, she took me in her arms—not as a lover, though she was that too, but as something that truly had no name but deserved all names—and held me tight against her. I shook and she felt me shake, and drew me in till the shaking was over. She pulled away just enough to look at me.

"I do love you, Steve," she said. "Whatever happens, I need you to know that. I need you to believe that. *Will* you?"

"Yes" was the only thing I could say.

And then, suddenly, with all the certainty I hadn't possessed until now, I understood that it was time.

Elena had called her office two hours earlier, only to be told that Yiannis was shutting the place early and would see her later at home. Those tourists who wanted to book a moto for tomorrow could wait for tomorrow. *Avrio* was the word, the Greek edition of *manana,* and I heard it a lot on Delfinos. Since it suited my desire to never let Elena go back—to that office, to that man, to that anything—I was all for it.

She'd turned down dinner. That would be too official, and of course too visible. Yet we did find our way, walking as though we barely knew each other, into a small square with only one street lamp and ordered *mezedes* with a glass of wine. Truth is, even had someone recorded our entire conversation that evening, I'm not sure they'd have gotten anything but a discussion of the stage, the music, the dances and the young dancers, now only forty-eight hours from their first real show time. Walking back toward the center of town, we looked the same as we had earlier, our heads mostly down, our voices only rarely breaking the silence.

I kissed Elena on both cheeks to say goodnight, watched her start up the street toward Yiannis' house and then sprinted up behind her. She stopped, surprised and confused.

"Elena, there's something I really need to tell you."

"I know." She seemed cold, as though she were trying to erect a wall against an enemy that was already inside. "You are in love with me."

"Yes, that. But there's more. And it isn't as nice." I was expected a sarcastic comeback but didn't get one. "When this is over—no, I mean, when this is settled, up and running, you know?" She nodded. "When this thing is up and running, I need to go back to America."

The words hit her harder than she surely wished me to see. But all she said was: "Of course."

"I have to because—"

"Because is where you belong, Steve? Yes, I can see. And maybe you wish me to come to port, say goodbye? We can make movie, perhaps—or they will make one for us—*Elena Says Goodbye to Her Lover*."

"No, Elena, it's not like that. *I'm* not like that."

"I'm sure it will be dubbed—dubbed, yes?—into *Russian*. It will be the next *Anna Karenina*, I think."

"Elena, please stop. You know me better than that."

"Do I?"

"Yes," I said. "Yes, you do." She was silent, waiting. "So yes, I have to go back to the States, but for only for a time. I have to speak with my wife. I do, Elena. There's no way out without doing that. And I have to get some—some—" I could say anything on earth and avoid this, but I didn't want to avoid this any longer. "I need some treatments, Elena."

"You are—ill?"

"I am. I don't know how ill yet. That is part of what I'm going for, so the doctors can figure that out. I may need surgery, I may need radiation. I may need chemotherapy."

"You have cancer, Steve." It was not a question.

"Yes, I have cancer. Prostate. They tell me it's very early, that it's not so bad. But I can't know as long as I'm—"

"As long as you're here? With me?"

"Exactly."

I was feeling lightheaded. But I felt lightheaded too soon. Elena pressed a fist against her mouth, shutting her eyes with what looked like her last ounce of strength.

"Steve." Her voice was different. Harder, stronger. "And when did you plan on telling me any of this?"

As I did not know I would speak until I was actually speaking, the truth is I'd never planned to tell anyone at all. Would it take care of itself, somehow? Would it all go away if no one knew? Or would it simply be better if I slinked away, into treatment or painkillers or death, without anyone knowing or caring or feeling the least bit sorry? It all made absolute sense to me now, asking myself such questions in a frenzy, but I also knew I did not want it for one second more.

"*Now*, Elena. I planned to tell you right *now*." I looked at her, an edge of pleading coming into my voice. "I just never knew when now would actually be."

I moved to take her into my arms, but instead she spun away and sprinted around the first corner she reached, me pursuing and calling her name and only afterward, each time I shouted, gazing up at the shutters to see if any were springing open to see us. I turned another corner, then another, and called her name one last time. There was a long, long silence, followed by a nearly whispered "I am here."

Elena was bent over in a splash of shadows, both hands tightly grasping her injured knee. When she looked up, all I saw was a grimace of pain.

"Jesus," she choked out. "Is damn shame when a girl can't run."

I tried to settle my hands on her shoulders but she shook then off, slowly letting go of her knee and straightening up. She had been deciding some things. I could tell. And I could see in her eyes, even before she said a word, I wasn't going to like what she decided.

"I wish you the best good luck, Steve," she said. "I am sorry you have cancer, truly I am. But I needed you to—"

"I told you—" Her raised hand stopped me faster than a stone wall.

"I *needed* you to tell me these things. Or maybe, to *be* the kind of man who *could* tell me these things. Otherwise, it is too difficult." She tilted her head as though to study me, or maybe as though to remember me when I was gone. "No, Steve Laros, my sweet, innocent boy, maybe you don't know this. But I do. I am sorry. But you are not *anything* I need in my life right now."

I sputtered out the word "But—" but decided against continuing, because Elena was already gone. This time I didn't follow her. It had to be the world's worst goodbye. I was afraid it was the only one we'd ever have.

Feeling lost, beyond ever being found, I walked back to the square and swilled a glass of tsipouro. With detachment from all around me, I watched the last of the workers pick up their tools, then I bought the rest of the bottle since the café was closing. I sat at the table alone, gazing straight ahead to absolutely nothing.

Hours later—I had no clue how many—I felt pounding behind my ear that wouldn't stop, until I came up from a fitful sleep in my bed and realized it was my mobile. I'd left it on my pillow, not even plugged into the charger. If the code for Greek Island Life popped up, I was letting it go to voicemail. But it didn't. It was another of those numbers that streamed off the end of the screen. "*Mr. Steve,*" a voice wobbled, and I knew, I knew the voice, and even that mode of address, but my foggy brain wasn't letting me connect any helpful dots. I mean, any. Then it was a question: "Mr. Steve?"

"Yes."

"It is Dimitri." He waited. But no, he wasn't waiting. The man with the voice on the phone was crying. "The son of Fotis."

In the minute that followed, I realized once against how little English the computer genius actually spoke. He talked, and I stopped him, then he talked some more. He cried some more too, a good deal. It all sounded distant, and very foreign. By the time we clicked off, there were only three words I was sure of: *hospital, boat,* and *bomb.*

39

I knew the way, the way you know how to reach a place you've walked past barely noticing every day. The Delfinos Clinic wasn't, by any stretch, a *hospital.* But it had doctors, and it had a few beds. And now, thanks to something involving a boat and a bomb, it had Fotis.

Dimitri was waiting inside the frosted glass door. He was not recently shaved, his former neatness and Athens office pallor long replaced by scruffiness and a deep tan from fishing. There were two women, one old and the other young, sitting side-by-side on the hard plastic chairs behind him. Both had been crying. They were passing a crying baby between them.

Grabbing my hands in both of his, bowing his head repeatedly as in church, Dimitri thanked me for coming here so quickly. *Of course*, I told him, or something like it. What I was beginning to think, though—the thought that had struck me as I jogged through the winding dark streets from my B&B—was that maybe *nobody* on this island should thank me. Before me, people here did what they did. It wasn't much, and it usually wasn't pretty, and it never paid worth a shit. But at least nobody tried to kill them for doing it.

"He is lucky," Dimitri said, forcing his lips into a worried smile. "Doctor say."

Considering his English, I knew trouble lay ahead on the road I wanted to take—needed to take. But I knew I couldn't wait for Fotis to tell me, as I had waited for him to tell me almost everything since my arrival. I wasn't sure who else might now.

"What happened, Dimitri?"

"By boat," he said, then shook his head, realizing that must make no sense. "Colonel Petrakis he come."

That, I knew, changed everything.

Dimitri exerted a visible effort to calm himself, to force his thoughts and feelings into a single narrative that might actually tell me something. "I have problem today. On boat, yes? Fishing? When I come home, my father say we must fix." Dimitri smiled a real smile this time, a bit of a proud smile. "No, he say *he* must fix. And I will help him. We work on beach by port. In light." He raised his right hand above his head, arching it so it looked like a work lantern. "Colonel Petrakis he come to him, my father, and say he must speak. Is urgent. Must go to house, beach house. My mother and wife there, with baby."

"What did they talk about, Dimitri?"

"They go. I go too, walk up from beach. But when we get to house Petrakis say he—he—take—"

"Arrest?"

"Yes, arrest my father. For doing work, for you, with no permit, no *paper.*"

"I have all the permits."

"He say." Dimitri glanced over at his mother, wife and baby, all of them now looking up at us. "Petrakis say he take to prison."

"To jail?"

"Yes, to jail. But he say prison, I think. And then my father he no see us again."

"Jesus," I breathed. "Why didn't Petrakis come see me? I could show him the fu—" I suddenly went shy, or maybe just civilized, at the word I knew came next—"I could show him a goddamn stack of papers."

"I know. My father tell him like this."

"What did Petrakis do to your father, Dimitri? *What*?"

The young man seemed confused. I nodded my head, once then again, the international symbol for "Go on," and by his own lights, Dimitri did.

"Mr. Steve?—yes, after time Petrakis shrug shoulders like this, you know? He seem very angry. I remember I thought he maybe wanted to kill somebody. Then he turn and go out, making the bad sounds at us, yes?"

I nodded.

"So by this, all the women are crying like crazy. They are frighten, Mr. Steve. So I go to them and hug them and try calm them. But my father—"

"What happened?"

"My father, he angry also. And he say something about police chief not keep man from feeding family. You know how he talk, Mr. Steve. And he go out of house too, and I know he going to boat, to fix anyway. And I must help him but I must help women also, and I stay one minute, two minute maybe. Then, from outside, there is *boom!*"

"That is the bomb, Dimitri? Are you sure it wasn't the motor?"

"You did not see, no? *I* see. I run to him, and light is blown out, and he is on sand but moving and making noises with mouth, pain noises. It was his *legs,* you see. This was not motor on boat. This was under boat."

"Bomb?"

"I think so very much, yes," Dimitri said.

A woman I took to be a nurse poked her head out the swinging doors that led deeper into the clinic, then told Dimitri something in Greek so feverish and fast I missed every word. He placed his hand on my left shoulder blade and pushed me toward the doorway.

"You may visit," he said.

There was a long hallway of rooms with closed doors, and the lights flickered greenly as I followed the nurse. She turned around once to make sure I was still there, but seemed too tired and drained of all color to care. Or maybe it was just the lighting. Another set of swinging doors waited at the hall's end. She stopped and pushed the right side open for me, then let it slip back into place when I was inside.

Fotis lay on a table, a terrible flashback to Avery Graham at the police station. There was one tube disappearing into one of his nostrils, another going into a hole in his throat and several more connecting at various points along his left arm. There were no official covers, nothing formal or tucked in, simply a white sheet tossed over him that showed me his feet and legs were covered in bandages. Based on the patches of blood I saw seeping through, it was time to change both bandages and sheet.

I moved up beside the bed, pressing deeper into the zone of beeps and blips from machines at the other end of tubes and wires. I saw a huge purple bruise along the right side of my friend's face, filled with welts and wrinkles and cuts, perhaps where some piece of the boat had hit him in the blast. His face looked uneven, twisted, his mouth dipping on the right and fading at the right corner into the bruise. Fotis was looking up at me now, his eyes cloudy with painkillers and, no doubt, with pain. I was happy to see he was alive. It was good to see *someone* alive.

His lips smacked together dryly a couple times, and I heard a small sound trying to make it out. Though he barely could move his head, he did seem to nod in the direction of a tiny rolling table in the corner, where a plastic carafe sat beside a paper cup. Neither of us saying a word, I understood he was asking for a sip of water. This I got and held gently to his lips, being careful not to touch anything that would hurt when I knew that anything and everything would hurt. He raised his head just enough to run his lips around the edge of the cup, drawing in a few drops, then letting his head fall back onto the small, stiff-looking pillow.

His arms and hands, lying on either side of him, were bandaged too. But once I'd set the cup back on the table I found a bit of arm that had no bandage or burn. I set a hand upon it without pressure and saw what I thought was the briefest smile. It went away, though, letting my friend's eyes fill with fear.

"Be—" Fotis struggled, as though speaking were the hardest thing he'd ever done. "Be—" He closed his eyes tight. Then he opened them again, with startling determination to tell me something important. "Be—very—careful," he whispered. "My friend."

When I finally did say goodbye to Dimitri and his family, having met with the doctor and assured him I would pay for any treatment that seemed best, the sun was starting to rise. Colonel Petrakis was waiting for me just outside the frosted front door.

"As you Americans love to say," he snorted, "*you* are under arrest."

That was my unofficial notification. The official one came from the shadows behind me, as three thugs grabbed my arms and started kicking, butting, punching and beating me until even the dawn couldn't keep the world from tilting into blackness.

I woke in the dark. My jail cell had a window. I had to figure it was night. There was a bitter, metallic taste in my mouth, a dark memory of anything and everything that involved blood. I had a left eye that felt like it would never open again and a right knee that gave way when I made my first effort to stand. Leaning my weight against a wall I could barely see, I slowly shifted this way and that, avoiding the positions that hurt just before I reached them. The knee still did its job, if painfully. When I reached my full height, I could look out between the bars, and I was shocked by what I saw. After weeks of clear weather, the bowl of stars above our heads blinked on and off behind fast-moving black clouds, some spreading flashes of lightning across the roiling night. I heard wind whistling between the buildings and over the rooftops, and somewhere the sound of some unlocked shutter banging again its window frame. The island's cats scuttled from door to fence to sill, yelping in distress, searching for someplace to hide from the storm.

There was no place to hide, I knew with finality. Not for me. Not for my friends. Not ever. Not anymore. I had done everything in my power, without understanding exactly why, to leave behind everything and anything that had protected me every day of my life. And at that moment, certainty itself switched on a blinding white light and stepped to the door of my cell.

"Our accommodations," Petrakis scowled. "Do they meet your standards?"

I made a show, if a painful one, of glancing around the small space. The bedroom was a cot with straw tumbling out of the lumpy mattress. The bathroom was a bucket. Between the two, there was a dried river of blood, only some of its recent enough to be mine.

"Magnificent," I scowled right back.

He stepped closer to the bars, still holding back beyond anyplace I might get to him. I'm not sure what the man thought I might do. Then again, I was no doubt just another man in his captivity. I was not me. It would be nice, I thought, if me being me somehow helped me get out of here.

"So, Mr. Laros," he said, his eyes turning dark and angry, "ask me how long you can be held here without any charges being filed against you."

I asked him.

"This is Greece, not America," he said. "And ask me about that famous phone call you might wish to make."

I asked him.

"This is Greece, not America." The man was beginning to enjoy this. "And now, ask me about your right to have an attorney present to represent you."

I asked him.

"Again, Mr. Laros, this is Greece, not America. I warned you to go back there, did I not? I told you this was not a business for you, not a place for you. I told you it would be very bad for you if you stayed. Did I not?"

I nodded.

"And yet, Mr. Laros, here you are."

"Here I am."

Petrakis shook his head, as though almost sad about all the terrible things that were surely going to happen to me, all because I'd chosen to disobey him. The colonel was not used to people disobeying him.

"Now tell me," he said, "do you know why you are here?"

I thought, remembered, struggled my way back, to Fotis and his son, at the hospital, somehow only hours before. "Something to do with permits, yes?"

"Bravo. Yes. Indeed that is why you are being held. But there are other things, other suspicions. There is the suspicious death of your friend, Avery Graham, who might have been competition for the winery you wish to build—"

"That's crazy. He—" Petrakis silenced me with his hand. I could tell where this was going.

"Mr. Laros, please. And then, there is the suspicious explosion that nearly killed your friend Fotis. You may, it seems, have wished to take over your business." There was much I could say, but it wouldn't have made any difference. "These are suspicions, you understand, not criminal charges. Greece is, after all, a civilized country, yes? But as long as these suspicions remain, we can hold you on the permit problems and investigate. For a good *while*, I'm afraid."

"I have permits, from the municipality."

He chuckled. "Not in Delfinos, you haven't. Not even in Greece. And besides, sir, I see no permits here."

"They are in my room. I raced out to see my friend."

"Mr. Laros," he stared through me, pronouncing the words as slowly as a death sentence read atop the gallows. "*I—see—no—permits.*"

As promised, I did not hear a charge, make a phone call or meet an attorney over the next 24 hours. The weather outside my window was terrible, dark even during the day as the hours ticked by toward our event. The worst rain since my arrival bombarded the window and everything else on Delfinos, kicking up a cold mist that filled the air to wet my face, my arms and my clothes. By the time the sun went down, there still was no sun.

I wondered what the people of the island were doing that night without me. Maybe staying home, I thought darkly. Maybe, if they were smart, pretending I'd never turned up here in the first place.

It was about an hour after sunset that I heard the first shouting, only some of it belonging to Petrakis. Through several thick walls, it rose in volume to near-fistfight, then got so quiet I heard nothing, then arched upward all over again. There was what sounded like repeated bangings of thick hand on metal desk. A long silence was prelude to a seething Colonel Petrakis swinging open the heavy door to the cellblock, followed by Father Michael and a small, balding man in eyeglasses and a dark suit. Petrakis looked tired and defeated, but also defiant.

"You may go," he muttered, using a key on a thick chain to unlock my cell. "You may thank these gentlemen for that." He glared first at the man in the suit, then at Father Michael. "I myself will thank them *later*." There was no emotion in his voice. "Every way I possibly can."

"Steve," said Father Michael. "You must follow us now."

"What happened?" I asked, filled with fear that someone else I knew had died.

"You are free."

I shook my head, trying to clear it of mangled thoughts, wishing I could make my legs simply get me the hell out of there. "But how?"

"Those permits," the other man said, with a small voice and a strong Greek accent. "They were not *necessary,* you see. Since 1933, the square in Delfinos has been the responsibility of Father Michael's church." He smiled. "It is the *church*, not the municipality, that has paid for all upkeep of the square. Therefore the permits you need must come from the church, not from the municipality. And Father Michael has been kind enough to deliver those permits as of now to Colonel Petrakis. As a citizen, in the interest of right and reason, of course."

The colonel grunted.

"So Father Michael *brought* you here?"

"I came from Athens, yes," the attorney said, starting to grin. "It is a very long trip."

"I can't believe he has an attorney in Athens."

"Oh no," the priest interrupted, "I am not the client here."

"Well, who is?"

The attorney's grin was absolute. "In Athens, we have rendered to Caesar, as our good Lord suggested," he said, rubbing three fingers together until I understood, then turning to lead me from the police station. "My client happens to be the Greek Orthodox Church."

I was running, running and limping and gasping for breath, pain flowing out of every pore. I took the ragged turns in the streets as though I'd lived on Delfinos every day of my life. What I had never done before is run while trying to listen to voicemails. I had twenty-seven of them, two of which really mattered and one of which I'll never forget.

The phone had been a snarling parting gift from Petrakis, along with my wristwatch and wallet. I'd checked everything on instructions from the attorney, but it all was as I left it. The attorney had held back outside the police station, needing to speak with Fr. Michael, who promised to catch up with me on the square. I could listen and delete quickly without losing my stride, so that's what I did to anything that was an inquiry about tonight's show. That's what everyone called it, a show, and making them *not* was clearly a battle I was destined to lose. The messages were in six languages—Greek of course, plus Italian, German, French and English, plus something I took to be Russian.

Now that was something none of us had thought of: who the hell could actually talk to all these people. That, however, was a problem for another day.

Right now I had to get to the square, and that meant not slipping and killing myself on stones made slick by all the rain. Rivers ran along one side of the street or the other, once in a while along both, and sometimes waterfalls spouted from second or third-floor balconies, baptizing me when I wasn't paying attention. The drains were clogged with falling branches.

"Hey Steve, I got some bad news, man," said the voice of Chef Miguel, phoning from the corporate offices of Shimmering Seas. "I just heard from our Ops people, man, and we can't get in there tonight. The seas are too rough to use the tenders. But hey, man, they like the *idea*. They want to do it as much as we can, when we're around there, you know. But not tonight."

Another time, I would have called him back. Another time, I would have worried. Another time, I would have poured myself a large glass of Maker's Mark. But this was now, not another time. All I knew was we had a show to do. And if all anybody wanted from Delfinos was a show, a show we would give them. I had to be there to help, I simply had to be there—until a final voicemail stopped me wheezing at the intersection of the final two streets.

"Mr. Steve Laros," the French-accented voice said, breathing with too much emotion. "It is Marcel. The husband of Roxanne Dupre." A terrible shiver took hold of me. I don't know if I shook physically or simply lost control everything inside me. "She tell me I must call you. I am sorry. But she is in hospital now. The doctors are trying to find what is wrong, so far, it is not possible. She tell me we cannot make it to Greece, and that we are sorry." There was another long, breathy pause. "She say tell you there is always next time."

Father Michael caught up with me in that place, my back pressed against a plaster wall, rainwater from an unseen roof cascading down around my tears. Without any drama or pretense, he wrapped an arm around my shoulders and led me slowly out into the square.

The place, for the most part, was a mess. Several strands of lightbulbs had been blown down and now slept coiled at the base of lamps and trees. There had been banners saying welcome in as many languages as we could think of, but all the banners were gone. The lights in the square, even in the buildings looking out onto it, had been switched off, leaving the only illumination to torches that burned at each end of each rough wooden.

Near the slick-wet stage, I saw an elderly couple chatting amiably with Irini as she gathered up the last of the plates, even as one of the village men refilled one glass each with local wine and the other with tsipouro. There was another table of six off to the side, filling most of a table on the side facing the stage. We had an audience of eight.

The small cruise ship deposit would pay some of our bills, but I knew I'd have to work hard to keep from having to give that back. Too late now, I told myself, over and over. *Too late now.*

I heard a buzzing from above my head and I knew the follow spots were being switched on. It was dark on the stage, very dark, though I could see past it to the winding streets spreading out from the square. In the darkness, I heard music—it *was* music, though it began so softly it might have been wind brushing through the trees. It was a shepherd's flute, soulfully playing across a rocky hillside, the sound of island night and of loss and loneliness. Both spotlights came up on the small stage now. And where everything in me expected a line of young costumed Greek dancers, there stood before us only one.

Elena.

She raised her eyes, outlined with dark streaks of face paint, splashes borrowed from the ancient world, and then her left arm rose above her head, heartbreakingly arched, till her eyes worked their way up to her open fingers. She was dressed completely in black, a robe that drifted and filled and fell with her every gesture. The flute gathered strength and speed, almost without our noticing, as Elena swooped her body downward and began to turn, as slowly and thoughtlessly as the earth.

I saw pain deep in her eyes, as she struggled to protect her knee. The knee that had ended her dreams, and ended them much too soon. She, however, turned her pain into passion, even as the music picked up, joined in sequence by bouzoukia and the suggestion of primitive drums. Her turns were spins now, one foot then the other supporting her, each shooting out in a curve that finally tightened upon itself. There were kicks. There were leaps. Each thing she did was more dangerous than the thing before, but she did them, did them with all the anger she could find inside herself. She held none of it back from any of us lucky enough to be watching.

And then, as suddenly as it began, it was over. Elena stood before us, heaving to catch her breath, tilting slightly to ease the agony in her knee. The audience of eight stood up to cheer, as did Fr. Michael and I, as did everyone from Delfinos who had worked to make this night happen. There was no yesterday and no tomorrow after this dance. And the dance was our reminder that *there never really is.*

Elena stepped from the stage carefully, given a supporting arm by one of the workers. She gathered her dance bag from the shadows and walked quickly past the still-cheering audience to the place where she had seen me.

"Steve," she said, with no intention of staying. "It was Petrakis. He called the other dancers. And frightened them. I am sorry. They would not come."

"Elena, that was incredible."

"No," she said with immense sadness. "But it was the best I could do."

"Thank you. I feel—"

"Please, Steve. I must go."

She turned away from me, and in the turning I noticed the thick makeup covering her forehand and cheek, and before she could get away I carefully touched those places with my hand. Powder came away on my fingers, leaving her bruises no longer covered.

"Elena, what did he—"

She stood in silence, looking down, as I stepped around her and saw the pattern repeated on her neck and arms. Each place I touched I felt powder, and each time it brushed it off there was bruising.

"Yiannis was angry, when they tell him. About video." Elena said, answering the question she'd brushed aside at last. "He was—very cruel." Her eyes left the street to find mine. "He say—he *accuse* me of telling you everything. About his business."

"Elena, you didn't tell me *anything*."

She smiled with resignation. "I know."

There we stood, two people playing out one of the oldest, saddest scenes on the face of the earth.

"Please," I pleaded. "I can't let you go—"

"*Steve*." Finding her true voice, Elena spoke calmly but with finality. "Tonight you were needing the dancing. I danced. We should leave it at that, yes?"

"Yes," I said, before I could spend a lifetime thinking better of it. Yes meaning *no*. Yes meaning *never*. Yes meaning *please don't*. And really, all I said was *yes?* Perhaps it didn't matter. By the time I thought of twelve million better things to tell her, Elena was already gone.

I looked up from the stones after something resembling a lifetime, and the three couples from the table beside the stage were surrounding me. To my relief, they were smiling.

"You please are Steve Laros?" one of the men asked in halting English.

"Yes," I answered, halting a bit myself.

"We wish to thank you," one of the women said. "For this."

"Oh, you're welcome." My training was taking over. "We're glad you could join us this evening." I forced a smile. "Next time, I'll be sure to put in for better weather."

They laughed. "Yes, please do so," the woman said.

"But please," said another man, "You must understand."

I looked at the man full on. He was deeply tanned from his shaved head to his feet in leather sandals. In the poor light of the street, it occurred to me that all six of them were tanned much the same.

"We are Russian," the first woman explained. There were nods all around. "And you must know: we are here for to love *Greece*."

"*Not* here for to love Russia," the third man said.

"And now we can see," continued the woman, "that you are also. We wanted to say to thank you."

After that, the best I could do was ask if they needed a ride somewhere. We'd arranged for a dozen donkey carts in advance, but this group had not made use of one. Besides, *their* side of the island was best accessed by car. They assured me they had a rental and wandered off down a side street to find it.

The cleanup had already begun. Irini and a group of ladies were stacking plates into rubber bins and men were arranging things knocked down by the storm for repair or replacement. I went over and did my best to be helpful, but the men and women of Delfinos, almost sadly, waved me away. Without making a scene, I pulled Irini to the side and told her to make sure all leftover foods went home with the people who'd helped. As I'd paid her for it already, this might have been the best news she and they had heardall day.

Feeling empty inside, I worked my way around the stage, viewing its edges and angles from all sides and finally taking a seat out in front. I stared at the platform, at the men cleaning around it; and while I felt in some ways that this island was my home, I understood that nothing I could do would ever make these people less strangers. I could learn their language. I could adopt their traditions. I could dress and eat and drink as though I were one of them. But when the show was over, on this or any other night, I would always be *this* guy, the one sitting by himself in the seat our front, belonging neither here nor anywhere else.

Eventually I stood up to head for my B&B. It was only for another day or two before I could move into my father's house. And with that move of virtually nothing I possessed here it would no longer be his house but my own.

Pulling up short at the edge of the square, I spotted the elderly couple from front and center table. They were talking with each other in a concerned way beside a cart with a donkey but no driver. I went over to see if they needed help.

"Do you know," the woman asked, by way of answering, in a soft British accent, "if this cart will be heading down to the port? We were counting on it somewhat, you know. We've taken a flat there until the Thursday ferry."

In response, the best I could do was glance around. I couldn't guess, after all I'd been through, who'd ended up driving any cart at all.

"Climb in," I said.

I shimmied my way painfully up onto the driver's seat and picked up the reins from the floorboards. "Student Driver," I laughed over my shoulder, and the donkey lurched forward onto the road that led those three kilometers down to the water. By the time we left the last houses of Chora, donkey, cart, passengers and even driver had settled into a rhythm. The clouds were starting to break open, and a few stars were coming out, etching our slow progress against the darkness.

"Where are you two from?" I asked.

"Britain," the man offered, his voice as gentle as his companion's. "The countryside south of London, actually. Though I worked in the city for a time. Enough of all that, I say. Either *it's* too young or *we're* too old."

We shared a warm laugh at that truth, then rode in silence a bit longer.

"I'm curious," I said, gazing ahead to where the road flattened to reach the starlit sea. "How on earth did you all hear about this?"

The woman fielded that one. "We read about it in the newspapers, of course."

Of course. I would have to light a candle at church for Roxanne Dupre. I actually might consider lighting several thousand of them.

"And then we simply *knew*," the man picked up. "Didn't we, dear?"

"We knew we had to come here."

"We'd never visited, you understand" the man continued. "And my brother-in-law had always spoken so fondly of this island. It seemed like the right time, is all."

"And my brother, Mr. Laros," offered the woman, "said so many wonderful things about you."

I understood.

"Your brother—"

"Was Avery Graham." Her eyes glistened in the starlight. "Frankly, our family never understood what he saw in this place. Now, perhaps, we are beginning to see. Tomorrow, at his request, we'll be spreading his ashes over the vines, and we knew we'd need to ask your permission."

"I don't see why," I said, confused. "His vineyards were lovely."

"Yes, of course," the man said, turning to his wife in hopes of assistance. "But he doesn't seem to understand, does he, dear?"

"No, I don't believe he does." The woman placed her hand on my shoulder. I turned from the silver road to meet her eyes. "My brother didn't wish his ashes spread across *his* vineyards, Mr. Laros. He made us promise to spread them across *yours*."

43

"Steve," the voice said, crossing an ocean to make its way into my cellphone. "It's Jerry."

It was the middle of Holy Saturday, one day before Greek Easter and therefore two days before I sailed away from the island of Delfinos, every cell in the body vowing it wouldn't be forever. There were many conversations to be had at the other end of my journey, many of which might go very poorly. I had to speak with Beverly about our marriage. I had to speak with Nick about my job. And I had to speak with Jerry—Dr. Jerry Hallam of Baylor College of Medicine—about my cancer. Except that Jerry was speaking to *me* right now.

"It doesn't look good, Steve," he said matter-of-factly.

"I was afraid of that."

"The blood samples you sent—I mean, your PSA is through the roof from last time, and it's only been—what?—like two months?"

As best I could tell, *that* had been a lifetime.

"We'll check it again when you get here" the doctor said. "But I think you're looking at surgery or radiation. I mean, I think they have an excellent chance of success. We caught it early, thank God. But you'll have to choose."

"What do you mean *I* choose? Aren't you the doctor?"

"You bet. But it's a choice you'll need to make—you know, talk it over with your wife." Sometimes you just have to let things go. There was so much Jerry didn't know. Hell, there was so much *I* didn't know. "So Steve, call me when you get here. I'll set you up with two of the best, one a surgeon, the other a radiation guy. I'm sure they'll give you everything you need to make a good decision."

"Thanks, Jerry."

"But wait, Steve. I just need to tell you this. This isn't one of those things you can just go away and think about. It's getting worse, you hear me. Time is your enemy. If you don't do something about this, I promise you, it *will* kill you."

I sat without life at a table beneath the trees, until the café owner offered to get me a coffee. All I could do was wave him away. Then I wanted to apologize, but it suddenly seemed that nothing and nobody in the universe cared all that much about what I wanted. For several minutes, I stared at my phone on the table as though even touching the damn thing would be fatal. Then again, fatal is what far too many things had suddenly turned out to be.

I let my left hand wander across the screen, enough that the surface lit up, and then I let that inspire me to pick it up. Somehow that first phone call connecting me to Houston required a second, and it was unavoidable, whatever the time differences, that now I should make it. I hit the speed dial, the signal starting across the ocean to Beverly.

It seemed to ring forever, more than I remembered it ringing, and I wondered if that was something she could make it do. And then I wondered, all of a sudden, what I should leave as a voicemail. And then, just as I had a workable script in mind, Beverly picked up.

"Hey, Bev," I said. "It's me."

In the drawn-out moment that followed, I again heard glasses clinking and muffled conversation, the kind my professional life knew all too well. It was the sound you *wanted* in my business, especially at night. Which it was right now in Houston.

"Steve," she said, "is everything all right?"

Now *that* was a question.

I wanted, I think, some resolution, or at least the beginning of some. Perhaps the beginning, or the beginning of the end. But also I wanted a connection with someone who knew me, who still loved me at least a little, even if only in the retreating past.

"Bev, have you got a minute?"

Another silence, then the scratching sound of hand covering phone and voices, one female and one male, both sounding like strangers to me, and finally fading into something akin to quiet.

"Okay," she said, trying to keep her tone breezy. "It was so noisy in there. I came outside. What's up?"

Why did all her questions sound impossible to answer?

"Look, I just wanted you to know." So then maybe *I* could know? "I'm coming back to Houston, for a while. I don't know how long, really. And I'll stay at the apartment, okay? I don't want you and Chloe to worry. It's just a medical thing. Jerry says—"

"*Jerry*?" Beverly knew what Jerry did for a living. She didn't say anything for a long time. Then, "Steve, I'm really sorry."

"Me too." I made an effort to laugh. "And I thought, you know, when I'm back, we might find some time to talk."

"That would be good. I've really been wanting to." That last sounded more serious than I wished. "There's a lot going on here, Steve. In my life, I mean. There's a lot we need to talk about. And you haven't, well—you haven't been *here*."

I knew what she meant. With cascades of sadness and regret, I knew I hadn't been there for my wife for a very long time. "I'm so sorry, Bev."

"You don't have to be, Steve. It's not your fault, and it's not my fault. It just something that, well, happens to people."

All the muscles in my throat contracted, not letting me speak. I forced the sound out anyway.

"*What* happens, Beverly."

Maybe she was having the same throat problem. "I've—I've met someone, Steve." I said nothing. "I mean, please don't go all emotional on me, okay? He's a nice man, and he's wonderful with Chloe. That's where we are. He's interested in me, and I guess I'm interested in him. We haven't *done* anything."

Yet. When in the course of human history has anybody saying those words not "done" something eventually?

"He's waiting inside now?"

"Yes. I told him it was you, that I needed to take the call."

"I—I appreciate that."

"Of course."

"So yes." It was my turn trying to fake breezy. "I guess we *do* have a lot to talk about."

"There's never a good time to tell somebody, huh?"

"I guess not."

"But we'll talk. As much as you want, as much as you need. I'm not angry, Steve. I want you to know that. It's just—it's just—I don't know—it's what happens."

"Yes, I suppose it is."

"And you'd better take care of yourself. I mean your health, Steve. A lot of people need you in this world."

"Well, I'm not so sure about that. But I caught myself thinking, right before I called you, that of all the things a person might want to do in this life, the only thing required—first and foremost—is that they be *alive*."

"I think you're right, Steve. Really, hold onto that thought, okay?"

Beverly and I broke the connection a couple pleasantries later, letting her return to the man who wanted her waiting at her table.

I had never, I realized, actually pondered my life; I'd merely lived it. Yet there's nothing quite like knowing it might end soon to make your life worth pondering. It had been a good life, I figured, good enough anyway, and absolutely *normal*—the same life all my friends were living at that moment, from office to home to country club to church, filling each day and night with, well, *something*. We're handed our scripts when we show up, we're pointed to our places, and then, day after day, night after night, we play out our little parts. Nobody ever told me there was anything wrong with that. But nobody ever told me there was anything more.

On this island—I was crying at my table by this point, and I didn't care who saw me—on this funny little no-place of an island, I'd *found* that something more: in this dry and impossible place, among these dry and impossible people, in the eyes of a woman who might or might not be crazy enough, ridiculous enough, brave enough to actually love me. I'd stumbled upon more work, more pain, more decisions, more danger, more love and more life than I ever knew existed. Before the end of my life, whenever it came, I *needed* to know I'd stumbled on something and someone worth living for.

44

The sun went down and the lights flickered on among the thick branches. The people of Delfinos gathered, greeting each other, buying each other glasses of wine. It took only a glance in my direction to scare them away. They knew I was going away now. It took no genius to know that in this life, not all partings are "till we meet again." Some actually *are* "goodbye."

Ultimately, as the night wore on, I did let the café owner bring me that coffee, along with a small dish of *loukoumades*, the round sugar-powdered dough balls crispy, hot and golden from the fryer. I ate one, swearing it would be enough, and then I ate the rest. He smiled in victory.

I thought about many things, and after a time, those things took on importance outside of me. There was so much to be grateful for. Fotis, for example. His legs were staying despite the damage. It would take time and surgeries, but the doctor felt confident my friend's legs would someday be fine enough to fish, fine enough to drive his taxi, fine enough to walk through a vineyard where most of his family and more than a few of his friends were gainfully employed. It would not be my success, but *ours*.

The Russians weren't going away, of course. Why would they, at least until they were good and ready? They still had virtually all the money that existed on Delfinos. But something elemental *had* changed, and I'd been a part of it, making me more rooted on this island and this island more rooted in me. As long as our island freed itself from Russia's corruption, the *people* of Russia were welcome to visit as often as they liked, to leave behind as many rubles as we could possibly take off them. They're here for *Greece*, they'd told me, my Greece. All we had to do was make sure, years into the future, that the Greece that was mine was here for *them*.

A day earlier, I'd spotted a tiny story in an Athens paper, reading the online English edition on my laptop on the square. A body had been found on the rocks of Delfinos, a body that had gone down from the square the way pirates had always wished to come up. It belonged to one Yiannis Mariotis, and Colonel Petrakis was quoted as ruling the death a suicide. "He was depressed," the police chief told reporters. Under the colonel's watchful eyes, Delfinos was fast becoming the suicide capital of the western world.

I called Elena three times after reading the news, but as I expected by this point, she neither answered nor returned any of my calls. It was eleven-thirty by the time I'd thought about these things enough, helped along by three more coffees. I glanced around me. The square was full.

The people of Delfinos were out in their Easter finest, such as it was. Men milled about in boxy suits and too-wide ties, women in dresses that seemed sewn with a baseball bat. Boys and girls, miniature versions of their parents, raced excitedly among the legs that filled the square. At the insistence of one couple, a small boy wearing a ragged black tie stepped reluctantly to my table and gestured that I should follow him.

It was time—I understood that, somehow. I rose from my far-too-familiar position looking out over this life and moved into the very center of it. The crowd closed around me until, in the oddest feeling of all, I couldn't tell which one was me.

Without warning, all the lights of the town went out. There was a rush of murmuring in the darkness, followed by silence.

We waited. The heavy door of the church creaked open after several minutes, and I recognized Father Michael. He was wearing a long white robe. In his hand he held a single flickering candle. The priest moved to the edge of the crowd and lit one small girl's candle with his own. The girl lit three more around her, and then the steps began to glow. The glow spread outward as all the men, women and children of Delfinos whispered something to each other that I couldn't, it seemed in a very long lifetime, begin to understand.

In the distance behind me, I heard my name, but it *couldn't* have been my name. It surely was only the whispering. Then I heard it again, close and quiet, almost lost among the spreading of flames and prayers.

"Steve," the voice said softly. "You really *do* need one of these."

I turned. In my hands I held nothing—until Elena handed me an unlit candle. I looked down at it, slow to comprehend. For a long moment, I couldn't look at anything else.

"We must light," she whispered. "And I must say, '*Christos anesti*, Steve. It means 'Christ is risen.'" She reached her own candle forward and I tilted mine against it until it flamed. "And say you to me '*Alithos anesti, Truly He is risen*'" She smiled. "It is, in our country, how this is done."

"*Alithos anesti,*" I repeated.

Eventually, the Easter ceremony ended and the crowd began to disperse. Each family moved out of the square toward home, until the stones held only Elena and me, just the two of us, holding our small and flickering candles.

"So," she said finally. "I am told you are leaving me."

"Not leaving *you,* Elena. Simply *leaving.* And coming back. That I *am* doing. As soon as I can."

"I see." She sought and held my gaze. "And you will settle things with your wife?"

"Yes, I will."

"And you will decide things with your brother?

"Yes, I will."

"And you will cure your cancer?"

"Yes, I will. ""And you will come home to me?"

"Yes, I will, Elena. If you are here, this *is* my home."

"I am here." Thus, with so few words, we took on so much more to care about in our lives, and so very much more to lose. "Perhaps, Steve, I *will* come to your boat when you go. We could make our movie, after all."

"Movie?"

"*Elena Says Goodbye to Her Lover*."

"Oh, that one." I giggled. "Yes, we could. But then the title would be completely wrong."

"What do you mean?"

"It won't be *Antio*. It will be *Sto epanidin*."

She brightened. "Not Goodbye. Only—Till we meet again?"

"Exactly."

"*Bravo, Stelios Laros*." Elena cocked her head to one side, studying me up, down and then back again. "There may be a little *hope* for you yet." We laughed. She stopped laughing before I did. "You know, Steve, this will not be so easy, I think. I'm a bit of a—of a—*mess?*" She smiled at the word. "I'm sure you have not noticed this. But it is true. I must get better, slowly-slowly. I will surely require of you oh-so-very-much time."

I saw her face lit by our candles, the entire town, the entire island, the entire universe lit by our candles, and I felt a warm breeze rise up around us, scented with something far away and impossibly sweet.

"All I've got is time, Elena."

"Me also," she said.

ACKNOWLEDGMENTS

I suppose the thank you's for *New Wine* begin with Anthony Quinn, the actor with the Irish surname and the Mexican birth certificate who first showed me on the big screen what it means to be Greek. How many times throughout my teens and 20s did I watch white-suited, ever-reluctant Alan Bates make his British way through *Zorba the Greek* to the point at which, having lost everything, he could say simply, "Zorba, teach me to dance." Similar gratitude could be expressed to Jules Dassin, the American film director who responded to the McCarthy Era Hollywood blacklist by going to Greece, making a movie called *Never on Sunday* and falling in love with his leading lady, Melina Mercouri. After decades of politics and personal turmoil, Mercouri remains even in death some mysterious essence of the feminine Greek soul.

Down at ground level from the movies, I should thank Cleo Nathan—the woman who rented me a room just off her roof garden in Athens in 1974, left me a braid of sweet bread with a boiled egg inside for Easter and suggested I make my way to the Orthodox Cathedral that midnight to celebrate the Savior's resurrection. My lifelong love affair with Greece got serious in that darkened square filled with believers. I began writing the end of this novel that night.

Specifically, many intelligent and generous people on both sides of the Atlantic took me by the hand throughout this project, explained things I should have understood more quickly, and never seemed to tire of my probably naive enthusiasms. These included Manolis Giamniadakis and Evan Turner on Greek wines and foods, Peter and Rebecca Work of Ampelos Cellars in California for pointing me toward Folegandros (the most important island model for Delfinos), and Peter's sister Anne, her Greek husband Fotis and their son Theo of the Ampelos Resort there. All three spent time taking me around the island, telling me about its many characters and, as always in Greece, explaining things that made no more sense afterward than before.

On the island of Crete, I learned much about the underbelly of Russian real estate investment, plus got memorable insights from Minas Liapakis of Hersonissos and his capable right hand, another Manolis, who effortlessly became "Fotis" in the book. On Santorini (Thira), Angeliki Geogantopoulou was quite helpful, as was Lefteris Zorzos of the Hotel Voreina in Pygos. In Athens, I'd like to thank Elena Lissaiou of YES Hotels, who shared her own love of these islands, her passion for storytelling via theater, and of course her given name.

At the editorial level, *New Wine* had several early readers, including Austin food and wine professional Nancy Marr and David Cordua of the Houston-based Cordua Restaurant Group, the latter for talking candidly about pressures that develop when restaurant families become restaurant corporations. Houston

Greek-American restaurant icons like Dimitri Fetokakis of Niko Niko's and the Demeris barbecue dynasty contributed both wisdom and food. Fellow author Holly Beretto gave the manuscript its most intense read, offering many elemental suggestions and improvements. At Bright Sky Press, big thanks go to editorial director Lucy Chambers, managing editor Lauren Adams, designer Marla Garcia, business manager Fiona Bills and public relations manager Eva Cox Freeburn for handling all the tasks required so this book could be, well, this book.